W9-ACQ-293

Date Due

Books by J O N   G O D D E N

A WINTER'S TALE

1961

MRS. PANOPOULIS

1959

THE SEVEN ISLANDS

1956

THE CITY AND THE WAVE

1954

THE PEACOCK

1950

THE HOUSE BY THE SEA

1948

THE BIRD ESCAPED

1947

A WINTER'S TALE

A WINTER'S TALE

JON GODDEN

1961

ALFRED A. KNOPF/NEW YORK

L. C. catalog card number: 61–53445

This is a BORZOI BOOK *published by* ALFRED A. KNOPF, INC.

Manufactured in the United States of America.

Published February 17, 1961
Second Printing, March 1961
Third printing, April 1961

Part One

I

Snow had fallen all night and the house in the woods was already cut off from the road and the village by a four-foot drift at the bottom of the lane. Snow lay along the branches of the firs that made a dark ring round the house, and the lawn was a smooth white lake.

As the sun came up behind the hills, the back door opened then closed again. One of the house's three inhabitants was now abroad in the morning; the cold air filled her lungs and cleared the last mists of sleep from her eyes. She shook her head, as if in amazement at the white world which confronted her, and moved cautiously round the side of the house keeping close to the walls. Every few steps she paused to look suspiciously across the untouched expanse of snow into the recesses between the trees. Nothing moved. Nothing threatened. On she went, moving more quickly now, until she had completed her customary morning circle round the house, the greenhouses, the garage and the sheds, and was back where she had started. All was well: smoke was rising from the two chimneys; she could hear Peter whistling as he raked out the furnace; a smell of coffee came from the kitchen window, which was now open a crack. With a quick upward glance, she noted that the curtains were still drawn over the bedroom windows, and that, too, was right and usual. Jerome, as she very well knew, was not an early riser; another hour must pass before she could stand beside his bed to give him her morning greeting and to remind him once again that she, his Sylvie, was there.

Turning her back on the house and putting it and all domestic thoughts and duties behind her, she took a few steps out where the familiar lawn should have been, refusing to show her surprise at the new white coldness round her feet. Above her, the sky was as blue and clear and cold as a huge aquamarine. As she faced the woods, standing with one paw lifted and her head raised, sunlight topped the trees and the snowy branches, the white expanse of lawn sparkled and shone. On the frosty air was the resinous scent of the firs, a tang of woodsmoke, and a new heady unaccustomed something—the scent of snow. Her sharp sensitive ears heard faint sounds from the village, which was nearly two miles

4

away; nearer, snow sliding from a branch deep in the woods and a pheasant stirring. Suddenly her long body tensed. Her eyes shone and she crouched, her tail held stiffly. Then, like an arrow from the bow, a spear from the hand, she sprang forward into the new exciting morning and into the woods which were her domain. Behind her she left deep narrow tracks, blue in the crisp whiteness.

The winter sun was well above the hills and the tree shadows were shorter on the snow when the back door opened again. A voice called, "Sylvie! Sylvie!" and a high-pitched, metallic whistle pierced the cold air, reaching far into the woods. Minutes passed before the trailing branches of a tree at the edge of the clearing were shaken, snow powdered down, and a dark form bounded out on to the lawn and stood, suddenly rigid, before the blank stare of the curtained windows.

The dark and shaggy spruce woods might have belonged to another age, or a less tamed land than England, and this creature, emerging abruptly from their depths, might have been wild, even ferocious; there was something wolf-like about the great pricked ears, long head and lolling tongue, and a faroucheness in the crouching stance; but this was no untamed animal of the forest confronted by the unwelcome sight of a human dwelling. A young Alsatian bitch stood on the snowy lawn, looking at her home.

She was three years old, full grown, and in full pride of her silver, black, and pale tawny beauty. Her alert strong legs were ready to flash into quick movement. Caked snow was on her black back and panting sides. Her ruff caught the sunlight and sparkled and shone with points of moisture. Her dark eyes were bright with youth and health, eager and confident with unquestioning happiness. An unmelted crystal of snow gleamed like a diamond at her ear.

The voice called again, "Sylvie! Where the heck are you? Come in, can't you? It's time," and a man came round the side of the house towards her. He was short and thin and at a distance could have seemed a boy, if it had not been for his bare grey head. He wore blue jeans and a blue turtle-necked jersey, and an old duffle-coat round his shoulders. From his walk, which was quick and slightly rolling, he might have once been a jockey or a sailor. The Alsatian crouched as she saw him and with ears back, tail held stiffly, began an elaborate stalk across the lawn, moving with exaggerated slowness while her eyes gleamed and the hair down her spine rose menacingly. Now the resemblance to a wolf was startlingly clear; but a wild creature from the woods had not sighted her prey. This was a familiar game, one played every day.

"Stop it, Sylvie," Peter said coaxingly, as he put his whistle back into his pocket. "It's breakfast time. Come in out of the snow." At the sound of his voice she abandoned her stiff crouching pose, and leapt into the air like a deer, all four feet leaving the ground, and flung herself into a dance, whirling and running, spinning in circles, sending the snow flying behind her. As she ran, she looked over her shoulder to make sure that he was watching her. Her white teeth shone as she threw her head up and

6

laughed the silent wide-jawed laughter of the happy running dog.

"That's enough for this morning," Peter said loudly and, turning his back, walked away down the snow-covered path to the kitchen. Enveloped in a cloud of shining snow, Sylvie made one last circuit of the lawn, unwilling to leave its fascinating cold whiteness, then, slowing to a sober trot, she followed him.

The disturbed snow settled again but within the dark stockade of trees the whiteness was now criss-crossed and crossed again by the marks of narrow running feet. The sun shone down on the clearing in the woods and on the low stone house with its slate roofs and blue smoke rising from its chimneys, on the haphazardly arranged out-houses and the neat rectangles of steamy glass which now housed nearly a thousand orchids, the extravagant exotic plants on which Jerome Holt had spent so much money, time and thought. All round the clearing the woods flowed to the rim of the shallow cup of hills and down the lane and along the road to the village. Beyond the hills, only a few miles away, were the tame fields and orchards of the English countryside; but here, in this apparently forgotten valley, the woods were unusually thick, untouched and dark. To-day, because of the snow, the house was truly cut off and remote, more than ever the safe retreat that Jerome had meant it to be.

2

The kitchen was comfortably warm and stuffy. It smelled of coffee, tobacco, onions, drying wool, and soot. Firelight was red in the open grate of the old-fashioned well black-leaded iron range which Peter still preferred to Calor gas or the Aga that Jerome had offered him. The ceiling was yellowed by smoke; a row of woollen socks hung drying above the range beside a bunch of onions. The sink was full of used cups and plates that Peter would get round to in his own good time. Sylvie's day-bed was by the armchair; both were covered with scarlet chintz patterned with blue stars and yellow flowers.

Although the kitchen had been modelled on the one Peter had known forty years ago in his mother's house near Liverpool, this was a man's kitchen, tidy in a man's way, and adequately clean; the table, old-fashioned too, was well scrubbed and the slate floor had been freshly washed. No thought or money had been spent on what Peter called 'frills'; there were no curtains at the window, which looked out at the dark trees and the distant shed that housed the electric-light plant, no formica or chromium or labour saving gadgets. A footstool sat in front of the armchair; an enormous pile of illustrated papers was on the small table beside it with two pipes and a tobacco jar. On the kitchen table, under the window, was a coffee grinder and three pots of orchids in flower, flagrant and curious spotted beauties, white, maroon, yellowish-green, with pouch-like lips, each as upright and highly varnished as a toy soldier. These were Cypripediums, three of the hybrids that Jerome did not care for, but which fascinated Peter.

The telephone and the large modern radio on the dresser were the house's main link with the outside world; they looked even more out of place in the kitchen than the orchids did. It was one of Peter's tasks to answer the telephone when it rang and to decide if it were necessary to switch the caller through to the extension in Jerome's workroom.

The door on to the back porch opened, letting in a shaft of ice-cold air. Peter's voice said, "Wait, Sylvie, can't you? Not all over my clean floor! Come here and get dried," but the Alsatian pushed past his legs into the room and ran to the door in the further wall. It was shut. She scratched at it delicately, touched the handle, turned her head and gave a sharp imperious bark, but Peter shook his head. "Too early," he said, as he hung his coat on a hook behind the door. "Not nine yet. Lie down, like a good girl."

When Jerome was back and settled down to a long spell of writing, Peter kept almost a ritual in the house. At eight fifteen he would open Jerome's bedroom door and let Sylvie sidle out on to the landing. Together they would creep down the stairs to the kitchen and the back door and off Sylvie would run to see to her own business, forgetting even Jerome once she was away from the house and in the woods, although she was always back in time to eat her own breakfast before Peter carried Jerome's tray upstairs punctually at nine o'clock. Now, as he took down a large towel and held it in front of the range to warm, Peter said, "Thought you were gone for good this morning. Bringing me out into the snow. Giving me the trouble to blow the whistle. I might have known better—not far off, are you, when he's here?"

He picked up her brush from the table and knelt down on the red hearthrug; at once Sylvie came to him. As he dried and brushed her, he talked to her, as he always did when they were alone together, in the monotonous, slurred and gentle voice he kept for her. "My clean floor—paw marks everywhere. Don't care, do you? Treat me like an old shoe, once he's back. Not a moment for poor old Peter. 'He's calling,' you say. 'Let me go, let me hurry to lie at his sacred feet.' Then, once he's away again, the kitchen's good enough for you. It's 'Dear Peter' then. 'Good old Peter, and good old kitchen and red armchair.' That's the woman in you—that's typical."

He put the brush down and reached out to the table for her new collar made of black leather and silver studs and lined with chamois leather. As he sat back on his heels, turning it round in his hands, Peter said to Sylvie, " 'Surely you aren't going to put that on Sylvie?' I said to the Captain, to Mr. Holt. 'All very well for Hyde Park, but this is country, real country, almost wild, and Sylvie's a real country dog.' 'Put it on her and keep it on,' that's what he said. 'It suits her, but don't let her into the woods in it.' " Peter shook his head and put the collar round Sylvie's neck and buckled it.

"Pleased with yourself, aren't you?" he said, looking into her face which, as he sat back on his heels again on the rug, was on a level with his own. "Anything new. Trust a woman!" Sylvie stared back at him.

The face so close to her own long furry and noble visage, with the beautifully marked brows, was one that no human being, except Jerome Holt who was used to it by now, could look at without quickly looking away again and suppressing, or not suppressing, a shudder. Even the regulars in the public bar of The Crown down in the village were careful never to look directly at Peter and they had drunk beer and played darts with him for years. Sixteen years ago Peter had been a good-looking man. Then a primus had exploded in a tent in the desert, as he was boiling a kettle for Jerome's tea. His body was still youthful and slim for a man of nearly fifty. His head, with neat ears and curling grizzled hair, was well shaped, but his face was scarred and pitted and, from chin to hairline, was an odd purple-red mottled with grey. His nose was hardly a nose at all and the mouth was nearly lipless. Only one side of his forehead and part of one cheek had escaped this holocaust, and here the tint of normal smooth flesh seemed by contrast more shocking than the rest. The eyes, miraculously unharmed between their thickened and lashless lids, were small and sharp and bright and an innocent sky blue.

No one knows what a dog sees, how little, or how much. Sylvie looked with calm affection into Peter's face and even when he brought it down within an inch of her own she did not turn away. She gave him a gentle absent-minded kiss, a quick touch with her moist and cool muzzle. "That's my girl," he said. "That's my Queen," and he put his hand for a moment on her dark head and ran it down her neck in a quick caress. Then he stood up and turned towards the range.

"Cupboard love!" he said, in his usual rather aggressive voice. "Breakfast, that's all you want, or all you will want for the next quarter of an hour." He looked at the cuckoo-clock on the wall, which was one of his treasures, compared it with his battered silver wrist watch, as he always did, and moved the pan of bacon on to the fire. "Here you are then," he said, as he took Sylvie's dish of liver and biscuit from the top of the oven where it had been keeping warm and put it down beside her blue drinking-bowl on the sheet of newspaper behind the armchair, which was her eating place.

"Go on then, of course you want it, after all that running about," he said to her. "Don't act the lady with me. You're as hungry as a hunter, and you know it."

Sylvie stood up slowly, stretched and yawned, and moved reluctantly towards her dish. Peter watched her as she nosed the contents, picking up a piece of meat and dropping it on to the paper, scattering the chopped biscuit fastidiously. This she did every morning, but he kept his eyes anxiously on her until she settled down and began to eat with her usual healthy young appetite.

As he began to get the breakfast tray ready, Peter looked out of the window at the snow piled thickly against the black side of the shed. The sun shone. The sky was brilliant above the dark green tops of the trees. The kitchen was warm with the scent of frying bacon, cosy between the sun-filled window and the fire; but he shook his head again and said gloomily, "Too cold. Don't like it. More snow to come. That drift will take a bit of getting through. We'll be short of everything if it goes on. A hunter is what you'll have to be, Sylvie, if this keeps up for long."

He crossed the room to the range and, as he put the bacon and tomatoes into their dish and lifted the kettle to fill the warm-plate under it, he said, half to himself and half to Sylvie, "Plenty of tinned stuff and flour. Plenty of coal and paraffin. Meat's the trouble. Sylvie won't eat tinned meat, couldn't expect her to, particular, that's what she is, naturally, with her breeding." He turned to the tray. All was ready: coffee over the spirit lamp, toast, honey, mustard, pepper, fruit and finger-bowl and napkin; only the usual pile of letters was missing. "Can't help that, Sylvie," Peter said, seeing in his mind the red-painted letter-box perched on its post on the wrong side of the drift beyond the gate. "Might manage to get down later to see how deep it is. Wonder if the post-van got through that far or not."

The clock whirred on the wall and out came Peter's little, busy bird to say, "Cuckoo, Cuckoo," nine times. Sylvie, leaving the rest of her food in the dish, ran to the door whining eagerly and waving her long plumed tail.

"No hurry," Peter said crossly. "He won't give us much of a welcome this morning."

Peter knew what to expect when he opened the bedroom door. He knew that Jerome had worked until after two last night and that half a decanter of whisky had gone. Jerome would tell him

13

to get out, to go to Hell. "It's all very well," Peter grumbled. "I'm the one that suffers if he's a few minutes late at his damn tread-mill, as he calls it."

Sylvie was not listening. Her whine had changed to a low moaning, as if she were in pain. She scratched frantically at the door and turned her head to look at him beseechingly.

"Go on, then," Peter said, as he flung the door open. "Go on, you poor silly!'

He turned back to pick up the tray and heard her feet pattering down the polished floor of the hall, skidding on the rugs and, clumsy with eagerness and love, running up the stairs.

3

Jerome Holt's workroom, which only Peter called his study, was in the right-hand front corner of the old part of the house. One window looked down a high steep bank on to the lane below and over the lane and the woods to a wide view of the hills. Jerome did not need a view when he was working, only enough light, and his writing-table was set sideways to the second window from which there was nothing to be seen except a strip of lawn and the close ring of trees. His chair had its back to the hills, and when he looked up from his work it was at a blank panelled strip of wall.

Every writer must have his own idea of the perfect place to

write in, but many will agree that too much space is distracting, that a sense of being enclosed and safely held apart conduces thought. Writers are perverse creatures and some find it easier to concentrate in a toolshed or a summer-house than in the most carefully planned and luxurious study; a cell with the door locked on the outside is, of course, the best place of all. Jerome had been writing for many years, but he was not one of those who can write anywhere, in a train, or a plane, a tent or a hotel bar. He liked to write here, in this room, in the corner of his house where he was as comfortable, at ease, and as at home as a badger in his sett, a fox in his den, or a snail in his shell.

The room was not large, but there was enough space for him to walk about in when he could not think of a phrase or a word, for movement helps words to flow. It was warm as, sitting still for hours on end, he needed it to be; an open fireplace faced the window and there were two radiators against the walls. Most important of all, it was quiet, shut-off and private; the only door, which opened on to the hall, was shielded by a black and gold Japanese screen. No sound from the rest of the house penetrated the thick old walls of the workroom. In the last fourteen years, no one except himself, Peter, Sylvie, and an occasional workman, a painter or a carpenter, had ever been inside it.

At twelve that morning, Jerome was sitting at his writing-table, which was large and solid and made of mahogany; when working he liked to put his elbows down and to have plenty of room. In front of him was a notebook, a china mug holding pencils and pens, and two piles of paper, one covered with lines of his small niggly writing and the other blank. On the table, pushed to one side, was the typewriter he seldom used for a novel until his first pencil draft was complete, a glass ruler, a bottle of ink still unopened, and a small carved stylized wooden owl, emblem of wisdom, that he had bought many years ago in an Indian bazaar. This battered and scarred object went with him everywhere, even to his London flat where it was known not only to his friends, but to his many acquaintances and hangers-on. "Old J's owl," they said, and he did not deny it when they also said that he could not write a word without it.

Sitting hunched in his chair, staring morosely in front of him through the horn-rimmed spectacles he used for work, he looked that morning a little like an owl himself. He was a big man, now perhaps a little too heavy. His head, with the high bald forehead, was large and his face long and dark with a straight fine nose and an ugly humorous mouth with a protruding lower lip. His eyes were almost black and, in spite of the pouches under them, they were beautiful, being large, well-shaped, with long dark lashes. He was wearing fawn cavalry drill trousers, a thick high-necked sweater, fur-lined shabby slippers and a shapeless brown tweed jacket. This was his writing-coat that he would sometimes change for a brown flannel dressing-gown with yellow spots, that was equally old and worn. He put his pencil down and picked up the wooden owl.

"Much use you are this morning," he said.

At the sound of his voice, Sylvie lifted her head. She lay in her customary winter place on the white sheepskin hearthrug where she would doze and dream, or simply wait until the long, immobile hours had passed, content to efface herself, to lie on the rug as unnoticed and undemanding as a shadow, perfectly content because he was there and she was near him. Sometimes her eyes would turn to the window and search the open sky beyond it. Sometimes her ears would prick, would move as delicately as the antennae of some great furry moth, questing the world beyond the room. Sometimes, as she slept, her feet would twitch as if in her dreams they were running, running, down the dark resin-scented tunnels between the trees. The cream and silver-black tail would lift on the white sheepskin and a small sound of longing, a faint eager whine, would escape from her throat, but never had she been known to desert her post or to abandon her self-imposed and happy vigil. She would lie with the firelight warm on her back and the sound of the flames to lull her for hours on end, all day if necessary, until Jerome said, "What? Still here, Sylvie? That's enough for one day. Let's go out, my love."

Jerome set the wooden owl down on the table, making a sharp sound. In the last hour and a half he had written two lines. He ran his hand through the thick dark hair at the back of his head, seized a sheet of paper, rolled it into a ball and hurled it in the direction of the fire. Pushing his chair back, he walked to the window.

"Oh, God! What's the matter with me?" he said.

In spite of the weight he had put on in the last years, he still moved as lazily and easily as a cat crossing a lawn, or a tango dancer of a few decades ago on a ballroom floor. Perhaps it was the contrast of this wholly masculine grace of movement and his odd ugly face with its habitual mocking and amused smile that made him attractive to women, especially to the discontented fashionable pretty women he laughed at and enjoyed. Now he hunched his shoulders, put his hands in his pockets, and kicked at the window-seat. Sylvie, head raised, watched him indulgently. This childish behaviour was familiar, nothing out of the way, and she lowered her head to her paws again and shut her eyes.

Last night, after days, weeks, of sterile effort, the words had suddenly come easily; for a short while before sleep and exhaustion came over him, they had spilled out, flowed, each one right and bright on the page, what he wanted and what he meant. He had gone up to bed in the small cold hours, feeling exhausted but still in the rosy glow of achievement, and he had fallen asleep before the reaction, that dive from star-filled heights to the depths of doubt and depression, had had time to set in. When he woke, he had been confident and cheerful and he had hurried over his breakfast, eager for once to begin again where he had left off. As always when he sat down to his writing-table, he had read the pages he had written the day before and still these few hundred words had seemed right to him; he had been surprised, almost awed, at their rightness, and he had picked up his pencil not only happily, but humbly. And then suddenly, for no reason, there he was again in the familiar slough, wading through mud. Not only did nothing come, not only was he stuck fast but, after the first hour, he no longer wanted to extract himself or to write a word.

This was the second phase, worse than the slough from which, with enough effort, something might in time have been drawn; this was the unutterably dreary soul-destroying phase when the shapes and colours of the mind become flat and grey, when every thought and word turns to ashes.

"Why?" he asked himself, staring across the woods to the hills. "For the love of Heaven, why?"

The hills, whose dark rough hair of trees was to-day sprinkled with whiteness, were indifferent and remote against the serene cold blue of the sky. Turning his back on them, he began to walk up and down the room between the fireplace and the window, pausing to touch an ornament or to pick up a book without knowing what he was doing, taking a cigarette from a polished wood box and lighting it, moving a chair. Possessed by the demon that writers know, that demon who suggests endless small ways of wasting time, he unconsciously avoided his writing-table.

Sylvie rose, stretching herself, and walked with him keeping by his side and turning when he turned until he stopped in front of the bookcase that filled the wall space between the window and the door.

The shelf on a level with his eyes was filled with his own work: the travel books that had given him so much pleasure: the novels which were his real work, with their many translations: two collections of short stories: the five plays that had made him famous but which he had never been able to take very seriously. He had always published his books under his first two names, John Jerome, while as a playwright he called himself simply,

'Jerome.' Now he stared at the shelf as if he could not believe that all these bound volumes had anything to do with him, with Jerome Holt, and took down the first book he had ever written and looked at it curiously. This was an account of a university climbing club's expedition to the Andes written while he was still an undergraduate. It was by chance that he had been chosen out of the team to write the despatches that were sent from the base camp to a London newspaper, and the success of the book written from these despatches had astonished him, as much as everyone who had known him. 'Like no other travel book,' the reviewers had said, exaggerating its virtues as they might as easily have exaggerated its defects. 'An astonishing and unusual talent.' He turned the pages, read a few words, and then put the book back on the shelf and patted it gently.

His first success had not gone to his head. He had taken his degree, a good second in law, continued to climb mountains when he could, and only when his second book, another tale of mountaineering written two years later, proved as great a success as his first, had he dismayed his uncle and guardian by leaving the family firm of country solicitors to make his living as a writer, a dyed-in-the-wool writer with no intention of being anything else as well. These young plans had been interrupted, perhaps luckily, by the war which in many ways he had enjoyed although he had always known that for him it was only an interruption, a slice out of his real life, and important only because it had given him the experience and background for his first and, as some still thought, best novel. Writing this novel had cleared the war out of his system and now all that remained to him of those years in the desert was his sheepskin jacket, a German Lüger pistol, which he treasured in memory of an exciting moment, and Peter.

Jerome ran his hand lightly down the long row of books as if they were the keys of a piano that might give back an encouraging and living sound to him.

"Fourteen years' hard labour," he said to the room. "Prolific fellow in his time, John Jerome, but now?"

He turned his back on the bookshelves and, lighting another cigarette, began his pacing again. He had bought his house which was then a four-roomed gamekeeper's cottage at the end of the war with his gratuity and the money he had made from his second book, which his uncle had carefully invested for him. He was thirty years old and he knew himself only too well by then; he knew that if he were to write the novel that was heavy in him as it deserved to be written, he must find a retreat far from the London of his leaves and far from his friends where he would be cut off from all temptations. To write this book was a necessity. He would have written it somehow, somewhere, even if he had known that when it was finished it would be taken away from him and never heard of again, but it was also the keystone of a plan, and a gamble. He was determined to put everything he had of talent, time and money into it in the hope that its success would allow him to live as he wanted to live by doing only the work he wanted to do. With a purposefulness that would have surprised his friends who, misled by his lazy affable slightly mocking manner, thought that he never took anything seriously, least of all himself, he made his plans and set about putting them in action. When he retreated to this house with very little money, three suitcases, a minimum of furniture, and Peter, who had been his batman and was now his responsibility, he had intended to live like a hermit in the woods, but only for a time. He had allowed himself two years.

His plan had succeeded, if not quite in the way he had meant. The novel had taken longer than it should have done because half-way through it he had been overtaken by an idea for a play, an idea that had seemed to him, quite rightly as it turned out, to be so original, so overwhelmingly sharp and witty, and so pressing that he could think of nothing else until he had given it shape. It ran in the West End for three years and the first draft was written in two weeks. When it was done, he had put it away and gone back to his novel; but he had taken it to his agent with his finished book.

Now Jerome, with Sylvie at his heels, came to a halt in front of the fireplace and stood looking down at the burning logs without seeing them. He knew that he had been lucky. Other writers thought well of his work and his plays had made him widely known, but there were better writers, and as hard working, who had not done as well for themselves; if he never wrote another word he and Peter could live comfortably on his investments and insurances for the rest of his life. The house and everything in it belonged to him. He turned and looked appraisingly round the room.

It was at its best on a day of wind and rain; this morning's insistent sunlight and the frosty shine of the snow invaded its winter privacy and dimmed the fire; but it was a pleasant room in any weather and by now it fitted him as easily as his old coat did. The walls were panelled, the ceiling was white, the floor was covered with the rugs he had bought in Karachi; the crimson cushions on the broad window-seat, which was Sylvie's summer place, were shabby and the curtains were a little faded. It held his most personal and cherished possessions that were a part of his life. In the wall cupboard by the fireplace were his ice pick and boots and crampons, the Lüger, carefully oiled and greased on its shelf, the silver cup he had won at his preparatory school. Disposed on the bookcases or chimney-shelf and tables were, among other things, the cigar box that had belonged to the father he could not remember, his mother's old jewel case which held a collection of half-forgotten trinkets, the jade horse he had bought in Hong Kong, a carved ivory fan that had been given to him by a girl in Ceylon. The only picture in the room was a snow scene, peopled by small dark skating figures; he had bought it in New York and had hung it here over the fireplace instead of in the sitting-room because he found its stiff puritanism and its greys and whites soothing and peaceful. All the colours in the room were subdued and the furniture, which had come from his uncle's house, was plain and sparse. Only the black and gold screen and the orchids gave it an air of richness, that touch of luxury and sophistication which amused and satisfied another side of his nature.

The orchids, which Peter had brought in only yesterday from

23

the hothouses, had a table to themselves close to the window. He crossed the room and stood looking down at them. The five earthenware pots stood in shallow Chinese porcelain bowls. The delicate blooms which rose up into the warm air of the room were more like a swarm of butterflies, extravagant insects, than flowers. Their fragile but fleshy beauty was to Jerome's taste, and their look of fastidious cruelty amused him. To transport these startling aliens to the house in the woods and to rear them there had given him much pleasure. At first they had been only an expensive and time-wasting diversion but now, after seven years, they paid for themselves. It was lucky that Peter should have fallen in love with the orchids. Jerome always told himself that it was for Peter's sake that he had enlarged the greenhouses, increased his collection of Cattleyas, Cypripediums and Cymbidiums, the cats, cyps, cyms, of the commercial orchid world, bought the van, and started this small but flourishing business with the wholesale florists of Maningham, the great manufacturing town sixty miles away.

To put off the moment when he must sit down at his table and pull the paper towards him, Jerome took a pint-sized china watering can from the bottom shelf of the bookcase, and began to water each plant slowly and with care. He was thinking of those first two years in the house, which had been shut up and neglected all the war and was damp and extremely uncomfortable. Then there had been an earth closet outside the back door, the only heat had come from the antiquated range and two small open fireplaces, while the only light had been two petrol lamps and candles. Peter had enjoyed those two years as much as Jerome had often hated them. It had suited Peter to live where there was no one to look at him and he liked hard work as long as he was left to work in his own way. Before the war he had been a ship's steward; in Jerome's house he was cook, housemaid, gardener, carpenter, mason, plumber, woodman. If it had not been for Peter, Jerome would probably have given up the house when he first began to make money. He had taken a long lease of a flat in Chelsea and for a time he had lived as he had always promised himself he should live if his book succeeded. Before long he had realized that if he wanted to go on writing in the way he had always hoped to write, the house in the woods was the best place for him. His mountaineering days, the war, and above all his two years of hard austere labour, had taught Jerome what the true sensualist knows by instinct: that the keenest delight lies in contrast: hard before soft, thirst before satisfaction, abstinence before pleasure. He had arranged his life so that, as far as possible, he should have the best of both worlds.

The greater part of each year he spent alone with his work and Peter. His descents on London were frequent but irregular and brief, unless he had work to do there for one of his plays. His secretary, Michael Johnson, lived in his flat and served as a buffer between him and the literary and stage worlds of London. He left all his business and most of his private affairs to this young man and to his friend and agent, Gilbert Stone; they, alone, knew the address and telephone number of his house. Michael would ring up almost every day to make his report and to send on messages from friends, usually through Peter. Three times in fourteen years, Jerome had unwillingly uprooted himself and had gone for about six months to Africa, the Himalayas and to the Far East, not for love of travelling or of seeing new worlds but because he intended to write a travel book of his own special kind. His last journey, except for short visits to Paris or to Rome and once to New York, had been made four years ago, the year before Sylvie had come to the house. These travel books and his novels brought him a steady income; three of the novels had been made into films; but his plays had made him a moderately wealthy man. He was generous to his friends and had a reputation for being open-handed, even careless with his money, but Jerome was cautious and in spite of his tastes his extravagances were few. For the last ten years he had kept a large and fast car, always a Mercedes; he had bought a few pictures, books and wine, and an annuity for Peter; but after he had rebuilt his house, putting in electric light, drainage and central heating, making himself comfortable in a modest way, he had saved money. He had never found it necessary to spend much on women. Martha Cleghorn, the actress, was the only woman he had ever wished to marry. Perhaps luckily for both of them, she had refused to take him seriously and she and her husband were now his closest friends. He did not think very much of women but at intervals, that grew longer through the years, they were still necessary to him. The trouble, he had found, was to keep his affairs as light and brief as he wished. Women were inclined to stick like burrs and then for a kindly and gentle man, as he supposed himself to be, life became too complicated and it was time to take refuge in the house in the woods again where no female, except Sylvie, was allowed.

Seven years ago he had installed his orchids with great expense and some trouble in his home almost as another man of his type might have installed a mistress, or a mandarin of ancient China a bevy of concubines. Jerome knew that if he were to work contentedly for long stretches of time in the house and to keep boredom and staleness away, he must have something in his everyday life apart from his work, something to indulge himself with, to rest in, something to divert him and keep him amused. The orchids were his safety valve. Sylvie, who had been brought to the house three years ago to keep Peter company, was now Jerome's loving shadow, indispensable as shadows are and as taken for granted.

Jerome gently touched a flower in the second pot with the tip of one finger. Peter had found this species disappointing because of its smallness and paleness, but the delicate spray of small flowers amused and enchanted Jerome because at the centre of each delicately frilled bloom was a wicked little cat face that might have been made of dark spotted velvet; this gave it that air of fragile sophistication that he found irresistible in women and in flowers.

"You are a pretty thing," he said, and bent his head to the plant, half shutting his eyes to breathe in a faint sweetness, a sweet moist green breath that reminded him of the great Brazilian forests. The first orchid he had ever owned had come from those forests, whose close sticky heat he had detested but where he now suddenly longed to be. He straightened himself and walked to the window where he stood with his hands in his pockets looking out at the woods. There was no need for him to live this lonely, often boring monastic existence. He could go where he liked, live as he chose, travel all over the world without any real need to turn all he saw and felt into words.

"Sylvie," he said, "this isn't life, for man or dog. The sun is shining. Let's call it a day and go out."

At the sound of the last word, Sylvie ran to the door but when she turned her head to look at him, her tail drooped. She saw that he did not mean it. The clock above the fireplace ticked on inexorably and she knew that it was not yet time. The habit and discipline of years would keep them both together in this room, prisoners of something she did not understand but accepted, until the allotted time had passed. Already she knew that he had forgotten her. Sylvie went back to the hearthrug and lay down.

Jerome looked at the clock. It was twelve; another three hours must pass before the time of his release. At three he always went to the orchid-houses after taking Sylvie for a brief run up the lane. To-day, because of the snow, she would have to content herself with a scamper round the house. Meanwhile, he told himself, if he went on walking about the room, something, a few words, might yet come. He had often been asked how he wrote his books, where he found his ideas. 'How do you *do* it, Mr. Jerome?' he had been asked only a month ago by a girl at a cocktail party. 'By hard work, my dear,' he had answered lightly, as he always answered this familiar question. He knew, of course, that this was not the whole truth. He worked hard for a naturally lazy man but he knew that hard work was not enough. The truth, of course, was that he did not know how he did it. The work was a fact but the rest was a mystery. He only knew that it was this hope of the inexplicable, the descent of the angel, that kept him in this room on a fine clear frosty day. It was this that he would miss if ever it deserted him. As if that thought were unbearable, he sat down at his table again and picked up his pencil.

The door opened and Peter carried a tray round the screen into the room, as he did every morning at twelve. The sleeves of his thick blue jersey were rolled up above his elbows and he was wearing a green baize apron. He put the tray down on a low table and pulled up an armchair.

"I made you some hot soup," he said to Jerome's back. "Just the thing for this weather. Do you more good than coffee, although I have brought that along, same as usual, with the cheese. You get the soup down first and then you'll feel better. Not going too well this morning?"

Jerome threw his pencil down and turned round in his chair. "You sound like a trained nurse," he said. "And you look like an out-of-date stage butler. What are you doing in that apron? Rubbing up the ancestral silver?"

"S'matter of fact, that's just what I was doing," Peter said. "I don't like to let those pieces your uncle left you turn black on the shelf."

Jerome pushed his chair back and walked over to the table. As

29

he sat down in the armchair, ignoring the tray but lighting a cigarette, he said, "Sounds like a waste of time to me. We never use it here. I should think that you have enough to do as it is."

Peter knelt down on the hearthrug and began to make up the fire. Sylvie moved her tail gently to acknowledge his presence, but she did not lift her head or take her eyes from Jerome's face. "You get on with your work and leave mine to me," Peter said. "I seem to be doing better this morning than you are. What's wrong?"

"What makes you think that anything is wrong?" Jerome asked. "But then you always know, don't you?"

"Knew soon as I opened the door. Room's full of smoke. When you're doing nicely, the ashtray's almost empty. Paper chucked all over the place. Can't you use the wastepaper basket?"

Peter got to his feet and began to pick up the balls of paper that littered the floor. "Can I put all this in the fire?" he asked. "Or will you curse me later if I do because there'll be something on one you want?"

"There's nothing on any of them worth a thought," Jerome said, as he took the lid off the soup bowl. "I don't know what's the matter with me this morning."

"Perhaps it's another play coming on," Peter said. "It might easily be. It's over two years since the last."

"Oh, no! God forbid—" Jerome said. "Not until I have this novel straightened out."

The two men stared at each other with something like dismay. Peter had never read one of Jerome's books, but he was proud of the plays and he kept a book of their press-cuttings. He seldom left the house except to go down to the village, or to drive the boxes of cut orchids to Woodstreet, the nearest town, and in the last fourteen years he had only braved the journey to London for his annual visit to the Orchid Show and to attend the first night of each of Jerome's plays. Wearing a blue suit smelling of mothballs, he would watch the stage critically from the back of a box and return to the house by the first train the next day. For Peter, a new play meant that the household would be upset for a least a week, meals at all hours, fetching and carrying, little sleep. Eventually it would mean that Sylvie would have to spend one night with Mrs. Robbins at the farm, and that he would have to trust the furnaces and greenhouses to Alvin, her youngest son, who worked for Jerome as gardener and handyman. For Jerome a play meant an interruption to his real work. All his plays had been light and pleasing, sharp as a needle, witty and gaily outrageous, and each had been written at the same speed. 'Jerome tosses them off,' his friends said. 'That odd bird, old J, shuts himself up for three days in that eyrie of his and there you are!' Jerome had never contradicted this irritating legend which ignored the weeks of laborious shaping and re-writing, usually done with Michael in the flat, or in the theatre itself.

"A play?" Jerome said crossly. "Not a hope! I haven't an idea in my head, not the ghost of an idea. I'm getting old, played out. I have dried up, that's the trouble."

"Heard that before," said Peter. "Don't you believe it. That won't happen, not to you. Perhaps it's the weather. Snow upsets some people, makes them restless. Went to Sylvie's head it did this morning. Quite wild she was. The trouble I had to get her to come in out of the woods."

"I like snow. It usually makes me feel settled and cosy. No, I'm fed up and bored, yes, plain bored."

"You've only been back a month," Peter said accusingly. "The trouble is, you didn't stay long enough, not as long as you meant. Surprised I was when you turned up, not even giving me a ring, driving too fast back up the lane, looking like thunder. 'Something's gone wrong,' I said to myself. 'The Captain usually comes back settled down, sleek and happy as a tom-cat full of cream!' "

"How revolting!" Jerome said. "And how often must I tell you not to call me Captain? If you want to know, I was running away, Peter."

"Doesn't sound like you. I don't want to know. Don't say anything you will be sorry for later."

"I'm always telling you things I'm sorry for later," Jerome said. He looked down at Peter, and said, "Do you know, I really believe that if I hadn't been such a righteous fool, or such a coward, I wouldn't have worked so badly all these last weeks or be sitting here now wasting my time."

Peter got to his feet and picked up the ashtray from the writing-table. As he emptied the cigarette butts into the fire and knelt down again to sweep the scraps of charred paper from the hearth, he shook his head and muttered to himself.

"I can hear you, you old misogynist," Jerome said, "but it is no use blaming everything on women. Forget it, Peter. I'm tired of slogging away, that is the real trouble. If I don't do better this evening, I will take the car out and be off."

"Not to-day, you can't," said Peter. "Not in this snow. You haven't put your nose out, but I tried to get down to the post-box. Thick in the lane, that's what it is, and there's a drift piled up against the garage door. Even if we dug the car out, it'll be deeper still down by the gate. No, we won't get the car or the van out for days. The wireless says that there's more snow to come, and they'll be right for once. Looks set fine and clear, all sun out there, doesn't it? But I feel snow in my bones."

Peter stood up and feeling in his trouser pocket pulled out a sheet of paper. "Mr. Michael rang up same as usual," he said. "Told me not to worry you. Nothing important. He sent off that American contract, he said, and there are some papers in the post for you to sign. He said to tell you that Miss Cleghorn sends you this message: 'Why haven't you told her why you left in such a hurry without a word to her? She hopes you haven't got into any mischief, and that Peter is looking after you.' Here, I have written it all down."

As he handed the paper to Jerome, Peter said, "I was forgetting —Mr. Stone rang up too. Seemed put out about something. Hummed and hawed a bit, and said not to disturb you, he didn't suppose it mattered."

"You seem to have had a busy morning. Has Alvin been up, or is the snow too thick?"

"He got through all right, later than usual. Made him bring in a lot of wood and he gave me a hand for a bit, although it's

Wednesday, his day off. They seem to think down at the farm that there's real bad weather coming. They're bringing the sheep in nearer. Mrs. Robbins sent up two chickens and some eggs with the milk."

Jerome glanced at the slip of paper before putting it on the fire, and Peter said, "Well, I'll be off. Eat up your cheese and drink your coffee and then, if I was you, give it up for to-day. Put on your long boots and take Sylvie out. If you go up-hill it won't be so bad. Do you good. Look as if your liver was playing up, you do. Never could stand much whisky, could you?"

"Oh, go away!" Jerome said. "Take the tray with you, I don't want any more. Here, Sylvie finish the cheese."

But Sylvie, for once, took no notice of him. She stood on the hearthrug with her head turned towards the window and her ears pricked. As they looked at her, she took a few steps out into the room and paused, one paw lifted, listening intently to something they could not hear; the long hair down her spine rose slowly. Suddenly she bounded on to the window-seat and rearing up against the glass looked down the lane. Her growl, deep in her throat, was muffled but her bark, when it came, filled the room with a wild angry clamour.

"Shut up, Sylvie," Jerome cried and Peter, putting the tray down again, said, "Now, now Sylvie, don't be a silly girl—it's only the post-van at the gate, if it's anything."

Their voices were lost in the tumult. The deep threatening bays rebounded from the walls and set the door shaking, but when the two men reached the window and looked out, there was no one below them in the lane.

"Be quiet," Jerome commanded and at once the barking stopped, but when he put his hand on her collar and tried to pull her down from the seat, Sylvie refused to move and braced herself against him.

"Peter is right, the snow must have gone to your head," Jerome told her. "There's no one there, Sylvie. Be quiet!"

Sylvie can hear what we can't," Peter said. "Wait a minute— she means it. She isn't just having us on."

He put his hand on Sylvie's back and leant forward to peer past her down the lane. "What did I tell you?" he cried. "There you are, look at that!"

Something had rounded the corner by the clump of fir trees and was coming up the lane towards them between the snowy banks; at that distance it looked rather like a bear, a dark shape moving heavily against the whiteness but, as it struggled on, the three watchers at the window saw that it was a girl wearing a fur coat.

"Oh, no!" Peter cried, and he looked reproachfully over Sylvie's head at Jerome.

Jerome was staring unbelievingly down the lane. He knelt on the window-seat, pushing Sylvie to one side, and brought his face close to the glass.

"Well!" he said after a moment. "I'll be damned—"

The girl had nearly reached the house. She was too busy trying to force a way through the snow to be conscious of the three heads at the window. As they watched, she staggered and fell on to her knees. Peter made a sudden movement, but Jerome put out his hand restrainingly.

"Not yet," he said. "Leave her alone. She is young and tough. No one asked her to come."

He was smiling. It was not a pleasant smile and Peter, who was watching him, shook his head again and muttered something under his breath. Jerome took no notice of him. He was intent on the girl who had struggled to her feet. Standing with her legs awkwardly apart and the heavy coat slipping from her shoulders, she was trying to wipe the snow from her dress. Suddenly she flung her wet hair back and looked up at the window; her eyes seemed enormous and dark in her white face. As Jerome opened the window and leant out, her mouth opened in a small cry that sounded like a mew.

"What are you doing here?" Jerome called down to her, and Sylvie, who had been watching from the window with surprised interest, looked quickly up at him and growled again.

The girl stared up at the window, and then held out her arms like a child. The wide fur cuffs slid back from her wrists showing gold bangles from which hung small dangling charms.

"You needn't think that I'm coming down to help you," Jerome told her, leaning his arms on the window-sill. "I didn't ask you to come. Turn your little fanny round and go back the way you came. It will be easier down-hill."

Her mouth opened again in astonishment. She flushed and,

pushing her hair back from her face, cried in a shrill voice, "Jerome, when I have come all this way! I have lost my shoes. I would never get back to the car. It's stuck in a huge drift. Anyway, if you leave me here I'll get pneumonia, I'll die. This is a wild place. There was a noise—a baying—sounded almost like wolves—"

Jerome laughed, and she glared up at him, beside herself with temper and fear. "Now you look exactly like an angry and bedraggled little cat," he told her. "Spitting won't help you. Nor will tears."

He stood back from the window and turned to Peter. "Better go and fetch her in," he said. "We can't leave her there."

"Fetch her in yourself, Mr. Holt," Peter said.

He took Sylvie's chain out of his trouser pocket and clipped it to her collar. "You come with me, Sylvie," he said. "The less we have to do with this the better. Apart from anything else, women mean trouble." Peter pushed the unwilling Alsatian off the window-seat and started for the door.

"Go and run a hot bath, bring brandy and blankets, and don't be a fool," Jerome told him. "Leave Sylvie alone. She can be trusted to behave herself and keep her temper."

He turned to the window again and, leaning out, said to the girl who stood knee-deep in snow with her arms hanging forlornly at her sides, "Listen, Una, go on a few yards until you come to a flight of steps. They lead to my front door. I will be waiting for you at the top—I'm not getting myself soaked for your sake."

37

Una looked up at him doubtfully. "Go on, you obstinate little donkey," he said, more gently, and she set off obediently along the front of the house, hitching her coat on to her shoulders and pulling her skirt up to her thighs. Jerome waited, smiling to himself, until she turned her head to see if he were watching her, then he shut the window quickly and turned back to the room. Peter had disappeared. Sylvie, her chain trailing, was standing in the middle of the room, looking at him uncertainly. The hair of her ruff was still raised and she growled softly once again as she turned from him to face the door.

"You stay here," he told her. "Sit now, and be good." He gave her head an absent-minded pat as he hurried past her into the hall.

4

Jerome opened his front door which was seldom used, turning the key and undoing the chain, and let a shaft of sunshine and a flood of cold air into the house. Snow spilled on to the door mat. As he stood shivering on the top step, he felt a light touch against his leg, a diffident and apologetic nudge; Sylvie, the usually docile and obedient, had followed him into the hall and now stood close beside him alert with feminine curiosity and possessiveness. Before he could rebuke her, the girl appeared below

38

them; he looked down on her pale silky head and at a small bare hand, that was blue with cold, clutching the iron balustrade. From this foreshortened view, she seemed very small and insignificant. As he stepped forward and held out his hand to help her she looked up into his face.

"I'm frozen," she said accusingly. "I'm soaked through."

"Serves you right," he told her, "I didn't ask you to come."

The sleeve of her coat was wet and heavy under his hand as he helped her into the hall. She shivered and he could hear her teeth chattering.

"Peter," he called. "Hurry up with that brandy."

As he pulled the wet coat from her shoulders, letting it drop to the floor, and turned her towards the sitting-room, she cried out and shrank back against him. Peter was standing at the foot of the stairs, holding a blanket over his arm and carrying a bottle and a glass on a tray; the light from the front door fell on to his face.

"It's only Peter," Jerome said quickly, and saw that she was not looking at Peter.

Sylvie, who was not used to strangers, had withdrawn when Jerome brought the girl into the hall and was now standing in the shadow of the stove watching the scene with a puzzled enquiring look; she was still ruffled but more bewildered than hostile.

"Keep that dog away from me!" the girl cried, as she held Jerome's arm. "It's enormous—like a wolf."

39

"You little goose," Jerome said. "Are you afraid of an Alsatian? That's my gentle, harmless Sylvie."

At the sound of her name, Sylvie moved out into the centre of the hall but, as if she realized that this was not the moment for polite greetings, she did not approach the girl. Una began to laugh, high shaky laughter that soon changed to sobs.

Peter hurried into the sitting-room, set the tray down on a table, spread the blanket over the big sofa which he pushed up to the fire, and turned to help Jerome.

"Hysterics," he said in a disgusted voice. "Better get her in here quick. I'll take her other arm. Trust a woman to make as much commotion and bother as she can."

Between them they half carried, half dragged the girl into the room and put her down on the sofa in front of the fire. Sylvie, pausing to sniff distastefully at the fur coat where it lay on the polished boards, ran after them. Never before had she seen a human being who behaved in this odd noisy fashion.

The girl was sitting on the sofa with her hands over her face. She was sobbing and catching her breath, but the laughter had stopped. Jerome was standing helplessly beside her holding a glass of brandy. As Sylvie, still puzzled but deeply interested, approached them, Peter said impatiently, "Give me the glass. Here, Miss, stop that nonsense if you don't want a good slap. Drink this at once."

To Jerome's surprise Una took her hands from her face. She accepted the glass meekly, emptied it, coughed, and gave it back to him. Then she pushed her damp hair behind her ears, took a handkerchief out of the neck of her dress, wiped her face and, holding the handkerchief now rolled into a ball between both hands, looked up at Jerome.

Her lips were still trembling but she managed to say in a furious voice, "Don't stare at me like that. Anyone would lose their heads after the time I have had. That dog of yours was the last straw. Why do you want to keep a great wild savage-looking thing like that? Frightening people out of their senses—there it is again, don't let it come near me."

"Sit down, Sylvie," said Jerome, and Peter poured out another glass of brandy.

Una pushed the glass away. "I don't want brandy," she said, looking round the room in a distraught way. "I want a comb. I left my bag and gloves in the car. I must have my bag."

"We will fetch it for you later," Jerome said soothingly, and she turned on him.

"How selfish of you, Jerome, to live in an outlandish place like this," she said. "Hiding yourself in all these trees, giving everyone so much trouble—"

Peter made a scandalized sound, but Jerome, looking down at her white shaking face and furious blue eyes, began to laugh.

"How dare you laugh at me?" she cried, and now she was shaking with temper as well as with cold. "I have had a terrible time, I'm frozen and starved. I drove all night and spent hours stuck in that drift and hours more getting up to this house, all because of you, and then you laugh." She started to weep again and, turning her back on him, threw herself down on the sofa with her face in its cushions.

Jerome ran his hand through his hair and, looking across the sofa at Peter, said, "What shall we do now?"

Peter shrugged his shoulders. "That's not for me to say, Mr. Holt," he said. "This is nothing to do with me. I ran the bath as you told me, must be cold again by now."

"Of course—she must get these wet things off, have a hot bath and some food." Jerome leant down and touched the girl's shoulder. "Una, did you hear me?" he said. "Come upstairs. You will feel better once you are dry and warm and have had something to eat."

She sat up slowly and with her hair hanging over her face said, "I couldn't walk another step. I won't leave this fire. Give me a towel and a dressing-gown or something."

Peter started towards the door and Jerome said, "Bring a comb with you while you are about it. We must do our best to seem hospitable, I suppose."

As the door shut, Una slid on to her knees on the hearthrug and held out her hands to the fire. Sylvie retreated behind the armchair but no one noticed her.

"I wish I could get right into that fire," Una said. "I didn't know anyone could be so cold. I'll never stop shivering again. Help me, Jerome."

She held out her hand to him and he took it reluctantly in his.

"Why should I help you?" he said. "I didn't ask you to come here."

At once she pulled his hand to her face and rubbed her cold cheek against it.

"Don't be cross," she said. "Be a little kind. I couldn't help it. I had to come. I couldn't live another moment without you."

Before he could speak or pull his hand away, Peter knocked at the door and, opening it at once, came into the room carrying a bath towel and a navy-blue padded silk dressing-gown embroidered with sprawling gold Chinese dragons.

"Will this do?" he said, looking at Jerome. "It's the one Miss Cleghorn gave you. You never wear it here—must have brought it back from the flat by mistake. The comb's in the pocket."

Peter turned back to the door. "What next?" he asked. "Do I run another bath or get some food?"

Una, who was rubbing her hair with the towel, answered him through the folds. "Food please," she said. "I have had nothing to eat except some sandwiches in a pub late last evening. Could I have some tea and bread and butter, and a steak, a huge steak and perhaps some potatoes?"

Peter said, "Anything else, Miss?" and looked at Jerome again, but Jerome only smiled. "Do what you can, Peter," he said. "And don't be too long about it."

Una looked up as the door shut. "I don't like that man," she said. "He is disagreeable and impertinent. There's something wrong with his face too. Who is he? A servant?"

"Not exactly," Jerome said. "He does his work and I do mine, mutual benefit. His name is Peter Baines but everyone calls him Peter." But Una was not interested in Peter. "Help me up," she said. "I really can't stand alone. You will have to help me get this dress off. It's shrunk or something."

Jerome pulled her to her stockinged feet and holding her by the shoulders looked into her face. "You little nuisance," he said softly. "I would like to give you a good shaking. Coming here won't do either of us any good."

She stared up at him defiantly. "I'm here," she said. "You can't get rid of me because of the snow. Why not make the best of it, Jerome?"

When he did not answer, she cried, "Be angry if you like. All I want is to get these wet clothes off and to be warm. I can't stop shivering."

She twisted her shoulders from his hands and turning her back on him tugged at the hem of her dress. It was a black dress that he had seen before and thought too old for her, although he had told her that it suited her, that it showed off her fairness. He wondered if that was why she was wearing it.

"Not a very suitable garment for such an expedition," he said as he watched her struggles. "Why are you so wet? You had a coat. You will never get that off without help."

"Then help me," she said. "Pull it over my head."

As he stepped back, holding the wet dress in his hands, Una picked the towel up and held it in front of her. "Go away," she said. "I don't want you here."

"Not very consistent, are you?" Jerome said. "The most sensible thing you could do would be to get the rest off and to let me give you a good rub-down. You look quite blue, not at all alluring at the moment, my dear."

"Must you try to make everything cheap and nasty?" Una said. "Go away. Leave me alone."

"Just as you like," said Jerome. "I will be in the hall, call out when you are ready. Perhaps when you have had something to eat you will feel better, more yourself. At the moment your emotions seem a trifle mixed!"

"Please take your dog with you," Una called after him. "I don't want her staring at me either."

Jerome opened his front door again and stood in the flood of winter sunshine looking out. Never before, it seemed to him, had the sky above the hills been so blue and clear; there was not a wisp, a hint of cloud; but it was very cold. His breath hung on the air before him and the snow had not melted in the strong sunshine; when he walked out on to the top step, it crunched under his feet. Sylvie ran down the steps waving her tail. He said, "Not yet, Sylvie," but he did not know that he had spoken to her. He was trying to decide if he would be glad or sorry to see dark clouds rise up above the hills and spread out towards the house.

He could not remember where he had first seen Una. She was a young actress and it could have been on the stage or at a rehearsal, perhaps of one of Martha's plays. He had noticed her vaguely at cocktail parties, but he had first become conscious of her less than two months ago when someone had brought her to the flat with the usual stage crowd, and then it had only been because of the way she had stared at him. She was a pretty girl, a pale blonde, but too thin and too intense for his taste; his instinct had been to leave her strictly alone. He avoided young girls as a rule. Although he enjoyed looking at them, they bored and terrified him, especially if they were earnest and intelligent as Una was. Women between thirty and forty, discontented wives, smart, bored and restless women, were the ones who came his way. He was not conceited where women were concerned and a young girl's adoration had surprised and flattered him as it would have flattered most middle-aged men. He had told himself that this girl knew very well what she was about, that a successful playwright can be of use to a young actress who still had her name to make, but he had known from the first that this fact had nothing to do with Una's persistence.

She had intrigued him. He had wanted to know what went on in that pale little head and, although he had not exactly encouraged her, he had taken her out, watched her, listened while she talked, as she loved to do. At first he had been amused and interested, then alarmed and even slightly shocked. When he had tried to reason with her, to withdraw, it had been too late. He had told himself that he was no seducer of young girls and that anyway she did not attract him sufficiently to make the trouble he saw ahead worthwhile. He had taken flight, left the flat hurriedly after a last scene that had shaken him. When he drove back to the house a month ago he had felt virtuous and also distinctly cross. He had been a fool, for his work's sake if for nothing else. A successful love affair always refreshed him. If he had taken what had been so openly, so honestly offered, he would not have thought of the girl again once he was back in the house.

Jerome looked back at the hall. Una's fur coat had disappeared and the hall gave no sign of the invasion it had suffered; it looked exactly as it had always done with its polished floor and rugs and the big white porcelain stove that burned only logs. Peter's treasured open-work brass lantern, brought back long ago from one of his voyages, hung from the ceiling; at night the chequered pattern of light and shade it cast on the floor still irritated Jerome but he had never had the heart to tell Peter to take it away. The door to the workroom was open. He walked quickly across the hall and closed it firmly, turning the key in the lock and putting the key in his pocket. When he went towards the sitting-room door, he no longer looked like a bored and sleepy owl; his eyes were wide open and alert and he was smiling.

Una was lying on the sofa with a cushion behind her back and the blanket wrapped neatly round her legs. She was wearing his dressing-gown with the cuffs turned back and the lapels folded across her chest. Her damp hair had been combed behind her ears and this made her look demure, even childish, but she was smoking composedly. She looked up as Jerome opened the door and smiled at him.

"I'm sorry," she said. "I behaved very badly but I was looking such a sight. I haven't been myself since I went to the flat and

Michael told me that you had gone. You could at least have written."

She leant forward and patted the sofa. Jerome sat down obediently and looked at her curiously. The first time he had really looked at her, two months ago, he had noticed that her collar bones were too prominent, a thing he detested in women. He had always disliked the way she dressed and her thin long-legged body had never excited him, but he had found her pale hair fascinating because it was very pretty and soft and she seemed to have so many ways of doing it. She had a nice little nose set at an unusual angle and her skin was unnaturally white. He had never seen her face as it now was, exposed, innocent of powder and lipstick, washed clean and shining by the snow. The eyebrows and eyelashes, which she usually covered with mascara, were so pale a gold that they were almost invisible; this made her seem strangely innocent and unaware. It was a child's face, sexless and touching. Now that she was not wearing the scent she usually used too freely, she seemed to him like a well-cared-for child, fresh and clean and wholesome, that gives out its own grassy faint sweet smell. Feeling ashamed of himself, he put out his hand and touched her cheek which was cold and firm. Her eyes, which he had always thought too light a blue, darkened as he looked at her.

"My dear child," he said. "What was there to write? I had said it all to you that last evening in the flat. I thought that I had made myself almost brutally clear."

"You talked a lot, a lot of nonsense. You said that I was too

48

young, that you were too old. That I ought to get married and have children, that I ought to work hard and think of my career. Then, when I told you that nothing meant a thing to me except you, you said that you didn't find me sufficiently attractive to make it worthwhile, that it would only lead to trouble for you. First you tried to make me think that you were being noble, refusing to take advantage of a young girl, and then you tried to be brutal and tough. I ended up by not believing a word you said. Why did you ever have anything to do with me, why did you encourage me, if you wanted to put an end to it before it had begun? Why did you start it?"

"I didn't start it," Jerome said coldly. "May I remind you that I found you underfoot everywhere I went and that in the end I had to run from your pressing attentions?"

Una laughed. "Poor Jerome," she said, "how pathetic! The truth is that you are a bit of a coward, and also a rather nice and scrupulous person. I think that you don't quite know your own mind, my dear. Well, I know mine and that's why I'm here. I'll show you how much I love you."

"Hush!" Jerome said. "I can hear Peter in the hall." He jumped up and moved away from her across the room; he had never liked a woman to know her own mind too well; persistence bored him and he found such open adoration too much, even ridiculous. As he opened the door, Sylvie sidled in giving him a reproachful look. He saw at once that Peter, who was carrying a tray, was in a temper and, suddenly furious himself, he said, "What have you been doing? You have been a hell of a time."

49

Peter only looked at him searchingly and then gave him one of his twisted grins. "What a morning!" Peter said. "Nothing but trays. Might as well be at sea again."

"Here you are, Miss," he said, as he put the tray down on Una's knees. "Best I could do. Two eggs, bread-and-butter and tea. There's a chicken for dinner, but any meat there is I'm keeping for Sylvie. Can't tell when we'll get any more."

Una, for the first time, looked directly at Peter. The firelight lit her face. She did not look away as most people would have done but stared up at him with frank horrified curiosity. Peter stared back at her defiantly.

Jerome shut the door and hurried towards them but it was Sylvie who created a diversion. At the sound of her name she came forward and stood beside Peter, looking up at him as if she were asking him for a sign that would show her how she was to behave towards this strange being, this visitant from another world who, since she was now eating here, had obviously come to stay and should be made welcome. Sylvie was inexperienced, bashful and uneasy, but she knew her manners. Getting no help from Peter, she essayed a greeting, putting a paw on the edge of the sofa.

Una, withdrawing her gaze almost reluctantly from Peter, turned her head and looked straight into Sylvie's face whose brown eyes were on a level with her own. As she cried out and shrank back, Jerome said, "Down, Sylvie!" and pulled the Alsatian away by the collar. Sitting down in his armchair by the fire, he held her between his knees.

"I'm being silly again," Una said. "I like dogs, really. I had a Yorkshire terrier once. It's just that this one is so big, so like a wolf. I seem to have wolves on my mind. It must be this place, all those trees and the snow, more like Russia or Norway than England."

"Sylvie is the most gentle of creatures," Jerome said. "She wouldn't hurt a hair of your silly little head, would you, my beautiful?"

"Don't be too sure of that," said Peter. "She's a female after all."

Una laughed. "Then the sooner we make friends the better for me," she said. "Let her go, Jerome. Come here, what's-your-name, Sylvie? Here, have some of my bread and butter."

She put out her hand and Sylvie politely took the proferred piece of bread, held it for a few seconds in her mouth, and dropped it quietly on the hearthrug.

"Couldn't show her feeling more plainly if she was human, could she, Miss?" Peter said.

His voice was harsh and Una flushed. "I'm sorry," she said uncertainly, but Jerome interrupted her. "That will do, Peter," he said. "I will put the tray in the hall when Miss Una has finished. Take these wet things and hang them in the kitchen."

Peter bent down and picked up the small pile of wet clothes from the hearthstone. "Not in my kitchen," he said. "I'll put them in the furnace-room."

As he opened the door, he said, "Better come with me, Sylvie. The sooner you learn when you're not wanted the better."

51

"Oh, go away, both of you!" Jerome cried, "I have had enough of this—out, Sylvie!"

Sylvie stared at him as if she could not believe what she heard and then walked with dignity to the door. As Peter closed it with ominous gentleness, Jerome turned on Una. "Couldn't you have pretended not to notice?" he said. "There was no need to stare. Peter won't forgive you."

"No one could help looking," Una protested. "He must be used to it. What happened to his face? No, don't tell me. It must have been something horrible and I don't want to know. Now you are angry with me again."

She lifted the tray and held it out to Jerome. "Please take this away, I don't want any more," she said. As he took it from her, she put her head down on her knees and said in a forlorn muffled voice, "I can't do anything right. I hate this place. I wish I hadn't come."

Her hair fell forward showing the nape of her neck which was white and tender and thin, a child's neck. Jerome, holding the tray, looked down at her, exasperated but moved by an uncomfortable sense of guilt and compassion. He put the tray outside the door and went back to her. After a brief hesitation, he bent down and put his hand on her head.

"I'm sorry," he said. "I shan't forgive myself. Don't cry, Una. I will get you away somehow and no one will ever know."

She sat up and looked into his face. "I had to come," she said. "I couldn't help it," and putting her arms round his neck she pulled his head down to her. "Get me away?" she said in his ear. "Oh, no! I'm here and I'm staying. You will be glad. I will make you glad."

Jerome sighed, but he let his face rest against her cheek. Her damp hair still kept the fragrance that he remembered, not a scent but an emanation of youth and health, the sweet cleanness of cut hay, of early summer, of the earth. He ran his hand over the dark silk of the dressing-gown and she made a sound, a little purr of satisfaction and triumph. At once he sat up, pushing her away from him and looking down at her said, "No, Una. We are not going to begin again. You needn't laugh, you shocking little humbug, I mean it."

He stood up and, taking a cigarette from the box on the chimney-shelf, began to walk up and down the room. It was far larger and more luxurious than his workroom but it, too, had been arranged to please himself and no one else. There were pots of orchids here too, standing on a long table in the window. He looked at the bookshelves, at his gramophone and radio, at the many pictures, at the table where he ate his evening meals, at the large soft shabby chairs. Una, lying on his sofa with her arms crossed behind her head, looked as out of place and unnecessary in this easy masculine room as the orchids did. She was watching him with a fond indulgent look that he had already seen that morning and that now exasperated him. He sat down abruptly in the armchair by the fire and said, "I think that you owe me an explanation. How did you find out where I live? I never use my professional name here, or my real name in London—I don't suppose you have ever heard it. This place is where

53

I work, I have gone to a lot of trouble to keep it a secret from my friends and my enemies. Only Michael and my lawyer know exactly where it is."

"And your agent," she said meekly, looking up at him.

"You wheedled it out of poor old Gilbert?" Jerome said. "You really are a little bitch, what a shame!"

"There is absolutely no need to call me names, Jerome," she said, sitting up and arranging the cushions more comfortably behind her back. "When I went to the flat I got no change out of Michael Johnson. He laughed at me and told me to run away and play. He said, 'Jerome is too busy for little girls.' He is a horrid young man but he thinks a lot of you. Then I went to Gilbert Stone's office and asked him frankly for your address. When I said that I meant your country address, he looked shocked and told me in that prim way of his that letters would be forwarded. There was a pile of letters on his desk waiting to be signed. The top one was to you. It began, 'Dear Jerome,' I could read that much upside down. I snatched it up and read the address his secretary had typed at the top: Jerome Holt, Esq., Badger's Farm Cottage, Woodstreet, and the rest. He was furious, but he couldn't do anything about it then, could he?"

Una laughed and, after a few seconds, Jerome laughed too. "Poor Gilbert," he said. "That was bad luck. He will be conscience-stricken. He might have warned me."

"He had no idea that I meant to come here. I let him think that I only wanted to write to you. I expect he thought that I was only another silly girl."

54

"You are an unscrupulous wily female."

"I'm not, honestly, Jerome," she cried. "Can't you see? This is serious for me, even if it isn't for you. I tried not to come. Even when I had the address I waited a whole day. Yesterday at that idiotic party I knew that I couldn't stand it a moment longer. I drove home, threw some clothes into a suitcase, and set out—I didn't even wait to change my dress or shoes. I drove all night. It began to snow. I reached your village early in the morning. No one was about but I knocked and knocked at a door until someone came and told me the way to this house. I wouldn't stay although they asked me to and told me that I would never get here because of the snow. I expect they thought I was mad or drunk or something. I was in such a fever to get to you. I found your gate and it was open, but then the car ran into that drift. The door wouldn't open and there I was. I was so tired that I just ran the engine to keep the heater going and went to sleep. When I woke up the sun was right up, the engine had stopped and I was frozen. It took me ages to get out of the car through the window—I had to push my coat out first. Getting through the drift was the worst part, and that hill. Why do you have to live in this outlandish place?"

"I have my reasons," Jerome said. "They seem good ones to me, but never mind that now."

He threw his cigarette into the fire and, leaning forward in his chair, looked at her searchingly. "There is more to you than meets the eye," he said. "This iron determination fills me with awe. It is worthy of a better cause. How old are you, Una?"

"Twenty-two. You know that."

"You often look much younger. Have you no one to keep an eye on you, to stop you doing this sort of thing?"

"But I have told you all about myself, Jerome," Una said. "You always seemed to be listening, but I don't believe you heard a word. My father is dead. My mother lives in a flat in Knightsbridge. She makes me an allowance and has given up worrying about me ages ago. She probably thinks that I'm still with Rosa who, as I told you, is on tour. I have no brothers, only two sisters. You have nothing to worry about."

"You think not? I have a conscience after all. Do you realize what kind of a man I am?"

"I know all about you, Jerome."

"I doubt it! Listen my child. I don't know what you have heard about me or what you have imagined, but I expect it is too highly coloured, far from the rather dull and sober truth. I am forty-five, set in my ways and selfish. I now live exactly as I want to live. I have no intention of letting any woman upset my life or my work."

"You have said all this before. Do stop being pompous."

"Very well, Una," Jerome said. "I give up. You came here at the right moment. Yesterday I would not have cared if you were here or not. As you know very well, you are young and attractive, a pretty warm little thing. I have no more scruples than the average man about taking what is offered to me on a plate, pushed under my nose in fact, but I want to make one point clear."

"I don't want to talk anymore," Una said. "I'm terribly tired. I want to lie here in front of the fire and go to sleep."

"You can keep awake a moment longer. If you stay here, you must understand that it is only because I can't get rid of you. I'm going down now to have a look at your car. If Peter and I can move her and the road is clear, you go back to-night, if not, you stay only as long as the snow does."

Una lay down and turned on her side. She pulled the blanket up over her shoulders and shut her eyes. "Run along then, dear," she said. "Take that dog of yours a good long walk. I'm so sleepy that I don't want even you."

Jerome stood up. He looked down at her, frowning and undecided. Then he made up the fire and walked softly to the door. As he reached it, Una sat up and said, "What about my suitcase? It's still in the car. My clothes won't dry for ages. I can't go about with bare feet and in a dressing-gown and blanket. And I must have my handbag, I simply must."

"Peter and I will fetch it," Jerome told her. "You go to sleep like a good girl."

"You can't miss the car, even if it's half-buried in snow," she said, as she lay down again. "It's a bright red little car."

5

The sun was close to the western rim of hills and the late wintry sunshine, slanting through the trees, laid their long blue shadows on the snow that under a powdery crust was as hard as ice. It was very cold, an exhilarating, bright sparkling coldness, spiced with the scent of firs.

Jerome leant on his ski sticks at the top of the long slope and looked down the fireline: a breadth of pure untouched snow between the trees. He was out of breath and his legs were aching from the steep climb through the woods, but he was feeling pleased with himself and glad that it had suddenly occurred to him to get out the skis he had not used for years and to take this roundabout way to Una's car. The small enclosed world of the valley lay below him, dazzlingly white, dark green and blue under the calm pale spread of sky. The house was hidden in a sea of trees to his right; only a blue twist of smoke showed him where it was. He could not see the lane where Peter, carrying a spade and pulling the wood sled behind him, must by now be making his slow way down to the gate, but a loop of the main road lay far below him, winding through the spruce plantations. Far away, under the opposite rim of hills, were open white fields and the roofs of the village.

This was his own small private world. He seldom left the

house except to walk in the woods but he was known and accepted in the village and the valley farms as Mr. Holt, Peter's Captain, Sylvie's owner, a writing gentleman, perhaps a little odd in his solitary ways but generous with his money and no trouble to anyone. This anonymity was precious to him. He knew that his writing name would mean little if anything to anyone round about but even here in this remote place, since the grid had come to the valley, every other house in the village and most of the farms sported the familiar spidery excrescence, and he had refused firmly to appear in any television programme. He wondered at which door Una had knocked early that morning. The thought annoyed him; he shrugged it away and looked down at Sylvie who stood by his side, ears pricked, looking out and down as he had done.

Sylvie showed no sign of the steep climb and was not even breathing more deeply. She was young and she climbed these wooded slopes every day; they were as familiar to her as his workroom was to him. How swiftly and lightly she had skimmed over the snow, running from tree to tree, weaving a quick pattern round him, glad to make him free of her world of the woods but impatient at his heavy slowness as he plodded upwards. In a moment, if he had not forgotten how to ski, he would astonish her and leave her far behind. She had been suspicious of his skis at first, these strange long extensions that his feet had sprouted, but had soon accepted them as she would accept any change he chose to make in his appearence or anything, however incomprehensible to her, that he would do.

"Here we are, Sylvie," he said to her, "on top of our world. Shall we go on and on, just the two of us, and never go back?"

Sylvie looked up at him, not sure what he wanted of her but eager to be on the move again, to be off, it did not matter where. He laughed at her eager look and sparkling eyes and said, "Come on then, Sylvie. Down we go—down, down, down!"

She barked joyfully, leapt up to touch his cheek with her cold muzzle and, tail waving, set off down the slope in enormous bounds. Jerome waved his sticks above his head, gave a loud yodelling cry, and plunged after her.

He had tucked his trouser legs into woollen stockings and was wearing his sheepskin jacket and an old green felt hat with a peacock feather stuck into the band. His ski boots, which he had fetched from the box-room with his skis, were stiff with old dubbin. He was soft and out of training, but he did not care. As he made his first christie he felt young and free and confident and happier than he had been for years. The cold pure air rushed past him, filling his mouth and stinging his nostrils, plucking the hat from his head. The trees flashed towards him, leant away and passed him. He swooped and turned, finding something of his old skill. Sylvie was far behind; he could hear her frantic barking, but suddenly here was the road and the end of the lane. The top of his gate-posts stuck up out of the snow and there was a gleam of red that must be Una's car. Jerome fell and lay sprawling, laughing and panting, with snow down his neck and in his eyes.

Sylvie was beside him, pawing frantically at the snow and whining with anxiety. He felt her warm breath on his cheek and then her tongue in his ear. As he sat up, she fell upon him, overwhelming him with her delight at finding him alive, covering him with caresses. He held her off with one gloved hand deep in her ruff and looked at her, struck as he so often was by her beauty. The broad and noble forehead was dark against the snowy background and the soft hair in the inside of her ears was thick with shining snow crystals. Round her neck and across the pale silver-cream of her chest were two broken necklaces of dark hair. Her eyes, usually as bright and clear as the water in the bed of a hill stream but now misted and dark with emotion, met his and he said with mocking tenderness, that did not mock her but himself, "My beautiful, my snow princess, diamonds become you, don't they?"

The affection in his voice was too much for her. Quivering with joy, she leapt on him again, pushing him down into the snow and licking his face.

"That's enough," he cried. "Let me get up. Stop it, Sylvie, do you hear?"

At once she darted away and as he struggled up, brushing the snow from his clothes, returned to lay his hat at his feet.

Peter in his duffle coat and knitted cap stood in the lane below them, knee-deep in snow, examining the car. As Jerome, holding his skis over his shoulder, slid down the bank to join him, Peter said, "I heard Sylvie barking up on the hill. You must have climbed quite a way. Do her good but you're not used to much exercise these days, are you? It will be all we can do to dig this car out before dark. I have cleared the snow off the windscreen and dug around the bonnet, but that's all I can do alone."

Jerome put his head through the open window. The interior of the little car was warmer than the outside air and it still smelled faintly of Una's scent. The windows were heavily frosted over and in the dimness the red leather cushions gleamed cosily. A silver medallion of St. Christopher hung from the ignition key and a thick nylon rug and a pair of gloves lay on the floorboards. The scarf, handbag, and packet of cigarettes on the front seat gave the small space an intimate air.

"Nice little car," he said. "It doesn't seem to have come to any harm."

"Expensive but flashy," Peter said scornfully. "Scarlet paint and chromium! Not my cup of tea, or yours really. If we dig round the wheels we'll soon have them clear and then we can push her out on the road. The road's swept. Must have sent the snow plough along this morning." He began to dig round the rear wheels.

"Better bring the spade here and clear this door," Jerome said. "We will get the suitcase out. The car can stay where it is, for to-night anyway."

Peter straightened himself and looked at Jerome. "But we could have the whole box of tricks out on to the road in no time," he said.

"I suppose you would like me to turn that girl out to-night in the state she is in?" Jerome asked him.

"As you ask me, yes, I would," Peter said defiantly. "I heard you say that you didn't ask her to come here. This isn't the flat. This place is different, it's where you work. I think you ought to keep it that way."

Jerome did not answer. He seized the spade from Peter and began to hurl the snow from the car door. Sylvie, quivering with excitement, ran to help him and dug furiously beside him.

"You don't know what you're doing, poor innocent," Peter told her gloomily.

"Shut up, you old raven," said Jerome, "and give me a hand."

"Have it your own way," Peter said, "but I'm telling you that if you don't get that car out now you won't for days. Clouds are coming up already and it's far too cold. There's snow to come, lots of it, can't you feel it?"

"No, I can't. It's getting dark, that's all," Jerome said impatiently as he pulled the car door open.

A large white calfskin suitcase lay on the back seat. Beside it sat a small square box in the same leather.

"All set for a good long stay," said Peter. "You look out, Captain, the determined ones, the ones that know their own minds, are the worst by a long way."

"Lucky you brought the sled," was all Jerome said, as he put the scarf and handbag into his pocket, "I should never have thought of that."

Peter leant through the door and picked up the suitcase. "I

63

know women," he said. " 'Just one little case, steward,' meaning a ruddy great wardrobe-trunk. I'm not pulling my arms out for any woman ever again."

He threw the case onto the sled and piled coat and box and spade on top of it and, shutting the car door with a slam, started up the lane.

"Wait a moment," Jerome said. "We must put the window up and empty the radiator. Drop that rope and come here. What a pity we haven't got a dog harness. Sylvie could have pulled the sled."

As Peter made his way round the front of the car to open the bonnet, he said, "Harness Sylvie? What do you think she is, a great coarse husky? I'm surprised at you, Mr. Holt."

"Don't be an idiot," Jerome told him. "Dogs pull milk-carts all over the Continent and like it. You would think it fun, wouldn't you, Sylvie?"

Sylvie looked up into his face and waved her tail, but Peter said obstinately, "She isn't a working dog. She hasn't been brought up that way and she isn't pulling any milk carts or sleds while I'm around."

As he shut the bonnet and, plunging back through the drift, picked up the sled ropes again he said, "Look at us, carting all this stuff through knee-deep snow on a bitter afternoon like this! Two donkeys are enough, if you ask me. No one is going to make an ass of Sylvie if I can help it."

Jerome laughed, in high good humor again. "You old misanthrope," he said, "take the skis and give that rope to me.

'Do your own dirty work,' that's what you are longing to say, isn't it?"

He took the ropes from Peter and gave him the skis. "As for Sylvie," he said, "she can carry the lady's scarf, or do you think that beneath her? Come on, Sylvie, catch!"

To Sylvie, who had been bewildered and then made uneasy by the unexpected sight of the car, crouching like a red monster in the snow, this was a welcome and familiar game. She leapt to seize the scarf in mid air, then threw it up, pretending to herself and to Jerome that this was no scarf smelling of woman but something warm, alive and wriggling, that was trying to escape from her jaws.

"Gently, Sylvie! Don't tear it," Jerome called after her as she bounded away up the lane. She looked at him reproachfully over her shoulder, as well she might, for never since the days of her ignorant puppyhood had she harmed anything that she was given to carry.

"Good Sylvie, sweet Sylvie, that's the way," he called to her encouragingly, "Don't take it into the woods," and he walked up the lane, moving in Peter's tracks at a fair pace pulling the sled behind him. Peter, carrying the skis on his shoulder, gave the abandoned car a last regretful look and trudged after him.

At that moment, in the house, Una woke. She sat up in the strange darkening room, and almost at once knew where she was. The house was very still and she knew that it was empty except for herself. Throwing the blanket back, she stood up and gathered Jerome's dressing-gown round her and went to the win-

dow. The lane was deserted. The two men must still be busy
with the car. If she were quick there would be time for a hurried
exploration; she very much wanted to know exactly what kind
of a house this was. Una was inquisitive and she believed that
a house can give away a great deal about the people who live
in it, that a few minutes of uninterrupted looking and prying can
disclose more than hours of talk. She switched on the lights
and made a brief survey of the room, and then went into the
hall, moving silently on small bare feet which soon became cold
although the house was warm. In the hall, she looked up at
the brass lantern incredulously; then put her hand on the stove,
glanced at the radiators and nodded her head approvingly.
She looked into a small cloak-room and then tried the door
opposite the sitting-room; it was locked; she shook the handle
and frowned, but did not waste any time. Upstairs, she made a
quick tour of the two bedrooms, box-room and bathroom, switching on all the lights, opening the cupboards, smiling a little at
the austere and simple furnishing and the undistinguished colours, looking at herself in the small mirror on Jerome's chest of
drawers. There was not much to interest her up here, although
she could not have said even to herself what she had expected to
find, and carefully turning off the lights, she glided down the
stairs again and made for the kitchen. The kitchen intrigued
her. As she stood in the middle of the floor staring round her,
taking it all in from the smoke-stained ceiling to the slate
floor, her small pink lip curled with scorn; she looked at the

66

range as if she could not believe her eyes and spent some time examining Peter's saucepans. The cuckoo-clock striking four made her jump as she was opening a drawer in the dresser.

Feminine instinct drew her down a passage to the storeroom where she found not only a Frigidaire but well-stocked shelves that met with her approval. Beyond the storeroom was the furnace-room. She looked doubtfully at the large furnace and the piles of coal and logs beside it, which made so much work for Peter and which he had steadily refused to allow Jerome to change for oil-fired central heating; the furnace supplied heat for both houses and the orchid-houses, but this, of course, she could not know. Her clothes were hanging from a line above an array of old coats, gum-boots and other odds and ends which, she had to admit, were neatly arranged. A door at the end of the passage opened on to a short path and a vista of greenhouses; she shut it hastily and turned away. It did not take her long to discover Peter's bedroom and bathroom, which led out of the kitchen, and she only looked briefly into them; she was not interested in Peter. Una went into the hall again and stood in front of the locked door of Jerome's room. She did not know that it was his workroom, but she shook the handle angrily and tried to see through the keyhole. That this door was locked was the only odd discovery that she had made in this surprisingly ordinary, rather shabby if comfortable house that was obviously lived in only by men. She was still standing in the hall gazing at the door when she heard the sound of Peter's high sweet penetrating whistling in the lane. It did not take her more than a few seconds to turn out the hall light and to arrange herself on the sofa before the fire again.

On the hills the snow was still bright but all colour and life had gone from the valley with the setting sun. Lane and woods were in deep shadow and darkness had gathered under the trees. A pall of cloud was slowly spreading over the sky from the direction of the village and it was ice-cold in the lane, so cold that it was difficult to breathe. The silence of the winter evening was intense and broken only by the crunching of foot-steps and the hiss of the sled's runners on the snow. With the coming of night all illusion of tameness vanished from the woods. Here in the deep lane, close to the house, a mile or so from the village, in the heart of this busy over-crowded much-used land, Jerome and Peter might have been walking through one of the enormous forests of Finland or Siberia, or the cold badlands of Canada, anywhere untouched and wild where Sylvie, running before them with her long loping stride, was no longer their familiar but an advance guard of the wolf pack. But at the top of the lane the warm house was waiting for them. Jerome pushed his hat with the nodding feather to the back of his head, straight-ened his shoulders under the sheepskin jacket, and began to sing; this was something he did, very badly and out of tune, only in moments of exhilaration and exceptional well-being and when he was excited and pleased with himself. "Journeys end in lovers meeting," he sang. "Youth's a stuff will not endure."

Sylvie, intrigued by this manifestation of high spirits, returned to his side and, still holding the scarf in her mouth, trotted beside him looking up into his face, but Peter scowled and gave the sled a kick.

Jerome turned his head to look at him. "Cheer up, my old one," he said. "There is no need to walk like a mute at a funeral. Whistle your famous whistle, Peter, drown the hideous noise I'm making. It's a fine night and all is well, very well. Sylvie and I are as gay as larks."

"So I see and hear," Peter said sourly. "Feeling very different from this morning, aren't you? There's nothing like a spot of exercise for the liver, of course."

Jerome laughed uproariously and the excited Sylvie danced along at his side. As if this gaiety had infected even him, Peter pursed up his scarred lips and began to whistle as only he or a blackbird could.

But now the house was above them. The lighted windows of the sitting-room shone rosily out on to the snow. As they looked up, someone moved across the room. Jerome laughed again and, throwing the sled's rope to Peter, ran up the snow covered steps to his front door.

Sylvie and Peter were left in the lane staring after him.

6

The wind rose soon after six o'clock. As he peeled potatoes for dinner, Peter listened to the sound it made in the narrow open passage between the back door and the shed. The kitchen, in spite of the uncurtained windows, was warm and comfortable and full of the smell of roasting chicken. It was lit by the glow from the range and the harsh light of the unshaded electric-light bulbs hanging one over the table and the other above the red-covered chair. On the table beside Peter was a list of the stores in the storeroom and the fresh food in the larder; he looked at it with gloomy satisfaction.

An untouched plate of meat and biscuits stood on the paper behind the armchair; Peter wiped his hands, picked it up and walked to the door. Then he hesitated, shook his head and, putting the plate down in its place, went back to the table. The electric-light shone down on the pots of orchids which he had moved away from the cold glass; their glossy flowers with the deep bag-like lips seemed to stare at him disdainfully. For the first time he looked at an orchid with something like distaste and, pushing the pots carefully to one side of the table, began to cut up the half loaf that he had decided, for the honour of the house, to spare for bread sauce.

In the sitting-room where the brown velvet curtains across the windows moved slightly as the wind moaned round the house, Sylvie, who had refused her dinner half-an-hour ago, lay at Jerome's feet on the sheepskin hearthrug, twin to the rug in the workroom. Her half-closed eyes looked into the fire but her ears moved uneasily as she listened to the incomprehensible flow of talk that passed above her between the two armchairs drawn up one on each side of the fire.

"I like this room," Una was saying. "It's not at all beautiful, and it's untidy and a bit shabby—it could do with new chair covers, couldn't it? I like it because it's like you, warm and comfortable and big and interesting. But something about it worries me, something is wrong."

"It's a very ordinary room," Jerome said lazily. "What do you mean?"

He did not care what she meant, but it amused him to watch her while she talked. She talked rather prettily, showing her small white teeth, waving a hand, holding her yellow head on one side. He lay back in his chair with his feet in his old leather slippers stretched out to the fire and looked at her over the rim of his glass. After his hot bath, he had put on the dark blue dragon dressing-gown over the flannel trousers and had tied a white silk scarf round his neck; now he felt relaxed and at ease, only pleasantly tired, although his whole body ached from the unaccustomed hard exercise.

Una sat at the back of her chair with her legs drawn up

under her and a glass in her hand. Her hair, which shone from hard brushing or brilliantine, was pinned up and wound round her head until it looked more like a shining gold helmet or an elaborate bee's nest than hair. She was carefully made up and looked much older than she had done in her dishevelled state; there was nothing childish about her now, nothing to make him feel guilty or uneasy. She was wearing a crimson wool dress with two pockets and wide loose neck; it was full-skirted soft and loose, but pulled in tightly round her waist by a crimson cord. The warm colour became her extreme fairness; it was obvious that she knew it and that she also knew that he was watching her. Everything about her showed her determination to please: her smile, the movement of her wrists, the way she had carefully arranged her long legs to show her unusually pretty knees. One of her ridiculous spiked-heeled shoes had dropped from her foot which, curled against the dark cushions of the chair, looked small and helpless. She was a pretty creature, Jerome decided, not beautiful, her nose was too short and her forehead too narrow, not physically very attractive, being too thin, too small-breasted; but she was taking and she intrigued him. He liked the way she moved her head to show off her round chin and he enjoyed her laugh that was sweet and gay, if a little tinkling. As he studied her, smiling gently behind his glass, he decided that her animation was unforced after all, and the obvious coquetry that she was displaying in every gesture was almost unconscious, a young girl's natural desire to please.

"Why are you smiling like that?" Una said suddenly. "What have I said?"

Jerome roused himself to say, "I have no idea. I wasn't listening, I'm afraid."

She looked taken aback, and stared at him with her mouth a little open. Then she laughed, "And I thought that I was being intelligent and amusing," she said. "Never mind. Can I have another drink?"

"I suppose so, though I don't approve of whisky for you, it's a truly adult drink. You ought to stick to milk and an expresso, or tomato juice. There is plenty of sherry, but I don't keep any gin here, gin is for parties I always think. Help yourself, if you must, and bring me one, with water, not soda. I'm too comfortable and lazy to move."

He watched her put her foot into her shoe and stand up, stretching herself. She did not take the glass he held out to her at once but, with her back to the fire, looked critically round the room.

"It's the orchids," she said at last. "You have them all over the house, haven't you? Even in the kitchen? I wonder why."

"Peter brings my favourites, and his, into the house for a short time when they come into bloom," Jerome said, looking up at her. "I like to have them with me, where I can look up and see them when I want to without the trouble of going to the greenhouses. Don't you like orchids?"

"I like them in their proper place," Una said. "In glasshouses or pinned on my dress, or in a nice little box covered with cellophane after a show. They ought to be in the flat, not in this house. They are all wrong here."

Jerome stared at her, surprised and interested. "Now what makes you say that?" he said.

"This is a man's house," Una said slowly. "It's warm and plain, a little frowsty and a little doggy, if you know what I mean. It has everything it needs. It's all of a piece, true. It doesn't need anything added to it. Orchids don't suit it, and they don't suit you."

"Why not?" Jerome said, "Am I too large, too shaggy, not sufficiently sophisticated?"

Una looked at him. "Now you are laughing at me," she said. "I mean it. In spite of everything, you are kind and gentle at heart, I know you are. Orchids are cruel and heartless, and a little nasty."

As Jerome laughed, her eyes filled with tears. He stood up hastily and took her glass from her. "You know nothing about orchids or about me, Una," he said lightly. "You have been warned."

The sofa had been pushed far back into the room and the drink table stood beside it. Jerome poured whisky into the two glasses, added water and soda, and turned back to the fireplace. "Here you are," he said as he put the glass into Una's hand. "Sit down, my child, and drink that slowly, and don't talk so much. Let me just look at you, that's quite enough."

Una flushed. "Is that supposed to be a compliment?" she

said. "If it is, then you don't know anything about *me*."

Jerome put his arm around her shoulders. "I know that you are a soft pretty little thing. That's enough to go on with. I also know that tears become you even less than orchids do me. If you want to please me, no tears. Keep this light."

Una turned to him and pressed herself against him. She was trembling, and he said quickly, "Be careful! You will spill your drink and mine. Whisky is precious stuff at any time, but especially in winter on a cold and bitter winter night. If Peter's forebodings are right and we are going to be cut off from supplies, we will need every drop in the house."

She lifted her face to his and he kissed her gently and said, "Sit down, that's a good girl. Peter will be in at any moment to lay the table. I am famished after all that exercise on your behalf. Everything in its own good time and place, Una. The whole evening, the whole night, are before us."

Una pushed him away. "You are very sure of yourself, and of me," she said angrily, and then, as he shrugged his shoulders and sat down in his armchair again, stretching his legs out to the warmth of the flames, she cried, "No wonder you smile! Of course you are sure of me. You can be, Jerome. Why should love make me so silly, and touchy, so prickly? Why have I been rude to you and critical ever since I came to this house?"

"Because you are a woman, and women are as perverse as cats."

"Perverse? All I want is to love you. I'm here alone with you, and that is all that matters. I won't be serious, I won't bore you. Yes, let's keep it light."

Instead of going back to her own chair, Una sat down on the hearthrug beside Sylvie. "Have a drink, Sylvie," she said. "We can't have you feeling left out."

Sylvie sniffed at the glass politely and then wrinkled her nose and turned her head away.

"Don't let the bubbles put you off, my dear," Una said. "Here, lick it off my finger." She held out a wet forefinger and Sylvie, after an uneasy look up at Jerome, put out her long pink tongue and touched it.

"Oh what a face," Una said. "Look at her, Jerome! Come, try again, Sylvie. You will like it in time."

"Leave her alone," said Jerome. "Spring water is her drink, cold clean water straight from the earth. She doesn't even like tap water out of a bowl. There is a spring in the woods, above the house—"

But Una only laughed and, kneeling up, put her face close to Sylvie's raised head. "Tell me, Sylvie," she said, "as one female to another, does he really know what you like or feel? He is a bully, isn't he? He never likes you to try anything new. Have another lick, you like it really." Dipping her finger into her glass, she wiped it down Sylvie's muzzle.

"Don't tease her," Jerome said, but his voice was indulgent.

The two bright firelit heads close to his knees made a picture that charmed and pleased him. The girl's pale hair, the dog's gleaming silver-and-black ruff, shone with youth and health. He

76

shifted slightly in his chair to view them from another angle. Sylvie's dark and noble profile, seen against the background of leaping flames, had a bold and austere beauty very different from the white delicately moulded planes of Una's face. It amused him to see that of the two Sylvie had the longer eyelashes.

Sylvie suddenly rose to her feet and, ignoring the girl, walked past her and lay down again on the other side of the fire, resting her forelegs on the fringe of the hearthrug and her head on her paws and keeping her watchful gold gaze on Jerome's face. Una laughed again and wriggled into the vacated place at Jerome's feet. Leaning against his legs, she put her head back on his knees.

"I was willing her to do that," she said triumphantly.

"You really are a little devil," he said severely, but he smiled down at her and put his hand on her head.

"What have you done to your hair?" he asked her. "It's full of hard little pins."

"Don't you like it done up this way? I took a lot of trouble over it."

"It's pleasant to look at, a very nice spun-gold confection, but at the moment I would rather have it soft and loose."

"Then you shall have it as you like it," Una said, sitting up. "Your comb is probably still in the pocket of that dressing-gown. Give it to me."

As she put both hands up to her head and began to pull the hairpins from her hair, the gold bracelets slid down her thin forearms.

"Why do you wear those tiresome things?" he asked her. "They are like fetters. There should be nothing hard or heavy about you."

Una put a neat small pile of blonde hairpins down on the slate hearthstone and shook out her hair, which came to her shoulders. "They will come off," she said. "Anything else wrong with me, while we are about it?"

Her hair, as she ran the comb through it, stood out from her head as if every hair were made of thin gold wire and had a life of its own.

"Look! The frost has got into my hair," she said, handing up the comb to him. "I can't do anything with it. See what you can do." She put her back on his knees again and released the catch of each bracelet in turn and laid them down beside her on the hearthrug. "I always wear bracelets," she said, holding her hands up to show her bare wrists. "My arms feel lonely and naked without them. Anything else I can do to please?"

"That will do for the moment," Jerome said, as he passed the comb slowly through the hair which lay in a fan across his lap. It was silky and fine and it gave out a faint pleasing scent that was new and strange in his house. He began to play with it, letting the pale stuff slide through his fingers. There was a loud knock at the door and Peter, wearing a white coat buttoned over his dark blue jersey, came into the room.

Jerome took his hand away from her hair, but Una did not move her head; she stretched her legs out on the hearthrug and

78

picked up her glass. "Sylvie seems to have had most of this in spite of herself," she said.

Peter, who had paused in the doorway to look at the tableau by the fire, said indignantly, "Sylvie? You haven't been giving Sylvie that stuff? It isn't right. She wouldn't eat her dinner. She's upset in her feelings as it is."

Una rested her arm on Jerome's knee and turned to look at Peter. "I was only joking," she said. "Your precious Sylvie hasn't had a drop, she just turned her head away."

"Lay the table, Peter," Jerome said. "If that is what you mean to do. Then you had better bring Sylvie's dinner here. She will eat it for me."

Peter walked across the room and slid back a square of the oak panelling to show a hatch into the kitchen. Una sat up to watch him. "So you do have a hatch," she said. "I was wondering—it seemed a bit suburban, and too easy and obvious for this house."

"What do you mean?" Jerome said, as he put the comb back into his pocket. "This is a house like any other."

"Oh no, it isn't," Una said, and she laughed. "It might have been like any other house fifty years ago. When I woke up this afternoon I prowled round a bit. You don't mind, do you? I like looking at other people's houses. It seems impossible that this house and your London flat could belong to the same person. Here everything looks years behind the times, not enough years to make it exciting but enough to be quite out of date. That ridiculous brass lantern in the hall! Really, Jerome! It's a nice house, too. You ought to take some trouble with it. I like the shape of the rooms. I could make it quite perfect. I should paint all this panelling. Some of the furniture is good, I like mahogany."

"Most of it was left me by my uncle," Jerome said, "and some of it came from Peter's mother's house near Liverpool."

"Yes, I should use a lot of paint," Una said. "White paint in the hall too, I think. It's all rather dark. Those trees need cutting back. I should throw out that prehistoric range, of course, and put in an Aga, and change to oil-fired central heating, much less work than that old furnace. Do you use that great stove in the hall? It must eat logs. I see that you still have fireplaces in the bedrooms as well as the heating and that the one in your room is laid and ready. What a lot of work!"

"You don't know Peter," Jerome said. "He is as obstinate as a mule and he is a glutton for work. He won't let me make life easier for him. I have offered him an Aga, company electric-light, and a new system of central heating, besides humidistats and thermostats and sprays, that would halve his work in the orchid-houses, but he will have none of them. The only concession he has made is a little device that rings a bell in the kitchen and his bedroom if the temperature in the greenhouses falls too low or climbs too high, and that he does not always rely on because he wants to save electricity and switch off the engine at night. He only accepted it in the first place for the orchids' sake, not for his."

"How do you cope, Peter?" Una asked.

"The house is as we like it, Miss," Peter said. "Mr. Holt and I, we have our own ideas of comfort and have never found the need to consult anyone else."

"He means that you must take us as you find us, my dear," said Jerome. "That will do, Peter. Get on with it, or we will never have any dinner."

Una settled herself against Jerome's knees again, but she watched Peter as he pushed the sofa still further back and set up an oval gate-legged table in the middle of the room. "Do you always eat here, Jerome?" she asked, as Peter turned back to the hatch. "It's too big a table for one but not big enough for more than two. What do you do when you have guests?"

"We never have guests here, do we, Peter?" Jerome said.

Peter did not answer as he moved round the table, spreading a white tablecoth, setting out silver, knives and glass, with an absorbed air.

"Well, you have a guest now," said Una, "and I must say that you are doing her proud, Peter! A silver candelabra! I do love candles."

"Guests are invited," Peter said suddenly.

Jerome smiled and looked from Peter to the girl, but he said nothing. In the silence they all heard the wind beyond the curtained windows. The flames wavered on the hearth and a log fell with a small crash. Sylvie stood up and walked slowly towards the table.

"She is hungry," Jerome said. "Take her to the kitchen, Peter.

If she still won't eat, bring her plate here and I will see what I can do."

As the door shut, Una said, "That man hates me. What have I done now? You might have ticked him off, Jerome. I mean, that was rude."

"You were not exactly tactful, were you?" Jerome said softly, as he glanced towards the hatch. "But Peter dislikes all women, not you in particular. His wife left him when he was in hospital. She saw him at a difficult stage of the skin-grafting and said that she couldn't stand it. He took it very hard, poor man. He refused to go on with the treatment, said it wasn't worth it."

"You can hardly blame her, can you?" said Una, with a shudder. "How you can bear him round you all day, I can't imagine. What happened? Why do you have to have him here?"

"He was my batman. We were in North Africa together. It's a long story."

"Oh, no!" Una said, turning her head to look up at him. "I simply can't have that—that won't do for John Jerome. Famous men's men-servants are always ex-batmen or reformed safe-breakers. You should have thought of something more original."

She waved her hand at the room and said, "The orchids are bad enough. Surely you know that all well-known recluses in dressing-gowns grow orchids? An ex-batman as well is just too much. I'm disappointed in you."

"But I like orchids," Jerome protested, and was surprised to find how annoyed he was. "And Peter was my batman, no getting away from it. As for his face, he was making a cup of tea for me on a cold night in the desert when my primus exploded."

Una turned round and put her hand in his. "I call that a silly sort of thing to happen," she said. "It was probably his fault for not keeping the sand out of the primus, but if you must be responsible for him, I should think of a more exciting story. Saving your life from Rommel, or Arabs, or a bomb going off or something."

She rubbed her cheek against his hand and said, "Still, it shows that I was right. You are kind and good, and responsible."

"Now, listen, Una," Jerome said, but Sylvie barked once in the hall and scratched at the door. Peter opened it and followed her into the room. He was carrying her enamel plate which, without looking at Una, he put down on the middle of the hearthrug; then he stood back and folding his arms across his chest said, "Not a mouthful, and after all that running about in the snow. It's not right."

"What a fuss!" Una said. "It never hurts a dog to go without a meal. She is jealous. That's what's wrong with her."

As Peter made an angry movement, Jerome said quickly, "You had better move, Una. Go and sit over there again and keep quiet." He put his hand under her elbow and when she was standing up, he pushed her gently towards her chair. Una shrugged her shoulders, as if to say, 'How ridiculous!' and sat down drawing her legs under her, and reached for a cigarette. Jerome held out his hand to Sylvie and said in a deep caressing voice, "Come here, my foolish one. Come, eat up your dinner. Eat it for me."

83

At the sound of his voice Sylvie came slowly to him. She moved as if she were uncertain of her welcome. Ignoring the plate of meat, she touched his hand with her muzzle and looked up into his face. "There's no need for this, Sylvie," he told her. "Silly Sylvie, silly girl." He knelt on the hearthrug beside her and put a piece of meat into her mouth. She took it and swallowed it, watching his face, and he gave her another bit. "Silly Sylvie," he murmured, as he fed the meat to her, piece by piece. "Sweet Sylvie, only one."

Peter, his arms folded, watched them solemnly; it was impossible to tell what he was thinking, but Una fidgeted in her chair and smoked jerkily. When the plate was empty and Jerome held it out to Peter, she said loudly, "What an exhibition! Really, Jerome! I don't know who looked the most ridiculous, you or that spoilt creature."

Jerome sat back on his heels and wiped his fingers on his handkerchief. As he looked up at Una's angry face, he chuckled. "Who is jealous now?" he said, as he sat down again and picked up his glass. "Second round to Sylvie?"

Sylvie was pleased with herself and showed it. She jumped up at Peter, put her forefeet on his shoulders and licked his face, and then, innocently overcome by her small victory, she tore round the room, ruff raised, tail threshing, pretending to snap at the furniture and barking shrilly. Jerome laughed but Una put her hands over her ears and shrank back in her chair.

"That's enough, Sylvie," Peter cried. "You'll have the table over in a minute. Remember where you are, this isn't the woods!"

At once Sylvie abandoned her antics and, walking soberly back to the fireplace, sat down at Jerome's feet and looked apologetically up at him.

"Too simple, my girl," he told her. "It's usually wiser to disguise one's feelings."

He looked over Sylvie's head at Una, and Sylvie, sensing his glance and moved by some impulse of generosity, or perhaps only remembering her fine manners, crossed the hearthrug and politely touched the girl's knee and offered her head for a pat.

Una hesitated and then laid her hand gingerly on Sylvie's narrow head. "There!" she said, smiling at Jerome. "Now we are friends. You and Peter had better look out. We two females may gang-up together, join forces, and then God help you!"

Peter laughed suddenly. It was an odd explosive sound, more like a snort than a laugh. "Sisters under your skins," he said rudely, "I don't think."

Turning to Jerome, he said, "What about your dinner? It's ready when you are. I don't want the soup to get cold so I won't put it in the hatch until you're at the table. There's a soufflé after the chicken."

"Chicken, soufflé, whisky!" Una cried, springing up from her chair. "Silver, white tablecloth, candles! The simple life! I think that you two are a pair of frauds."

"What did you expect? A few bones in a cave?" Jerome said as he stood up and put his arm round her waist. "We may live like hermits in the woods but we are not savages. Peter is a very good cook by now, and proud of it. We can even run to a bottle

85

of Burgundy for special occasions. There is one sitting in the hatch now, isn't there, Peter?"

Peter looked at them sourly and then made for the door.

"Wait a minute, Peter," Una said, "We must arrange a place for Sylvie at the table. I'm not going to have her left out. Please put a chair here, between mine and Mr. Holt's. I shall make her a wreath."

She pulled herself free of Jerome's arm and hurried to the table in the window where the pots of orchids in flower stood.

"Mr. Holt!" Peter cried. "Your Odontoglossum, the Golden Guineas! And that's the new hybrid!" But Jerome only laughed.

There are times in a woman's life, usually very brief, when, as far as one man at least is concerned, she can do no wrong. Una, flushed with excitement and her two drinks, looked over her shoulder at Jerome and knew that such a moment was hers. She tightened the cord round her waist, put her hair back and laughed at him. Even Peter, watching her in anger and dismay as she bent over his precious plants, made no attempt to intervene.

"Poor Peter," she said kindly. "Don't look so sad. I will take only one of these yellow and white sprays, they look like a ballet dancer's skirts, don't they? And perhaps this speckled pink one. The gorgeous frilled white thing with the purple lip is too big."

Like a large glossy crimson butterfly, she hovered over the plants, moving from the window to the table behind the sofa where a tall Cymbidium stood serenely in the place of honour beside the drink tray. Even Una did not dare to touch the two

86

long curving sprays of waxy flowers, the colour of palest jade or the green seen in winter sunsets; she looked at Peter, put out a hand teasingly, and went back to the fire. Her white hands moved expertly, twisting the two stems. "There, isn't that pretty?" she said triumphantly, holding up a small vivid flowery circlet. "Come and sit down, Jerome, and make Sylvie sit on the chair beside you. You can put the wreath on her head. She will wear it for you. Now we are quite ready. Dinner, Peter!"

Peter shut the door on the sound of her laughter and, swearing to himself, walked down the hall to the kitchen.

The candles wavered in the draught that in spite of the shut windows and the thick curtains was in the room. No one at the table noticed it; for Jerome and Una the fire burned brightly and the flickering candle-light showed them each other's face in a new and entrancing light. Peter moved silently behind the three chairs as he cleared the table. Dinner was over and he had to admit that it had been a successful meal. He had taken more trouble than usual, quite why he did not know. No London restaurant, he was sure, could have produced a more tender and succulent bird. Soufflés were tricky, but never had one of his been so light—a sugary lemon and egg masterpiece—which was odd considering the rage he had been in when he made it. It had all been a waste of his time because he doubted if these two would have noticed if he had put sawdust before them.

Every time that Peter came back to the table from the hatch, he looked commiseratingly at Sylvie who sat on her chair with the wreath balanced between her ears. "Get down, Sylvie," he whispered to her, for it hurt him to see her sitting there unnoticed while they talked across her. He knew that she was suffering not only discomfort but hurt pride; but Jerome had told her to sit where she was and nothing, neither Peter nor wild horses, would make her move until Jerome told her to get down. She sat on, with her feet uncomfortably close together, looking straight before her like a statue that keeps its stone dignity unimpaired.

Peter wanted to take the cloth away, but Jerome had both elbows on it as he leant across Sylvie towards the girl. "He's besotted," Peter whispered to himself, his thin lips barely moving. "And with what? A white, bony little thing, a piece of yellow hair and two doll's eyes. Hundreds like her about." He looked at Jerome's absorbed and smiling face and shook his head. "She's too young," he muttered to himself. "What's her mother doing, letting her run loose like this? It's too bad. I'm surprised at the Captain. Came here just at the right time, she did, that's the answer."

Una looked up suddenly and met his eyes. Her smile vanished and she put her hand on Jerome's arm.

"What do you want, Peter?" Jerome asked him. "Stop muttering to yourself. What is the matter?"

"I want to take the cloth off and to have my own dinner in peace," Peter said crossly. "I don't want to hang about all night, getting in your way. It's time Sylvie got herself down from that chair. You ought to be ashamed of yourself, keeping her sitting there."

Jerome looked from Peter to Sylvie. He put out his hand and took the wreath of her head and laid it on the table. "What are you doing there?" he said to her sternly. "Get down at once."

When Sylvie looked back at him, bewildered and offended, he touched her gently on the shoulder. At once she jumped down, ran to the fire, and stood in front of his armchair as if she were on guard. He laughed and standing up pulled Una to her feet.

"I can smell coffee, Peter," he said. "We will have it by the fire. Just put the tray in the hatch and we will help ourselves. Where did I put that brandy? There's a bottle somewhere about."

"In the bookshelf cupboard, with the glasses," Peter said, as he picked up the wreath and began to unwind and straighten the stems. "What about Sylvie? It's snowing, but she ought to go out again."

"Snowing?" Jerome said.

He went to the window and drew the curtains back. Against the darkness the white flakes drifted down, unhurrying in spite of the wind which carried them against the glass. The dim light in the room reached only a short distance into the night. They all heard the sighing that came from the acres of dark trees standing shoulder to shoulder over the breadth of the valley.

Jerome let the curtains fall back into their place and turned to face the room. He put his hands into the pockets of the dark blue dressing-gown, on which the gold dragons gleamed faintly, and smiled at Una. His eyes were shining and there was a curious absent expression on his face as if he were, in spirit, a long way from the room. "Working up for a blizzard, I wonder?" he said. "It's coming down thick and fast again. How right you were, Peter. It looks as if Miss Una was here for keeps."

Una laughed suddenly; it was a high nervous laugh, and Jerome crossed the room to her and put his arm round her shoulders.

"Bless the snow," he said, smiling down at her. "I'm glad, do you hear, Una? Think of it, coming down out there, millions and millions of white feathers covering us up in layer after layer, a huge soft eiderdown between us and the world!"

Peter picked up the candelabra and put it on the bookshelves. As he began to fold the cloth, Jerome said, "You still here, Peter? Leave the candles, leave the table. Where is that brandy? Better bring three glasses. You must have a drink with us. 'In such a night as this'—"

"I'll have a hot toddy in the kitchen, thank you," Peter said. "The brandy and glasses are on the drink table, and now I'll let Sylvie out of the back door. She won't go far in this weather, and then she can run straight up to her bed. Well, I'm off. Come on, Sylvie."

He walked to the door and Sylvie, knowing what was expected of her, followed him. With his hand on the door-handle Peter hesitated and looked back at the two by the fire.

"Snow doesn't last long in these parts, Miss," he said. "It soon goes as if it had never been and leaves a mucky sort of world, a nasty mess, behind."

He looked defiantly at Jerome and said, "Well, good-night."

7

Jerome's bedroom was above his workroom and here the thick walls of the old house made little of the wind. Behind the drawn curtains the two windows were carefully wedged and gave out only a muted rattle when a fresh gust or flurry of snow beat upon the glass.

He fastened the cord of his dressing-gown and, crossing the room, drew the dark blue curtains closer and put his hand on the radiator under the windowsill. Before he put the central heating in it had often been unbearably cold up here, but now the fire was an unnecessary luxury; even when it went out the room would be warm.

As he looked round he realized that this room had changed less in the fourteen years he had known it than any other room in the house. The low white-painted ceiling reflected the flames which burned brightly in the open grate. The walls were still rough and whitewashed and on the polished oak planks of the floor were two faded rag rugs that had belonged to Peter's mother. The only furniture beside the large old-fashioned mahogany bedstead and the bedside table which held a shaded lamp, a candle and matches, cigarettes and a pile of books, was the chest of drawers and a straight-backed Victorian chair covered with faded woollen embroidery. He had enlarged the fireplace, built in two cupboards and exchanged his original camp bed for the bed that had belonged to his uncle, but the room was in essentials the same room he had slept in alone for fourteen years.

Sylvie's couch, raised a few inches off the floor and covered with a blue blanket, stood in winter and summer at the foot of his bed; it had been introduced into the room less than three years ago but was by now part of it, as Sylvie herself was. She lay facing the fire, extended and at ease, with her head resting on her forepaws and her eyes half shut. Suddenly, she raised her head. Her ears pricked, and she sat up facing the door; as it opened she growled softly.

Una, in a white wool dressing-gown, hesitated in the doorway looking at Jerome. "Lie down, Sylvie don't be silly," he said, as he walked across the room to the girl. "What ages you have been, Una. What have you been doing?"

Una shut the door behind her and slipped past him to the fire. She pulled the straight-backed chair up to the hearth and sat down. As he followed her and stood with his arm on the chimney shelf, looking down at her, she said a little breathlessly, "Have I been long? I'm sorry."

The firelight threw a rosy glow on her white skirts, touched her cheek, and turned her pale hair to gold. "Why are you smiling like that, Jerome?" she said, "It makes me uncomfortable, as if you were having a secret joke. You have been doing it on and off all evening. What are you thinking of?"

Jerome laughed. "You make me sound like the Cheshire Cat," he said. "Was I smiling? I was thinking how delectable you look sitting there in the firelight, pink-and-white and sweet and warm, good enough to eat, just the thing for a cold night like this. How astonished this room must be to have you here. I wonder if it has ever seen a woman before. Certainly not in my time."

"This house is a monastery, then," Una said, "and you and Peter are two hermit monks? The only thing is, I can't imagine why."

"I tried to tell you, to explain to you what this house means to me," Jerome said. "If you can't understand, I will put it more simply. I have found that work and play don't go well together."

"Play!" Una said.

"Pleasure then, if you would rather—"

"I would rather call it love."

Jerome said nothing and Una looked away from him to the windows and then in her turn round the room. "The wind seems further away up here," she said, "but I can hear it roaring in the chimney. What a night!"

"It can't reach us here," said Jerome. "This is our cave, our hole. Here we are tucked away safe under the snow. Let's forget the wind, Una."

He put his hand out to her, but Una did not take it. "Does Sylvie have to sleep here?" she said.

93

"She always has."

"I don't think that a dog in a bedroom is really healthy."

"Don't you?"

"No, I don't. Anyway, why must we be here instead of in the other room?"

"Because this is my room, because it has the bigger bed."

Jerome bent down and picked up the tongs. "I'm going to make up the fire," he said. "With luck it will last until the morning. I'm not going to stand here talking all night, Una."

He knelt down and, as he banked up coal at the back of the grate and put on a log to make a blaze, he said, "A fire in a bedroom is one of the pleasures of life—what about the one in your room?"

"I didn't touch it. What is the point if we are going to sleep here?"

"You will need it in the morning. We don't want to embarrass Peter when he brings up our breakfasts."

"I think that is silly. He must know."

"Of course he does, but it will be easier for all of us if he finds you at breakfast in your own room."

He stood up and turned to her, but Una said quickly, "Sylvie is watching us. She is watching every move you make."

Jerome swung round. Sylvie lay in the same position with her head on her paws facing the fire, but her eyes were wide open and fixed on him. "You turn over and go to sleep," he said to her, and bent to give her a last quick good-night pat, as he always did. His hand did not recognize the tense watchfulness of her body and when she lifted her head to him he had already turned away.

As he took Una's hands from her lap and pulled her to her feet, the lights slowly dimmed. In the shaded bulb above the chest of drawers the filament glowed redly and disappeared.

"It must be the wind," Una cried. "It's getting worse. It's a blizzard by now."

"It's not the wind, it's Peter," Jerome said impatiently. "Unless I'm working late he often turns the electricity off at midnight when he goes to bed."

"I didn't know that you made your own electricity. This place must be the back of beyond."

"In a way it is, but we could have been on the grid years ago. Peter refuses to change. He likes his engine and he likes work. Damn Peter, I forgot to tell him, but he might have thought—"

"Does it matter? I like it better with only the firelight."

"The firelight doesn't reach far. I'm going to light a candle. I like to see what I'm making love to."

"Please don't," Una said. "Please leave it. It will be easier for me this way."

"Easier? What do you mean? Isn't this what you came here for?"

He put his arms round her and said, "Stop this nonsense, Una. It's too late to change your mind, and you don't want to change it, do you? Then why are you behaving like this? You have a lot to learn, my child. Never mind, I will see that you learn it, we will have plenty of time. It will snow all night—I know it will—it will snow for days."

"Wait a minute, Jerome," Una said, pulling away from him.

"What is the matter now?"

"It's that dog. I can't—not with her here."

"Don't be absurd. Sylvie is asleep."

"She isn't. She is sitting up, watching us."

In the red glow of the firelight, which danced upon the ceiling, Sylvie sat upright on her bed. Her dark, large-eared shape was as still as a rock and had something as implacable about it.

"Lie down, Sylvie, lie down at once," Jerome said sharply.

Sylvie obeyed him, flattening her long body against her blanket and laying her head on her paws again.

"She isn't worrying about us," Jerome said. "The wind is making her uneasy."

"Put her out on the landing, please Jerome."

"I can't do that. She wouldn't understand. I will take that log off the fire. The room will be dark. She will forget all about us and go to sleep."

"She won't. It wouldn't make any difference. I would know that she was there.'"

"How can you be so silly. She is only a dog."

Jerome tried to put his arm round her again but Una pushed him away. "Look, she is sitting up," she cried. "She won't take her eyes off us. She hates you to touch me, I know she does. If you don't put her out, I'm not staying here. I will go back to my own room and lock the door. Please, Jerome, it will be quite different when she has gone."

"Of all the hysterical nonsense," Jerome said furiously, but he turned to Sylvie.

Sylvie stood up. She looked into his face and moved her tail uncertainly. "Get off that bed," he ordered. Then he said, more gently, even apologetically, "It's your own fault, Sylvie." When he dragged her bed across the room and opened the door, she hesitated by the fire, staring unbelievingly after him.

"Outside!" he said, and for the first time in her adult life she did not obey him at once, but when he called her name from the dark landing, she hurried to him without another glance at Una.

Jerome pushed Sylvie's bed against the warm radiator under the landing window. "Lie down," he commanded her, and pulled the curtains back. Not waiting to see if she obeyed him, he turned quickly to the firelit room and shut the door on her.

8

Sylvie stood for a long time on the landing facing the bedroom door. Round her the darkness gathered and swirled, ebbing from the grey oblong of the window to settle and thicken over the stairwell. A door creaked; the window shook in its frame as the wind, sweeping up the valley and pouring through the gap in the trees, met the solid block of the house. The rug on the polished wood floor lifted in the current of air that flowed with the darkness from the window and down the stairs to meet the warm breath rising from the great porcelain stove in the hall below. It was not cold on the landing but Sylvie shivered as she stood with her head lowered and her tail touching the floor; her legs trembled down their length; a shoulder muscle twitched uncontrollably. She made no sound, or, if a whine did escape her, it was lost in the noise the wind was making. At last, moving stiffly, she turned away and walked slowly to her bed, her nails clicking forlornly on the floor-boards.

The landing was large for the size of the house. Once it must have been another room, one of the four of the old building; the four doors to bathroom, bedrooms, and box-room, were firmly shut, as were the doors into the hall below; but, as Sylvie lay staring into the darkness with her back pressed against the warm radiator, a pattern of sounds came to her under the overriding sweep of the wind. No human being could have heard what her ears caught and magnified: the sighing of the house as it braced itself against the blizzard, a complaint from wood and stone. All over the house the fires were dying down. Somewhere a long way off, perhaps in the coal shed, a door banged shut. A log split suddenly on the hearth in the sitting-room. Mice, excited by the wind, danced everywhere behind the wainscotting. Radiators and pipes gave off their own peculiar water-chuckling; furniture creaked, cracked, like the joints of the very old. Clocks ticked on and in the kitchen Peter's little cuckoo called once, then twice. She heard Peter's snores and the comfortable purring of the range. From the room across the landing distinct sounds had reached her, but these had given place to the soft breathing sounds of sleep. The snow piling up against the window-panes above her made no sound at all, but in the woods, she could hear the trees lamenting. As she lay unsleeping, looking wide-eyed into the darkness and listening to the house, her nostrils caught and held scents that made another pattern in her brain, one more complicated and diverse than that of sound and, to her, of greater interest and importance.

First she recognised the familiar everyday scents that made up the composite smell of the house: woodsmoke, furniture-polish, tobacco, leather and wood and steel, dust, coal and oil; the aroma of meals eaten hours ago: roast chicken, coffee, liver. Above these rose scents that were more intriguing: the green heavy scent of the orchids, a whiff of talcum-powder from the bathroom, Una's scent, the smell of warm sleeping bodies, of breath. As Sylvie's nostrils quivered, savouring, recognizing, exploring, her sore and bewildered heart was comforted by this familiar world of the senses. Before the clocks could strike again, her eyes closed and she slept.

Towards dawn the blizzard lessened. There was a lull in the wind and the snow ceased to fall. From a clear patch of sky the moon looked down. It shone with a cold pure light on the snow-filled cup of the valley, on the white rim of its hills, and over the sleeping countryside beyond to the far distant sea. It laid the peaked shadow of the house on the white lawn and, slanting through the landing window, made bright patches on the polished boards. Sylvie, waking, looked up and saw the moon. She

99

put her head back and pointed her muzzle to the sky, but awe and training prevailed over the urge in her blood; instead of a deep mournful howl—ancient wolf-music to the moon—all that came from her throat was a sad little whine. Clouds tore again across the sky; the brightness vanished and the landing was dark once more. Sylvie stood up on her bed, scraping and ruckling her blanket, and moved round and round on the axis of her hind legs, as if she were treading a new sleeping-place for herself out in the woods among last autumn's fallen leaves. She lay down again, sighed deeply, and curled herself into a ball.

As the snow came down again beyond the window, Sylvie, in her dreams, was deep in the woods. Gone were the tame scents and sounds of the house, left far behind her with alien thoughts and unnatural misery. All about her was the clean whiteness of snow and the tang of firs. The only sounds were the wind in the branches, the sigh of descending flakes, perhaps a sudden flurry and squawk in the trees above her from a disturbed and half-frozen bird. All remembrance of the warm close house had left her. Now she was no more hampered by loyalty and love than the dog fox who lived on the hill above the spring and who, re-turning to his burrow from his hunting, had barked twice at the moon. Free as the wind, clean as the snow, on she ran deeper and deeper into the trees. She whimpered as she ran and bared her teeth as her muzzle dropped to the trail; in her brain was the old knowledge of warm blood and flesh waiting for the huntress at the edge of the woods. Now the dark shadows of the trees closed round her as she passed into the healing wilderness and unknowing peace.

The stormy night gave way to a bleak grey dawn. The window-panes were opaque with frost, covered with a new pattern of strange ferns and frosty flowers. It was cold on the landing but Sylvie, deep in her blanket, paws and nose covered by the soft plume of her tail, slept on until in the morning Peter found her there.

♪❋♪❋♪❋ *Part Two*

Jerome had said of the falling snow that it was a huge soft eiderdown, 'Millions of white feathers between us and the world.' In the week that followed, the house and its four inhabitants were wrapped away into a hidden world of their own not only by the warm covering of the snow but by their own preoccupations. The blizzard, after its brief lull, blew for two days and for another twenty-four hours snow fell steadily. The house itself became more remote, truly alone among its trees; not only had it disappeared from sight under its white covering, if anyone had been abroad to look for it, but by the end of the second day it was cut off from all contact with the outside world. The aerial broke in the storm of the first night and, next day, Peter could get no sound from his set or the set in the sitting-room. For another day it was possible to ring up the farm or the village, but by that evening the telephone, too, was dumb.

During these first days, when all that could be seen from the windows of the house was a white whirling shifting curtain of snow, no one ventured more than a yard or two from the back door. Peter, grumbling to himself, tied a scarf over his head and, wearing his old duffle-coat and gum-boots, groped his way between the house, woodshed, orchid-houses and the shed that housed the electric-light plant. Sylvie did not attempt to reach the woods, though wind and driving snow did not confuse her as they did Peter and there was no chance of her losing herself; the needle of the compass that she carried in her brain swung surely to her north of home wherever she went and however deep she might penetrate into the wind-tossed darkness of the trees. As for the cold, her heavy black and silver coat would have protected her, and once across the open lawn in the shelter of the woods she would have forgotten her troubles. There she would have been free to make a way for herself through the piled snow, to pounce, perhaps, on a crouching hare, or to nose a bird, dead of the cold and fallen from its perch; but Sylvie was chained to the house by love and jealousy as firmly as she would have been if Peter had fastened her by her heavy steel chain to the ring in the kitchen wall by her bed, a thing he had only done once or twice in her life. Peter had to force her out of doors and, once

106

there, she did what she had to do in the shelter of the outhouses and hurried back to the warm kitchen again. There she would lie most of the day on her bed, dozing uneasily, jerking awake at every sound that came to the kitchen from the rest of the house. When she heard voices in the sitting-room, she would run to the door and look over her shoulder at Peter, asking him to let her out into the hall. Her humble, even abject look infuriated him. "Haven't you any pride?" he said to her, but he always did as she asked. "Go on, then," he said, "much good will it do you," and he would stand looking after her as she ran down the hall to scratch at the sitting-room door. When it was opened, as it always was eventually, he would go back to the kitchen and look at the untouched food on Sylvie's plate. Since the morning when he had found her on the landing, she had refused to eat. Every evening, to please him, she drank a little of the dried milk he mixed for her but she would touch nothing else, even when Jerome offered it to her. On the second evening, when she turned her head away from the piece of meat he held out to her in front of the sitting-room fire, Jerome said, "Take it away, Peter. I'm not going to coax her. She will stop this nonsense in time, when she is really hungry," and Una, from her chair by the fire, said, "She is jealous, of course. Poor Sylvie."

Jerome and Una spent most of those first days in bed. They would wander down to the sitting-room to eat the meals that Peter prepared for them, hungry, but noticing nothing of what they ate. They would sit for a short while by the fire, talking, talking, as only lovers can when they are possessed by that engrossing, but often fatal, urge to explore each other's mind and past as they did each other's body; kind and gentle with satisfied love, they would spare a few words and caresses for Sylvie, that silent undemanding, and therefore unresented, third in the room. After the first day, whenever they came downstairs, they would offer to help Peter with his work. "Let me dry up at least," Una would say. "Let me lay the supper-table," while Jerome would suggest that it might do him good to fetch in some logs or to stoke the furnace. When Peter refused their help brusquely, saying that he wanted no one messing about in his kitchen and that fetching in the wood was his only chance of a breath of fresh air, they did not insist. Una would sit on the hearthrug leaning against Jerome's knees while he talked of his travels, of the war, of his childhood, telling her stories, boasting a little, showing off, talking of anything and everything, even of his work; or they would stand silently together, looking out of the windows at the falling snow and then, laughing a little, would turn back to their absorbing private world. Few lovers, Jerome told Una, were so lucky in their choice of time and place for a honeymoon. Here there was no chance of any outsider intruding upon them by even a glance. There could be no question of their going out for a good walk, or of any guilty feelings about visiting a picture gallery or friends whom they ought to see. Here, well-fed and provided for in familiar surroundings, they were happily and snugly wound about by the snow into one chrysalis, and forced to know the pure unadulterated essence of love. Una, when he said this, looked at Jerome doubtfully and asked him if, perhaps, he was growing a little bit bored, and added that if he wanted to get back to his writing, to work for an hour or two, she would be quite happy reading by the fire. When he laughed at her, calling her his snow goose, a warm white sleek little goose but a goose none-the-less, she cried out that she understood very well that he never took anything except his work, certainly no woman, seriously. "It's only the snow," she said.

On the third evening, as the blizzard reached its peak before blowing itself out in the night, they came near to a quarrel.

Una, looking at herself in the little mirror above Jerome's chest of drawers, said suddenly that she was not fit to be seen, that she must wash her hair. This she did when she took her before-dinner bath. Wearing her white fluffy dressing-gown, she knelt on the hearthrug combing her still damp hair in front of the sitting-room fire. Jerome, looking down at her from his chair, said, "You have changed, Una. Even in these few days you have grown fatter and sleeker, and it suits you. You are softer, rounder, the sharp edges rubbed off. Love becomes you, my dear. You look blooming—yes, that is the right word, in flower."

"Love becomes any woman, doesn't it?" Una said. "As long as it's a happy love, but don't let's talk about other women. Talk only about me and you. You look better too, Jerome. Younger— are you happy?"

"Of course I am. I'm purring—can't you hear me? Or I would be if I were not too lazy and satisfied to move. I feel like a cat full to the brim with cream and canaries."

"You could put it more elegantly, if you tried," Una said.

Jerome was not listening. He lay back in his chair, holding his glass of whisky, and smiled to himself.

"Please don't smile like that, Jerome," Una said. "It makes you seem suddenly miles away. What are you thinking of?"

"Of a story I heard in the war."

"Tell it to me."

He told it and, after a moment, Una laughed.

"That reminds me—" he said. "Here is another, and this one really happened to me."

This time Una did not laugh.

"What is the matter?" Jerome said, looking at her face.

"Was that supposed to be a funny story?" Una demanded. "Should I be amused?"

"Of course you should. It's a very funny story. Silly, but funny."

"It's vulgar and pointless, and you shouldn't have told it to me, here in this house. Who do you think I am? Would you have told it to Martha Cleghorn?"

"Martha? She was the first to hear it—I suppose I should have remembered that you are a prudish little schoolgirl with a stiff little mind."

Una put her hair back and glared up at him. "You are horrible," she began; then her mouth trembled and tears came into her eyes. "How can you call me a prude?" she said.

She put her hand on his knee, "Don't be cross," she pleaded. "I can't bear it. It's only that I don't want to hear about the war or other countries or other women. I only want to talk about us, here in this house."

Jerome looked down at her flushed earnest face and felt ashamed of himself, but he said, "There would soon be a limit to that—it would pall after a time, you know."

"You are getting bored, you see," Una said sadly.

"I will be bored if you start to cry. Your hair is dry, better go and put on a dress. I'm tired of that dressing-gown."

"You haven't complained of it before. You said you liked it."

"You should never remind a man of what he has said. It's always a mistake, my child. You still have a lot to learn."

"I'm not sure that I want to learn it, not from you."

"That's not true is it?" Jerome said, and he put out his hand and touched her hair. At once she put her head down on his knee. "Of course it's not," she said in a muffled voice. "Don't let's quarrel. We mustn't spoil it."

"Nothing is spoilt," Jerome told her. "All lovers quarrel. They can't help it. Tension is a part of love. Run along and dress, Una. Make yourself beautiful. You might even think of yet another way of doing your hair to delight and amaze me."

As Una lifted her head and smiled at him, he said, "And let Sylvie in, she has been scratching at the door for some time. We need some more logs. Before you go upstairs, you might tell Peter."

Peter, during these three days, minded his own business and went doggedly about his work, cleaning, cooking, carrying trays, fetching in wood and coal, keeping up the furnace, running the electric-light plant and guarding the orchids from the cold. He got up while it was still dark and went to bed at midnight and arranged his day carefully and methodically, as if it were regulated by the sound of a ship's bell instead of a cuckoo-clock. After breakfast he would go to the storeroom and make a careful check, sighing to himself, although there was enough tinned food, flour, potatoes, oil, coal and wood to last them all for at least another week. The only shortages were fresh meat, vegetables and milk and, as Sylvie ate nothing and Una and Jerome did not appear to notice what they ate, this worried nobody but Peter. Every afternoon after luncheon he went earlier than he usually did to the orchid-houses, as if he found it necessary to get away as soon as he could from the intense atmosphere in the house. The long range of the glass-houses was divided into four parts; the first and smallest, facing the side door of the house, was kept as a packing and potting room. Here Peter would rest for an hour in his old basket chair, drawn close to the hot pipes, facing the glass inner door through which he could see the bright green leaves of the Cattleyas arranged on their side benches and centre tier. He would read or just sit, listening to the wind or watching the falling snow on the steamy glass. Sylvie always accompanied him at this time and lay by his side on a bit of old blanket that he had found for her.

During these days Peter talked less to Sylvie than he usually did when they were together. The situation in the house was so distressing to them both that it was impossible to comment on it.

Delicacy prevented him from commiserating with her in her un-happiness. As they sat together or, opening the glass doors, wandered down the aisles between the orchids, he would put his hand on her head and say, "It will blow itself out. Too violent to last. It won't go on forever."

As for the orchids they flourished in their gently warm, faintly sweet-smelling world that, thanks to Peter, remained exactly as it always was. The thermometers and the humidity gauges showed the correct readings; the green fleshy leaves did not feel the wind; the bud sheaths opened in their own good time; petals and sepals unfurled, colours deepened and the strange cat-like flower faces looked blandly out at the snow-smeared glass or at the man and dog passing between them. It was, of course, nothing to the orchids that Jerome in four days did not visit them but this neglect affronted Peter. To him it was a betrayal and he continued to give Jerome the orchid news as he had always done saying, perhaps as he laid the table for a meal in the sitting-room, "That Oncidium is in bud. The Cymbidiums are almost at their best—pity we can't get that order off this week." Jerome would nod absently or say, "Good. I must come and see them. There will be time when the snow stops. Keep the furnaces going, won't you?" and then apparently forget that Peter had spoken. If Jerome had noticed that the morning after Una had made a wreath for Sylvie the pots of orchids had disappeared from the sitting-room, he said nothing; in four days he did not open the door of his workroom to see that, in the one room that Peter considered inviolable, the orchids were still there.

When the wind dropped on the third day, the silence in the house was uncanny. Voices and footsteps seemed unnaturally loud and any movement too sudden. Una and Jerome went downstairs soon after eleven and Una found that she was tip-toeing across the hall. As they sat by the fire in the sitting-room, they talked in whispers and then fell silent, holding hands and looking into the flames. Sylvie was restless. She wandered through the house asking for a door to be opened for her and then scratching at it, asking to be let in again. Her nails clicked along the hall and up the stairs to the landing; she explored each room but did not stay long anywhere until, at last, she settled down on the window-sill in the sitting-room where, resting her chin on the window-ledge, she could watch the falling snow. In the kitchen, Peter stood by the table, idle for once, looking out of the window as if bemused by the steadily descending whiteness. Then he shook himself awake and planned for himself an even fuller day than usual; but in the afternoon when he had washed up the luncheon dishes, he suddenly gave up and, going into his bedroom, for the first time in his healthy adult life lay down fully clothed on his bed, pulled the eiderdown up, and slept the blank still afternoon away. By mid-afternoon everyone in the house was fast asleep, Jerome and Una upstairs in their bed, Sylvie on the windowsill in the sitting-room. They slept soundly and dream-lessly as wild hibernating animals, such as bears, do, curled in their warm private holes deep under the snow. The house was dark when Peter woke soon after five. Yawning and stretching as if he had slept the whole winter away, he put on his shoes and stumbled into the kitchen to make up the range, to switch on the lights, to let Sylvie out of the back door, and to go to the orchid-houses to check the thermometers and to make sure that all was well. Soon the house was its warm self again; lights shining, fires burning brightly, the curtains drawn against the night. The smell of cooking dinner came reassuringly from the kitchen; Sylvie, back from her brief excursion into the outside air, shook the snow from her coat in front of the range; and in the sitting-room, Jerome put a record on his gramophone.

The snow stopped falling soon after midnight. Stars appeared in a clear sky above the house and it grew very cold.

The next day, which was the fifth that Una was to spend in Jerome's house, after an early morning of thick mist when the house was wrapped in mysterious veils that slowly lifted, the sun shone again on a world that was as dazzlingly fine and cold as the day Una arrived, but a whiter world. Never before, as far back as anyone in the valley could remember, had the snow been as deep. The trees showed only brief touches of their dark bottle-green; the house had almost disappeared under its white covering, and of the small red car at the bottom of the lane there was nothing to be seen. White and blue were the almost unrelieved colours of the day: blue sky, blue smoke rising from the chimneys, blue of the shadows and, after eight o'clock, blue in the footprints of man and dog in the snow.

After breakfast, which by now Jerome and Una ate together by the fire in her bedroom, a compromise that satisfied Jerome, made Una smile, and meant only one tray instead of two for

Peter, it was decided that an effort should be made to reach the farm which was less than a mile away. "Time we came up for air," Jerome told Una.

Una did not want either of them to leave the house. "Let Peter go," she said. "Let's stay, you and I, as we are a little longer. We have been so happy. Something might spoil it." When he laughed at her and told her that some fresh air would do them good, that if they lived this eiderdown existence much longer they would grow as fat and pale as a couple of cellar-stored potatoes, she ran to her looking-glass, looked at her reflection anxiously, and then said that perhaps he was right.

"Peter will take the sled to carry back any supplies we can get from the farm, and a couple of spades in case we come to a soft patch under the trees," Jerome said. "It's freezing hard and the snow ought to be firm, but you had better wear a pair of Peter's gum-boots over all the socks you have, luckily he has very small feet. Run along and dress in your warmest things and put on your fur coat and a scarf. I will lend you some dark glasses, the sun will be dazzling on the snow."

"Will Sylvie come too?" Una said, as she opened the bedroom door.

"That is a silly thing to say," Jerome said severely. "Surely you didn't think that I would leave her behind?"

Such a possibility had not occurred to Sylvie; when they left the house by the back door, she was waiting on the path that Peter had dug past the sheds and the orchid-houses to the garage and the lane. As the little procession with Peter pulling the sled in the lead moved out from the shadow of the house into the brilliant sunshine, she barked once, a high ringing bark that sounded on the cold air like a hunting-horn and echoed back to them from the ranks of snow-muffled trees. Then she ran ahead towards the garage and the lane waving her tail, whining with eagerness, and looking back to make sure that they were following her.

In the bright sunshine and against the white background, it was obvious that Sylvie was not the sleek proud beauty that she had been. Jerome stood still to look at her. "Sylvie is very thin," he said to Peter. "How can she have lost so much weight in a few days? Her coat looks dull and staring."

Peter shrugged his shoulders. "What do you expect?" he said. "Eaten nothing, and she's fretting." He jerked at the sled ropes and walked on.

Una, at Jerome's elbow, said, "Perhaps she will eat after a good walk. Dogs need exercise, don't they? There doesn't seem much wrong with her, look at her now."

Sylvie, her troubles forgotten for the moment, plunged joyfully into the snow, throwing up a white cloud about her, making a detour through the trees and returning to urge them all on. From the house the lane went up through the woods and over the brow of the hill and down towards the farm and its open fields. At first they made good progress, although it was heavy going as their feet sank through the crisp white surface before they met the hard packed snow beneath. Then the brilliant sunshine, the high blue sky above them, and the thin air, sharp and cold as a diamond, as exhilarating as champagne after the closed days in the house, went to their heads. They walked as if they were all a little drunk, staggering up the hill in their heavy clothes. Peter marched ahead without looking round, but whistled loudly and melodiously as if he had not a care in the world. Jerome, wearing his sheepskin jacket and his green feathered hat, kept bursting into a tuneless song. Una, encumbered by her long fur coat and Peter's boots, soon found the gentle slope almost too much for her and had to pause every few minutes to get her breath while she leant against Jerome, panting and laughing. These halts worried Sylvie; she stood and barked impatiently up at them, showing her white teeth and her long pink tongue. Her coat by now was thick with snow and her eyes gleamed below a fringe of ice-coated hair.

"Sylvie looks a wild creature," Una said. "I shouldn't like to meet her out here alone. I don't believe that Alsatians and wolves are different species, whatever you say. Doesn't she look exactly like one?"

"You and your wolves!" Jerome said. "Come on, slow-coach. Sylvie is running rings round us."

"It's all very well for her," Una protested. "These are her woods and she isn't wearing Peter's boots. She would look as silly as I do now if she had to walk down Piccadilly on high heels."

Jerome laughed and put his arm round her shoulders. "Don't look so cross," he said. "I don't expect you to compete with Sylvie on her own ground. Come on, it's too cold to stand here. You should see your nose—it's a beautiful bright pink."

Una stood still. "I'm going back to the house," she said.

"Oh, no you are not! You are going up this hill if I have to drag you there."

Peter was waiting for them at the top of the hill. Beyond him the lane, going down again between the trees to the farm, had been cleared of snow. The roofs of the farmhouse and its barns showed below them at the edge of the woods. Sheep, a dirty white against the snow, were moving across an open field. Here was the outside world, a vista of snow-covered fields, orchards, distant buildings, a blue horizon. Una and Jerome stood holding hands and looking down as if this view disconcerted them, as if they were explorers come back from an unknown country or space travellers returned from the moon or a further star. Peter looked at them curiously.

"Better get on, if we want to be back for lunch," he suggested. "Easy going from here but it will be a long pull back."

"I'm not going any further," Una said. "There will be people down there. I don't want to see anyone. They would spoil it."

"But the whole point of this expedition is to reach the farm," Jerome said. "We hope to get some news, as well as mutton, butter, milk and fresh eggs."

"Let Peter go, and come back with me, please Jerome."

"And how is Peter to get the sled back up the hill?"

"I will manage," Peter said. "Alvin or one of the boys will give me a hand up as far as this, and then it will be easy down to the house. I will be back by one but perhaps you would put my pie in the oven, Miss, it's in the larder." He started down the hill with the sled sliding at his heels, grinned at Jerome over his shoulder, and said, "So long, mutton for dinner. Coming, Sylvie?"

Jerome looked after him, and then turned to Una. Before he could speak, she cried, "You wanted to go. You look furious. I shouldn't have stopped you."

"Don't be silly. I had thought of trying to telephone to Michael but it can wait. Just as well, I dare say, it might have been difficult explaining you to Mrs. Robbins. I have a reputation in these parts to keep up! Look at poor Sylvie, she doesn't know what to do."

Sylvie, who had followed Peter, was racing up the slope again. She liked going down to the farm. Mrs. Robbins always gave her a tit-bit and fussed over her; there were exciting smells about the yard and barns, plenty to interest her, but now she hurried back to see what was keeping Jerome. When he told her to go with Peter, she could not believe it. She ran a little way after the sled and then ran back again, confident that he would soon realize that he had made a mistake. When he spoke to her more sternly, she looked up at him with beseeching eyes and lay down at his feet in the snow, fawning and supplicating.

"You need a longer walk," he told her patiently. "This little amble isn't enough for you." He squatted down beside her and stroked her head. "There now," he said. "Go on, be off with you, silly girl."

Sylvie rolled over on her back as she used to do as a puppy when she knew that she had done wrong, but this undignified gesture did not help her. Jerome stood up and said in a voice that she knew must be obeyed, "Go with Peter, Sylvie."

Jerome looked after her as, with her tail between her legs, she hurried down the hill. When she reached Peter, Jerome turned away and took Una's arm.

"There's obedience for you," he said lightly. "I can't imagine any woman obeying me like that, doing what she least wanted to do because I told her to."

"Would you like her better if she did?" Una asked him, as they set off together down the hill towards the house. "I rather doubt it. . . ."

Peter did not speak to Sylvie until he had turned the corner of the lane above the farm. Then he said, "You shouldn't have run back to him. You should have gone with me, without a look round, if you wanted to help yourself."

As they reached the farmyard he looked down at Sylvie, now trotting soberly at his side, and said, "Cheer up! There's such a thing as choking a cat with too much cream."

That evening Sylvie ate a little of her dinner of fresh mutton in the kitchen. Perhaps, as Una had predicted, her long walk had done her good, but it also seemed as if she had understood Peter's words and had decided to take his advice and to change her tactics. She absented herself from the sitting-room and sat with Peter by the range until nearly midnight when, of her own accord, she climbed the stairs and lay down on her bed on the landing.

The next day after luncheon, Jerome suggested that the time had come for Una to visit the orchid-houses.

Una agreed eagerly, although she would rather have stayed comfortably by the fire. She had noticed at once that the pots of orchids had disappeared from the sitting-room, and had wondered if it were Jerome or Peter who had taken them away. She had not dared to ask. Since that first evening when she had made a wreath for Sylvie, Jerome had not mentioned the orchids.

"Get your coat," he said. "You will have to cross the yard. I will be waiting for you outside."

When Una opened the side door of the house, she heard Sylvie barking excitedly. Jerome was standing in the snow in the afternoon sunlight with Sylvie dancing round him. He was wearing his sheepskin jacket again and his old green hat, tied on with a woollen scarf. Una stopped short as she saw that he was carrying his skis and sticks. Peter stood in front of the greenhouse door; although his face could show no expression, she knew that he was furious.

"There you are!" Jerome said, "I have asked Peter to show you round. He knows more about orchids than I do." He came to her and took her arm.

Una hung back. "I don't want to see the orchids without you," she said. "You promised—"

"Of course you want to see them, anyone with eyes would," Jerome said impatiently. "We haven't cut a flower for nearly three weeks and they make quite a show. Come on, you will enjoy yourself."

She pulled her arm away from him, and he looked down at her with his mocking smile. "Promise?" he said. "The only promise I made was to Sylvie. I promised her this morning to see that you were happily engaged while I took her out for a long walk. She and I both need exercise."

Before Una could protest again, Jerome walked away from her past the garage with Sylvie running in front of him; she watched him bend down and put his skis on at the entrance to the lane. He turned to wave briefly at her, and then he was gone."

Peter laughed disagreeably. "Time Sylvie had a look in," he said. "Mr. Holt never can say no to her when she's really set on a walk. Well, are you coming or not? It's cold standing out here."

Una looked past him at the glass-houses, shining in the sunlight. She was sure that Peter was willing her to go back to the house, and she said at once, "I might as well come. I have nothing else to do, have I?" Through the glass she caught a glimpse of green and suddenly she was curious. "I have never seen orchids growing," she said, more graciously. "Mr. Holt would like me to see his plants."

Peter said nothing, but held the door open for her.

Una looked round the small bare glass-enclosed place, at Peter's old basket chair with its faded green cushions, and at the pile of newspapers and Sylvie's blanket beside it.

"This is where we do the potting, among other things, and sometimes the packing," Peter said. He went to the big wooden table. "This is Osmunda potting fibre," he said, showing her a handful of dark dry stuff, that looked to Una rather like frayed and decayed string. "And this is sphagnum moss—we make a mixture."

123

"Osmunda—what's that?" Una asked.

"Japanese fern," said Peter. "Look, I'll show you. We take a pot, like this, and pack in the stuff, down hard round the new roots, using this short thick pointed stick—"

"Which looks like an elephant goad," Una interrupted. "Let's skip all that. If you say that orchids live on that dry stuff, I'll believe you, unlikely as it seems. I want to see the orchids themselves."

She took her coat off and dropped it on his chair and then turned to Peter. "You were sitting reading here, weren't you?" she said. "Having a bit of peace. I don't want to disturb you. Sit down again. I will wander round by myself."

"Oh, no," Peter said at once. "Mr. Holt said to show you round and I'm going to do it."

"I don't believe you trust me," Una said, and gave a little laugh. "I promise I won't touch anything."

"I don't trust you, not a yard, not an inch, why should I?" Peter said as he opened the second door. "Well, here are the Cattleyas."

The long glass-house, the first of the three that led one from the other, was divided down the centre by a waist-high tiered and slatted bench on which the pots of orchids stood in orderly rows, holding their bright green and fleshy leaves towards the glass roof. Running down each side were other benches holding still more plants. Here and there among the green were vivid splashes of colours: purples, mauves, strange pinks, yellow, shining white. Una followed Peter down the narrow concrete path between the benches, looking where she was told to look: at the hot pipes, down at the beds of dark earth under the benches, up at the ventilators, open a crack even on this cold day, at the shades partly drawn over the glass roof to protect the plants in bloom against the bright sunlight.

"It's not a bit like I imagined," Una said, interrupting Peter's explanations. She sounded disappointed and he turned to look at her.

"It's so quiet and so neat," she said, "almost like any other greenhouse. Every pot with its little ticket."

"What did you expect?" Peter asked her. "A jungle? Creepers and tree-ferns, parrots and squawking tropical birds?"

Una laughed. "I suppose I did," she said, "something like that, something far more exotic anyway. I certainly thought it would be much hotter than this, steamy and hot and lush, with things hanging down from the roof—"

"This is the hottest part," Peter said. "The Cattleyas like it round seventy to eighty. Next door, where the Cymbidiums are, it's cooler. And it's wet enough. We keep it moist by going down the walks several times a day with a mist-nozzle on the hose, spraying under the benches and down the walls. Look, here's the humidity indicator."

Una was not listening. She put her hand out and touched a plant gingerly. "These roots hanging out of the pot look like fat white worms," she said. "I don't like them, and what are those fat swollen things below the leaves?"

"Those are the pseudo-bulbs," Peter began. "I'll re-pot this plant, divide it here, directly it has finished flowering. Look, here's a bud sheath," but Una had turned away. "I expected masses of colour," she said, looking past him down the aisle, "more colour than green, and a heavy scent. There is no real scent at all, only a wet, earth smell."

"Lots of orchids are scented," Peter said indignantly. "There's one behind you—Cattleya Walkeriana. As for colour—you haven't begun to look yet. What about this pinkish-mauve with the darker lip, and here's a deep magenta for you. If we never cut a flower, there would be masses of colour—they last for weeks. As it is you're lucky, there's far more to see than there usually is because of the snow. We ought to have sent off a big order the day after it started. Mr. Holt and I grow most of these orchids to sell. Usually we send them off after we have enjoyed them a few days, although I have known him to stick in his toes and refuse to have one touched."

He moved away from her down the aisle and said, "Look at this one here, lovely isn't it? Just about perfect blooms, nearly six inches across, I would say. Look at that great wide frilled lip, and the ruffle on those petals and the way the sepals stand out straight. An aristocrat, that's what this one is, and each of those gorgeous things will end up in a corsage, tied up with a bit of fern on some silly woman's shoulder."

"Poor Peter," said Una. "When you put it like that, it does seem a shame. It certainly is gorgeous, and so is this snow-white one."

"That's a Bob Betts," Peter said, gloomily. "Come round here, there are more on the other side."

"Don't tell me their names," Una told him. "I never remember names, the Latin ones anyway, and the others sound to me like racehorses. What's through that door?"

"The Cymbidiums, I told you," Peter said. "They are just about at their best. Come and see."

As he shut the second glass-panelled door behind her, Una cried out with pleasure. "Talk about colour!" she said, staring up at the great curving sprays which on the highest tier of the central bench almost touched the glass roof. "These are truly wonderful. Like huge moths or like miniature birds, green and gold, red and pinkish brown birds, sitting close together along the branches. Look at that pale pink one, it shines like silver. How lovely, Peter. How clever of you!"

Peter refused to show that he was pleased. "Let's get on and look at the rest," he said. "There are some species over here that Mr. Holt thinks a lot of."

"I should like to see some of those little frilly ones, you know, like the ones I picked that first evening."

Peter smiled, almost as if the remembrance now amused him. "The Odontoglossums?" he said. "Those are Mr. Holt's favourites. Very well, you shall. Come over here."

"They really are fascinating," said Una. "What extraordinary shapes. They make me think of pink and white and yellow feathers and butterflies, or of lace. I like this dark-pink one here with the flat pansy face."

127

"That's a Miltonia; 'Cat face,' Mr. Holt says," said Peter, but Una had darted away into the last greenhouse and he walked after her.

"Look at these big flat white ones on the long stems—I do like these," she said. "I like the way they bend out and their short leaves. You should have more of these." She bent down to peer at them more closely. " 'Phalaenopsis,' " she read. "What a mouthful. 'Serenity,' that's better."

Peter said, "The Moth orchid, they call that. Now come back here. There's one, a species, that you must have a look at because it's got a scent, for one thing."

"So it has," Una said, bending her fair head to the plant. "Faint, but a real scent. What an odd-looking thing, though. It sticks out its chin doesn't it, as if daring anyone to touch it?" She put out a finger and touched the thin dull yellowish petals blotched with purple. "Lucky for it that it has that big white and mauve lip. I suppose it has some jaw-breaking name."

Peter chuckled. "It has," he said. "Zygopetalum Mackyi. I thought that would make you pull a face. Come and look at my Cypripediums. Mr. Holt doesn't like them, but I think you will—"

For the rest of the short afternoon there was peace between Una and Peter. If anyone had been there to watch them as they went together down the aisles, stopping to examine a flower minutely or to read a ticket that showed not only the orchid's name but the date of its flowering and of its last potting, he would have said both of them were equally interested and absorbed and perhaps he would have been right. Only when, nearly an hour later, they came back into the bare small potting-room again, did Una show any impatience.

"Now I'll show you how Mr. Holt and I pack the orchids for market," Peter said. "Quite a business it is. Each flower has its own glass tube of water and we have to fix them in the box on a layer of paper and shavings by wooden batons so that they can't be shaken about in the journey. Wait here a minute while I fetch one of our boxes."

"Oh, no, Peter!" Una cried. "It must be nearly tea-time. We have been here for hours. Look, it's getting dark."

As she picked up her coat, Peter said in his usual rather surly voice, "He won't be back yet, if that's what you're thinking. Run along then. There's plenty I can do without wasting any more of my time."

Una stopped with her hand on the door-knob and looked back at him. "You haven't wasted your time," she said. "I enjoyed myself, really I did, Peter. It was a treat," but she saw that he was not to be mollified.

"Very well then," she said stiffly. "Have it your own way, I shall only say what it's up to me to say. 'Thank you very much, Peter.'"

Peter watched her through the glass as she hurried across the yard, running through the snow to the side door. Then he looked at his watch, straightened the cushions in his basket chair, and a few minutes later followed her.

Jerome and Sylvie had the woods to themselves for nearly

two hours. Together they climbed up between the trees until, once more, they could look down on the valley, and then one behind the other they descended the steep slopes. The clean clear air, as always, went to their heads. Sylvie ran and barked, laughed her silent laughter, ran again, and threw herself down on the snow beside Jerome when he paused to rest. Jerome laughed with her, calling her all her pet names, rolling her over and over in the snow, caressing her, throwing her pine cones to retrieve and giving her his hat to carry when he set off again, climbing still higher. Forgotten was the house; forgotten the day and time; for Jerome and Sylvie, the whole world was the woods and the sky above them. Only the sun dropping redly behind the hills brought them back. At the moment that Peter closed the greenhouse door and started across the yard they turned unwillingly towards the house, and that evening before dinner in the sitting-room Sylvie, with fresh heart and courage, made a determined stand.

After Jerome had taken off his ski boots and left his skis in the back porch, he stayed for a short time in the kitchen smoking and warming his hands at the range while Peter rubbed Sylvie down.

"When the sun goes it's colder than ever," Jerome said. "I wonder how much longer this is going to last."

Peter looked up at him. "No way of telling," he said, sitting back on his heels and picking up Sylvie's brush. "May go on for weeks." He jerked his chin in the direction of the hatch and said, "I took tea in some time ago and told Miss Una not to wait for you as once you and Sylvie were loose in the woods, there was no knowing how long you would be. She's there now sitting by the fire, not too pleased, if you ask me. It's growing dark."

"How did you two get on?" Jerome asked. "Did she enjoy the orchids?"

"I thought so at the time," said Peter, looking down at Sylvie again. "Seemed interested enough."

As he spoke the cuckoo-clock on the wall wheezed once and the brown bird said cuckoo five times.

"Better hurry—" Peter said. "I'll bring you in a fresh pot of tea directly I have finished Sylvie."

Jerome threw his cigarette butt into the grate and walked to the door. "Don't worry," he said. "I will go straight up for a hot bath. Keep Sylvie tied up until she is really dry and then give her her dinner early. She will eat to-night, you will see."

But Sylvie refused her meal when Peter gave it to her, at six, her usual time.

"What are you up to?" Peter asked her. "You know that it's no use my letting you into the sitting-room now, there's no one there."

Sylvie knew what she wanted. She ran straight across the hall without a glance up the stairs and stood impatiently in front of the sitting-room door until Peter, grumbling to himself, opened it for her. When Jerome came into the room, he found her waiting for him on the hearthrug close to his armchair, sitting upright with her back to the fire, her front feet close together, watchful, tense and bright-eyed.

"What are you doing there? What are you up to?" he said to her, much as Peter had done. "You look very purposeful—why don't you lie down and relax? She won't be down for ages."

He helped himself to whisky and water from the tray on the table behind the sofa. He was pleasantly tired, but glowing with his hours of hard exercise followed by a long soaking in a hot bath in which Una had insisted on putting a handful of her bathsalts to take any stiffness away. He had put on his ancient fur-lined slippers and his favourite green socks, old fawn trousers and a dark brown velvet smoking-jacket that he had found in the back of his cupboard and that he must have bought years ago and never worn. He felt benign and comfortable and younger, much younger and more vigorous than he had done for years. He wandered round his room, smiling to himself as he touched a book, straightened a picture, ran his hand over his polished gramophone cabinet, putting off the delicious moment when he would sink into his armchair and stretch his feet out towards the blaze. He knew, vaguely, that something was missing from the room; but he could not think what it was. He looked at the empty armchair on the other side of the fireplace but Una was still in her bath. She had been a little cross and reproachful when he had found her waiting for him behind the tea-table and, as he bent to kiss her, he had told her gently that she was becoming possessive, domineering and spoilt, an insufferable female. For a moment she had believed he meant it, and she had jumped up from her chair and had put her arms round him, anxious and repentant. Her face had been smooth and warm and scented against his cold roughened cheek. To please her he had drunk a cup of tea that he had not wanted.

Jerome walked over to the hatch and sliding it back called into the kitchen, "Peter, what have you done with the orchids that were in here?"

Peter came to the hatch, holding Sylvie's plate. "So you have noticed at last?" he said disagreeably. "Never mind the orchids, I put them out of harm's way days ago—look at this, not touched."

"You needn't sound so tragic. Sylvie ate quite well yesterday. Can't you see that she is only trying to make herself important?"

Peter snorted. "I can see how poor-looking she's getting, if you can't," he said. "None so blind as those that won't see anything except the carrot dangling in front of their noses. Well, take the plate and see if she will eat for you. I'm tired of this."

He thrust the plate into Jerome's hands and slammed the hatch shut.

Jerome carried Sylvie's plate across the room and put it down on the hearthrug in front of her, but he made no attempt to coax her to eat. He sat down in his chair, holding his glass on his knee, and looking down at her consideringly. Sylvie stared back at him.

"This is going too far. What are you trying to do, or be?"

133

he said to her, and now there was no mockery either of himself or of her in his voice. "There is no need of this dangerous silly jealousy. It's Peter's and my fault. We have spoiled you. Perhaps we have talked too much to you. Humans must talk. They forget that it worries animals. You are only a dog, Sylvie. Most beautiful and clever, but a dog. You must stay in your proper place, here on the hearthrug at my feet."

He put his hand on her head and felt a shudder run through her body and knew that it was a frisson of pleasure. "Oh, no, Sylvie!" he said.

He took her head between his hands, looked into her eyes, and knew that he need not really be dismayed. The dark brown-gold eyes, so luminous and candid, so lambent and warmly moist with love, held in their depths a saving spark of cold. It chilled but reassured him. Here, in Sylvie's eyes, was the wilderness, the inviolable secret pride of the wild, which no man could touch, where he could never go. Jerome sat back in his chair, gave her a firm friendly pat, and said briskly, "Go on, eat it up." As Sylvie, obedient to a tone she understood, bent her head to her plate, Una, glossy and fresh and sweet smelling from her bath and wearing her red wool dress, came into the room.

"You two look very cosy by the fire," she said. "Am I interrupting?"

Jerome put his hand out to her and drew her on to the arm of his chair. He turned his head, pressing his cheek against her side.

"How nice and firm and warm you feel," he said to her. "I like that dress."

"Do you, Jerome? I'm glad," Una said. "I haven't seen that velvet coat before. It suits you, makes you look like a writer, even like a distinguished playwright, but it doesn't go with those awful old trousers and those socks. Not to mention that jersey! I have taken a lot of trouble over myself this evening to please you. I think that for dinner at least you might put on a tie."

"What a shocking idea," Jerome said. "In my own house I dress to be comfortable. Stop trying to make a silk purse out of a contented old pig, my child, because you can't do it. Get yourself a drink and go and sit down where I can see you."

" 'And be quiet,' you might as well say it as you did on our first evening," Una said as she stood up. "But I must talk sometimes, I'm human after all. If you want silent adoration, there is always Sylvie."

"I want rational behaviour from you both, but I suppose that is too much to ask!"

"That depends what you call rational behaviour," said Una seriously. "Sylvie and I would both like to please you—how should we behave?"

"You should sit still in your chair with your hands folded in your lap, looking your prettiest and listening to me if I feel like talking, and just sitting if I don't. As for Sylvie she should eat her dinner."

"What a pasha you sound! But what is the matter with Sylvie? She ate yesterday. I thought that she had decided to put up with me. She can't be jealous still!"

Una knelt down on the hearthrug and picked up Sylvie's dish.

"Not touched," she said. "Dogs can go a long time without eating, but she does look wretched, poor Sylvie. Can't you do anything about this, Jerome?"

"I could turn you out into the snow, I suppose," Jerome said. "That's what she would like me to do."

Una looked up at him. "I wouldn't put it past you," she said. "Smile if you like, but you are nearly as silly as Peter is about this animal. Do you know what I think? I think that it is wrong to treat a dog as you do Sylvie, to talk to her as if she were a person, to make such a fool of her."

"You do, do you? Leave Sylvie alone. She is not your dog."

"If she were, she would be healthier and happier. She would eat what she was given and like it. She would sleep outside in a kennel. I would see that she was mated. Puppies would give her something real and natural to think about all day instead of you."

"You are very eloquent all of a sudden on Sylvie's behalf," Jerome said. "You should see yourself kneeling there, pink with self-righteousness! What a busy little know-all, you are, Una. First you would like to redecorate my house, then you would see to my man servant and my clothes, and now you turn your attention to my dog."

"How can you be so unkind and unfair? I was only trying to help."

"Don't try. Mind your own business. No one asked you—"

Una put her hand on his knee. "Don't say it, please Jerome," she said. "I know that you didn't ask me to come here. I came, and I have been happier than I thought that it was possible to

be. I refuse to quarrel with you, even if that is what you want me
to do. I'm too grateful."

"Grateful?" Jerome picked up her hand and held it in his.
"My dear, I'm a brute," he said. "I'm sorry. What can I say?"

"Nothing. It's over now. Let's forget it." Una jumped up and
smoothing her red skirt walked across the room, helped herself
to a drink and lit a cigarette. She moved self-consciously as if she
knew that his eyes were following her.

Jerome watched her thoughtfully as he stroked Sylvie's head,
pulling the long soft fire-warmed ears between his fingers. "Before you sit down," he said at last, "you might put this dish in
the hatch, she won't eat now."

Una put her glass down on the table. "Why don't you try and
make her eat it," she said. "She might, if you really insisted."

"No, I'm not going to force her. She has a right to leave it if
she wants to."

"Poor Sylvie," Una said as she knelt down on the hearthrug
again. "It must be horrid to be so jealous. We won't enjoy our
dinner if we know that she is hungry. Let me see what I can do."

Taking a piece of meat in her fingers, Una held it under Sylvie's nose. "Come on, Sylvie," she said. "Just to please Jerome."

Sylvie drew back, pressing herself against Jerome's knees and
turned her head disdainfully towards the fire.

"Be careful, Una," Jerome said, as he felt the hair of Sylvie's
ruff rising against his hand.

Una only laughed and held the meat nearer. "Be careful?"
she said. "Of what? The saintly Sylvie? Make her come out here

where I can reach her, Jerome. You are in the way. Very well, if you won't, I will. This is too stupid—"

Before Jerome could stop her, Una knelt up and stretched her arm across his legs and put her hand on Sylvie's collar. "Come out here," she said. "That's my place anyway."

Sylvie's low growl gave no warning. She struck as swiftly as a snake and her long head, with the flattened ears, had something snake-like about it. Leaving blood-filled marks of her teeth on the white flesh of Una's arm, she sprang out from the shelter of Jerome's knees and stood on the hearthrug in front of the fire, legs braced, hackles raised, and showed her teeth in an angry snarl. Gone was the familiar of the house, the graceful gentle creature that they all knew; in her place was a menace in the room, a wild thing from the woods.

Peter was making up the range in the kitchen when he heard Una's shriek. As if he had been expecting it, he threw his shovel down and, snatching up the heavy steel chain, rushed through the hall and into the sitting-room.

"Sylvie!" he shouted, as he saw the group by the fire. "Stop it, Sylvie."

Una was crouched by Jerome's chair, holding her wrist, while Jerome, leaning forward, had one hand on Sylvie's collar; in his other hand he held the poker.

"Don't touch her," Peter cried. "She doesn't know what she's doing. Wait, I'm coming."

He ran forward and, pushing Jerome aside, knelt down on the hearthrug and fastened the chain to Sylvie's collar. "What have you done to her?" he said furiously, looking up at Jerome who had risen to his feet. "I never saw her looking like this. Stop it, Sylvie. Quiet now."

"Done to her?" Jerome said. "I like that! She has just attacked Miss Una."

"Then Miss Una asked for it," said Peter. "She teased Sylvie into this, she's been at her ever since she came. I know, I have been watching."

"I wasn't doing anything. I was only trying to help. She flew at me—oh, look at my arm!" and Una burst into tears.

Peter looked briefly at the arm she held out to him. "Better sit down and tie your handkerchief round that to stop the blood," he said. "I'll bring my First Aid box in a minute. All the same, you began this, Miss—must have done."

He swung round on Jerome. "It's your fault," he said. "Amused you to see them at each other's throats, doesn't it? I know you—all this week you have been egging them on, setting one against the other."

"Don't talk nonsense," said Jerome. "Give me the chain. I'm going to give Sylvie a good beating."

"With that poker? No, you're not."

"Of course not, don't be stupid. My slipper will do."

"You can't—you won't—Sylvie's not the sort of dog you can beat, with a slipper or anything else."

"She has drawn blood. What do you expect me to do? A dog who bites must be beaten, really beaten. It's the only thing to do."

"Then do it in the hall, not here in front of her," Peter jerked his head at Una, who was sitting on the sofa, nursing her arm and sobbing noisily.

"I shall do it here, on the scene of the crime," Jerome said. "Sylvie must understand what she has done."

He took off his slipper and handed the end of the chain to Peter. Sylvie, now quiet, dignified, herself again, looked up at him. As a puppy she had often been slapped for small offences and while she was learning her lessons in obedience, to come to heel, to sit, to wait, to leave the valley sheep strictly alone, she had known the sting of a light switch; Jerome had once cuffed her hard for rolling on a dead bird; but nothing in her three years of life had prepared her for this. As Jerome gripped her collar with a hand that had suddenly become alien and heavy, awful to her with a terror that she did not understand, her ears went back flat against her head and her tail curled between her legs. She did not flinch but when he lifted the ignominious slipper and the first blow fell, her lip curled back from her closely gripped teeth in a grimace of pain and shame, so brief that no one saw it.

Peter dropped the chain and turned his head away. Una held her breath and put her hands over her ears, but now Sylvie submitted to her punishment stoically, almost with an air of indifference. When it was over, instead of touching Jerome's hand forgivingly with her muzzle, as she had always done before when she was corrected, or leaping up at him to put her paws on his shoulders while she asked with eagerly waving tail and supplicating eyes for him to forgive her too, she walked without a glance at any of them to the door.

Jerome sat down and put on his slipper again. His hands were trembling. "You needn't look at me like that," he said to Peter. "I didn't really hurt her. I wish I had for her own sake. If she thinks that she has got away with this, there is no knowing what she will do."

"She doesn't think so," Peter said, looking at Sylvie. "It will be a long time before she can hold up her head again. A bad day's work, this is. Goodness knows what it will lead to."

"Take her to the kitchen and tie her up on her bed," Jerome told him. "Then bring that box of yours and some hot water. We had better see to Miss Una's arm."

As Peter left the room with Sylvie trailing after him at the end of her chain, he heard Jerome say, "Please stop that noise, Una, and pull yourself together. Have another drink. You are more shocked than hurt. The skin is just broken. Don't be so silly, of course you won't be scarred. Let me look—"

Peter smiled grimly to himself as he marched down the hall. As he opened the kitchen door, he said to Sylvie, "Not scarred indeed! You have left your mark on her all right!"

He fastened the chain to his armchair, pushed Sylvie on to her bed, and fetched his black tin First Aid box from its place on the dresser beside the telephone and put it on the table. As he lifted the kettle from the range, he said softly, "How could you do such a thing, Sylvie? How could you be so foolish? It was

141

wearing off, I know him—only a question of time. Now you have gone and spoilt it all. When he takes a good look at that arm he will be all over her."

He opened the box and inspected the contents. "Curse all women," he said. "Trouble, trouble all the time. Iodine, that's the thing!"

Dinner that night was much later than usual. After her arm had been washed and bandaged Una refused to go to bed, as both Jerome and Peter suggested. She sat in the armchair by the fire with a tray on her knees, eating with a fork in one hand, the other being in a sling made from one of Jerome's white silk handkerchiefs. Although she had swallowed the aspirins that Peter had given her with a second whisky, she looked very wide awake and she could not stop talking. Jerome had combed her hair behind her ears, fetched her eau-de-cologne and a clean handkerchief, put a cushion behind her back and cut up her food for her. He had drunk too much in his remorse and concern and, scarcely touching his own dinner, hovered near her in a maudlin fashion that made Peter grin scornfully whenever he came to the hatch, which was as seldom as possible.

As Peter ate his own meal on a corner of the kitchen table, he heard them go upstairs.

Sylvie lay on her bed with her eyes wide-open, staring at the uncurtained window. Peter had undone her chain long ago but she had not stirred since he had tied her on her bed. She made no attempt to follow him when he went through the hall into the sitting-room to clear the table and to rake out the fire. As he washed up and tidied the kitchen, he glanced at her but something, her attitude or her stillness, prevented him from talking to her as he usually did when they were alone together. When his work was finished, he sat in his chair in the glow from the open range, smoking his pipe, as he did every night.

For Peter this was usually the best part of the day, even better than the short rest-time he spent after luncheon in the orchid-houses; then he never knew what might bring him to his feet: a need to check the temperature and the humidity, to close or open the ventilators, a feeling that all was not well with some particular plant; he was as fussy as an anxious mother where the orchids were concerned, and he knew it. In his comfortable red armchair in his clean and tidy kitchen, he could be at ease and at peace for a short time before he went to bed. His work was done; the alarm would sound above the dresser if anything went wrong with the heating in the glass-houses in the night. Jerome would want nothing more from him until the morning. Sylvie would be in from her last run and either sleeping beside him, or else with Jerome. The doors of the house would be locked against the night. This was the only time that Peter really had for himself. He would pore over his football pools, read an old newspaper, listen to his wireless, write up his private accounts and his orchid-diary or, with a pencil in his hand, read the only book he ever read these days, which was Sander's Complete List Of Orchid Hybrids, the stud book of the orchid, take notes, and dream of the new and improbable hybrid that he and Jerome would startle the orchid-world with one fine day.

143

To-night Peter was not at ease. His wireless was silent; the book lay open but unread on his lap. He kept looking over his shoulder or at the window where the crusted snow was piled high against the black glass. Once he shivered as if a cold breath from the dark woods had penetrated into the room. Just before midnight, he stood up, knocked his pipe out and made up the range. Sylvie followed him obediently when he went into the porch and opened the back door. The light shone out onto the snow, showing the same white expanse he had seen for days. There was no wind and the stars were showing. As Sylvie slipped past him and vanished into the night, he stood listening; but there was nothing to hear except an owl calling a long way off.

Shivering, Peter went back to his chair and waited, with one eye on the clock, for Sylvie to scratch imperiously at the door, demanding to be let in. When twenty minutes had passed, he went into the porch again. There was no sign of Sylvie. He shone his torch towards the trees and taking his whistle from his pocket, blew it twice. He waited in the open doorway, huddled into his duffle-coat, but she did not come.

The light in the upstairs room had been turned out long ago, but at one o'clock Peter was still dozing in his chair in front of the range. At two, he got up stiffly, propped the back door half-open, pulled Sylvie's bed into the porch, shut the kitchen door and turning out the lights went to bed. The house was dark and silent under its covering of snow. Round it the woods stretched away to the hills.

In the morning when the sun rose, Sylvie had not come back.

Part Three

I

Jerome woke while it was still dark and, suddenly wide awake, switched on his bedside light. His clock in its shabby morocco case, which had gone with him on all his travels, showed that it was half-past six. He looked down at Una as if he were surprised to find her beside him in his bed, as if she were a stranger instead of his companion of the last six nights. Her face was turned towards him and one cheek rested on her bandaged arm. Her hair was smooth behind her ears and made a neat yellow fan on the pillow; her pale mouth was gently but firmly closed. As he looked at her, she frowned and, still asleep, turned over on her side away from the light, burying her head in the pillow and showing a bare shoulder. He pulled the blanket up over her and reached for the writing-pad and pencil which always waited on the table near the lamp.

Propping himself against the pillow and shivering a little he began to write. The fire had died to a small lingering glow and although the two radiators were on the room seemed cold to him. He thought anxiously for a moment of the orchids and wondered if Peter could have forgotten to make up the furnace; then, knowing Peter, he dismissed the thought. The vague idea that had floated in the back of his mind ever since he had set out on his skis with Sylvie, perhaps long before that—he could not remember the exact moment when it had first dawned on his mind's horizon—had taken shape and firmness during the night and appeared before him whole and ready when he woke. 'The Feathers Fly,' he wrote, and drew a firm line under it. This was how each of his plays had begun; with a title that set the key for all that was to follow and that had never needed to be changed.

As he put out his hand and felt for a cigarette on the table beside him, Una stirred and sighed. He quickly switched out the light and lay back against the pillow, rigid with annoyance and cursing to himself. She usually slept as soundly as a child and he felt aggrieved as he remembered how difficult it had often been to rouse her. "How exactly like a woman or a cat," he said to himself, as he felt her stir against him. "Never there when you call but always when you don't." When she was still and he could tell from her breathing that she was sound asleep again, he slipped cautiously out of bed and, clasping his pad and pencil and his packet of cigarettes, opened the bedroom door and crossed the landing to the bathroom.

The clothes he had worn the evening before were still on the chair by the radiator. He dressed hurriedly, washed his face with cold water and combed his hair back. The landing was dark but the dim light from the window fell on to Sylvie's bed; he saw that it was empty but at the moment this meant nothing to him. He went down the stairs, changed his velvet jacket in the cloakroom for his old tweed writing-coat, crossed the hall, and opened the door of his workroom.

Standing inside the door with the screen still between him and the dark room, Jerome paused. He was in a fever to get to his writing-table, but at the same time reluctant to move, to step round the screen and to commit himself to the hard labour that lay ahead. The air was close, stuffy, the air of a closed and unused room. He shut the door behind him and, passing round the screen, went to the windows moving quickly and surely between the furniture because he knew the room by heart. He pulled the heavy curtains back and, kneeling on the window-sill, opened the window, letting the ice-cold dawn air flow past him into the room. The sky was paling but above the dark line of the hills the stars still showed. "That's better," he said out loud and, leaving the window open a crack, he turned back to the room.

The matches were in their usual place in the blue bowl on the shelf above the fireplace. He lit the fire, which Peter had laid days ago, and knelt on the hearthrug watching the sticks catch and blaze and the flames seize on the coal before he got up and switched on the light. The room was exactly as it had always been: nothing had been moved since he had left it six days ago, although Peter, he knew, had given it its daily brush and polish. This was how it always was when he came back to it after a long journey, or a short holiday.

"Where have I been?" he said, and looking round guiltily, went to his writing-table and sat down. Now, as always after one of his travels, he knew that he was really home.

He pulled the manuscript of his novel towards him, read a few words, patted the written sheets into a neat pile and put it into a folder which he set down on the far side of his table, giving it a regretful farewell pat. Then he put a sheet of paper into his typewriter, squared his shoulders and, sighing happily, typed: 'The Feathers Fly. Act 1. Scene 1. A sitting-room. Snow is falling. . . .'

Peter, opening the door and coming round the screen two hours later, saw Jerome sitting at his table with the lights still on and the early morning sunshine slanting into the room.

Peter was dressed in his usual morning clothes: old trousers, slippers, turtle-necked blue sweater and leather waistcoat, and he carried a duster, but his hair was dishevelled and wet as if, a short time before, he had gone bareheaded into the snowy woods, as indeed he had. Normally, seeing Jerome at his table and hearing the clatter of the typewriter, he would have made up the fire as quietly as he could and then withdrawn to the kitchen to make a pot of strong coffee. To-day he walked across the room and said loudly, "Sylvie has been out all night. It's nearly nine and she hasn't come back."

Jerome frowned, but he took his hands from the typewriter and sat back in his chair.

"Do you have to bother me now?" he said, and then looking up at Peter's face he said more gently, "What did you say was the matter with Sylvie? Out all night? Don't worry, she will be back."

"How can you sit there and say that?" Peter cried. "For all you know she may have fallen into some hole and can't get out. She may be dragging herself along with a broken leg somewhere out there. She may be frozen to death, you don't know. But I don't think anything has happened to Sylvie. I think she has gone of her own accord."

"Nonsense, Peter. Why should she go, what do you mean?"

Peter put both hands on Jerome's table and, leaning forward, said into his face, "Sylvie doesn't care to stay in this house any longer, that's what I mean. I let her out as usual, near midnight it was. She went off without a look at me into the dark. In three years she has never been out on her own for more than an hour or two. She won't be back. It's your fault. You shouldn't have beaten her."

"Don't shout at me," Jerome said patiently. "As usual where Sylvie is concerned, you go too far. I had to beat her. There was nothing else I could do. If she is offended and hurt and has taken this way of showing it, she won't keep it up. When she is really hungry she will come back. Sylvie is young and strong. With her thick coat she won't freeze, and she won't lose herself—she knows these woods as you know your kitchen. There is no reason why she should have had an accident and there is nothing in the woods for Sylvie to fear. Keep your head and talk sense, that's a good chap."

"I know all that," Peter said. "Perhaps you're right, but I know that something has happened."

"If she doesn't come back in an hour or so, why don't you go down to the farm and see if she is there? What a nuisance it is about the telephone—she might have gone as far as the village."

"I thought of the farm," Peter said slowly, "but I don't want to let anyone know about this until we have to. It's dangerous, I tell you, to beat a dog like Sylvie. Suppose she turns savage? I mean, there's no knowing what she might do."

Jerome lost his patience and his temper. "Absolute rubbish!" he said. "Sylvie savage? You say that because of that silly scene last night. It seems to me that I know Sylvie better than you do. That's enough of this!"

He pulled his chair up to the table again and said, "Go away. Can't you see that I'm working? Bring me some coffee. Let me know when Sylvie comes back. Tell Miss Una that I will see her this evening. Leave me alone!"

Peter stepped back. As he turned away he said, "You and your work! Nothing else matters, does it? Miss Una! That one! I knew there would be trouble directly I set eyes on her. Why did she ever have to put her foot in this house? You tell me that!"

The sound of the typewriter, furiously driven, followed him to the door.

2

Una, in her white wool dressing-gown, was standing by her bedroom window looking out over the glass-houses and the path to the garage at the snowy woods when Peter knocked at her door and carried her breakfast tray into the room.

He was later than he usually was and she had been waiting impatiently for him for over an hour, walking round her room which was larger and more comfortable than Jerome's. To pass the time, she planned what she would do with it, if she had the chance: striped wall-paper, perhaps: new curtains, white-painted furniture instead of all this heavy wood. In the past week, Jerome had often shaken her awake just in time to allow her to run across the landing and to dive into her own bed as Peter climbed the stairs. This morning she had wakened early, as it was growing light, to find Jerome gone and the place beside her empty and cold. She had waited for him to come back, perhaps from the bathroom, and she had dozed a little; then she had put on her dressing-gown and had gone out on to the landing. Standing there with her hand on the banisters, she had heard Peter moving about the house and the sound of a door opening and closing below her in the hall. She had thought of going downstairs to look for Jerome but something, a new atmosphere, a strangeness in the house, had prevented her. She had gone to her own room, lit her fire, washed her hands, brushed her hair and powdered her face, as if she were preparing for an emergency.

If Peter was surprised to see her standing at the window he gave no sign. He said, "Good-morning, Miss," in the expressionless guarded manner he always used to her, and put the tray down on the table beside her smooth and obviously unslept-in bed.

"Good-morning, Peter," Una said, in a bright and slightly condescending voice. "Another lovely sunny day, isn't it? I'll have my breakfast by the fire, if that's not a nuisance. Let me hold the tray while you move the table. It's a shame to give you so much trouble. There is no reason why I shouldn't have breakfast downstairs."

"One reason is that it's less trouble for me this way," Peter said. "I do the sitting-room after breakfast. Yes, it's a fine day, but there's going to be a change. I can feel it. A thaw is coming. Call out if you want any more toast."

As he turned towards the door, Una said in her normal voice, "What is the matter? Something has happened."

Peter, with his hand on the doorknob, looked at her. His small angry blue eyes went over her from her newly brushed hair to the furry toes of her pink slippers. "Happened?" he said. "Nothing that would interest you—or perhaps it would. Sylvie has gone."

"Gone?"

"Yes, gone, gone, gone," Peter said rudely, mimicking her voice. "She went out late last night and didn't come back. That suits you nicely, doesn't it."

Una sat down in the chair by the fire and picked up the coffee pot. She said coldly, "There is no need for you to lose your temper. What do you mean by gone? I suppose you mean that she has run away. Don't get in such a state. Sylvie can look after herself. She will come back."

Peter came towards her across the room. "It's all your fault," he said. "No one asked you to come here, upsetting the house, upsetting his work, driving Sylvie out of her own home. Look at you sitting there, warm and comfortable and smug, drinking your hot coffee! Sylvie was out all night in the woods, and where is she now? Frozen and starved, for all you care. Well, now you have got what you want. You have him all to yourself, jealous scheming little bitch that you are!"

Una put her cup down carefully. She looked up at Peter and said, "The trouble with you is that you are not quite normal. If I thought that you were, I would go straight to Mr. Holt and tell him what you have just called me. You live too much alone, Peter, stuck up here in the woods with only a dog for company, and she is only a dog, you know, not a spoilt child or a fairy princess or even a precious piece of china. You are unbalanced about her, even worse than Mr. Holt is. It's wrong to treat any animal as you do Sylvie. It can't be good for her or for you. Take my advice, Peter, and go out into the world a bit more. See places and people and stop moping. If you can't forget about your face, do something about it."

Peter took a step towards her, but she lifted her chin and faced him calmly. "It's no use being furious," she said. "I'm going to say what I think. Mr. Holt told me why you wouldn't go on with the treatment, the skin-grafting and the operations. It was hard for you, about your wife, I mean, and I'm sorry, truly sorry, but I think that you ought to have gone on for your own sake and for other people's too. It's not too late even now. You could go back and start again. These plastic surgeons are even cleverer now. . . ."

"Be quiet," Peter said furiously. "You don't know what you're talking about. What a nerve. Leave my face alone. Mr. Holt had no business—"

"It's no use losing your temper again," Una told him. "I'm only talking for your own good."

Peter lifted his hand and Una shrank back in her chair; but he controlled himself and stepped back, smiling his twisted smile. "Thanks for the lecture," he said. "Know everything, don't you, Miss Clever? I shouldn't have spoken to you as I did, but I'm glad I lost my temper because now you know. Well, I'm off."

"Wait a minute," Una said. "Have you had something to eat this morning? You look terribly tired." She stood up and, going to him, put her hand on his arm.

Peter looked down at her hand, and then into her face. Una looked back at him without flinching and said, "Why not sit down and have some coffee and a piece of toast? Go on, sit in my chair by the fire. I'll get the glass from the wash-basin, you can use that instead of fetching another cup. I expect that you have been up all night."

Peter suddenly did what he was told. As he took the filled glass from her hand, he said, "I feel all-in this morning. I went to bed at last but I couldn't sleep, knowing Sylvie was out there and wondering what she was up to. Why should you wait on me like this, Miss, pouring me out coffee? What do you want?"

"What a suspicious creature you are," Una said, as she sat down on the edge of her bed. "All women aren't fiends, you know. A few of us can see when a man is tired and needs a cup of coffee. You have done a lot for me in the last few days, whether you liked it or not. Perhaps I'm grateful."

Peter looked away from her. "I don't trust you or any woman a yard," he said. "Under all these tricks you are always out for yourselves in one way or another."

Una laughed. "Tell me, Peter, what was your wife like?" she said. "Pretty? Fair? I imagine her fair, I don't know why."

"No reason for you to imagine her at all, Miss," Peter said. "If you want to know, she was the same colouring as me, black hair, blue eyes. I don't want to talk about my wife."

"You should have forgotten all about her and found yourself another girl."

"With this face? What a hope! Besides, once bitten twice shy."

157

He looked at Una and gave one of his snorting laughs. "All the same," he said, "Sylvie shouldn't have gone for you like she did. But you asked for it, didn't you?"

"I didn't do anything to Sylvie," Una protested. "I have been trying to make friends with her all this week. It isn't my fault if she is jealous."

"Of course it's your fault," Peter said. "Haven't I been watching you? Sylvie thinks the world of Mr. Holt. You might say that he is her sun and moon and stars. She doesn't care for anyone to be too near him, but she is sweet-tempered and she would have put up with you if you hadn't gone too far, gone out of your way to rile her. For instance, why should you, a grown woman, want to go sitting on the hearthrug? Because you know very well that it's Sylvie's place."

Una shrugged her shoulders. "What a fuss about nothing," she said. "I did nothing to make Sylvie dash out into the night in this melodramatic way."

"It's dangerous to drive anyone too far," Peter said, as if she had not spoken. "Pushes them off their balance. If Sylvie turns nasty, there's no knowing what she may do."

"Just because she bit me last night? Don't be silly. But if she felt savage, what harm could she do in the woods? There is no one there."

"There's more in the world than just human beings," Peter said darkly. Then he put his empty glass down on the tray and stood up. "Forget it," he said. "I had no call to say that. When you come downstairs I'll dress that arm of yours again—never asked you how it was did I? Well, I must get on with my work and take some breakfast into Mr. Holt."

Una let him get as far as the door before she said, as casually as she could, "Where is Mr. Holt?"

"In his study—his workroom, of course."

"At this hour of the morning? What is he doing there?"

Peter came back across the room towards her. His face could show no expression, but it was plain that he was triumphant. "Mr. Holt is working," he said. "Been at it for hours working on a new play. He told me to tell you that he would see you this evening."

"This *evening*? What about his luncheon?"

"You leave his luncheon to me," Peter said. "I'll see he gets it. When a play seizes him like this, I look after him like an old nanny, or a keeper. I might be either, I sometimes think. It's all right for me, got nothing else much to do with my life, but don't you worry about him. It's not worth it, not for a young thing like you that's got her life to make. You think of yourself, that's my advice."

Una was not listening. "What am I supposed to do all day until this evening?" she cried.

"I couldn't really say, Miss," Peter said. "But if I was you I should begin by sitting down and finishing your breakfast or the coffee will be cold. The fire will be lit in the sitting-room by the time you are dressed. I'll bring you your luncheon there. Pity about the radio, but you can always read—plenty of books in this house. Go for a walk, take another look at the orchids. Do anything you like, but if you know what's good for you, leave Mr. Holt alone."

"Thank you, Peter," Una said. "Did Mr. Holt say that I was to take orders from you? He can tell me all that himself."

"Go into his workroom?" Peter said, as she sat down again and poured herself a second cup of coffee. "Don't you dare. I tell you he won't thank you for disturbing him. No one except Sylvie is allowed to be with him when he is working."

"Go away, please, and mind you own business."

Peter came a step nearer to the table. He put his hands on his hips and looking down at her said, "Mr. Holt and I have been together in this house for a long time, fourteen years. I know him through and through. He came and took me out of the hospital and brought me straight here. If it was not for him, I should be in the Home now, the Home where they keep people with faces like mine. But never mind about that now, that's not what I'm trying to say."

He looked from her round the room, as if for inspiration, and then, gazing intently at her again, said almost beseechingly, "Listen, it's something after all to do what Mr. Holt has done. Not that I think so much of writers, it seems to me that practically everyone writes something or other these days. I look in the papers and it's books, books everywhere. But it isn't everyone who succeeds, is it, who brings in the money? You should have seen this place when we first came. Rough! Cold! I didn't think that he would stick it. It was all right for me, I was brought up different and I had nowhere else to go. 'Two years,' he said to me then. 'Give me two years, Peter.' I don't mind telling you now that I had my doubts. It seemed to me then that he would be better doing a real job of work somewhere. I didn't see what he was getting at, sitting there day after day scribbling away, with his bit of money going and nothing to show, while I worked round the place, like a black. 'I hope you know what you are doing?' I said to him. He knew all right. Look at us now, not to mention the London flat and the famous people he knows and the women chasing after him. Ruddy miracle that's what it is, and all out of his head."

Una interrupted him. "Mr. Holt has told me that he couldn't have done it without you," she said. "He owes a lot to you, Peter. You needn't go on, he has told me all about those first two years."

"Has he? I wonder what he told you. Do you know what he said to me once? An extra cold day it was, one of those days when nothing goes right. I took him in a cup of cocoa and he looked up at me, scowling, and said, 'I believe you are enjoying all this, you old so-and-so. Wonderful little woman knocking up a home out of a few packing cases and a yard of chintz in some outpost of the Empire, that's what you were in your last life, Peter.' "

Una laughed and Peter said earnestly, "No laughing matter sometimes, I can tell you. Living with someone who writes, who earns their living that way, is not so easy. Sometimes, even now, it seems to me that he is hardly human, and then I say to myself that he can't help it, that he is made that way and perhaps all these artists, painters and writers and so on, are all much the same. A vocation, that's the word for what they think they have, something the same as a nun or a priest. I read that somewhere and took the trouble to look it up in Mr. Holt's dictionary. 'Called to a task,' that means."

Peter looked at Una anxiously. "Takes a bit of understanding, doesn't it?" he said. "But Mr. Holt makes a lot of money out of all this, and that's something anyone can understand. Writers have their moods, same as anyone else. The only thing is, they don't seem to realize how lucky they are. I mean to say, after all, other people have to *work*. Take a doctor, for instance, or a miner, or a bus-conductor, after all there is some difference, but to listen to Mr. Holt sometimes you would think that no one had ever worked before. 'A partnership,' that's what he called us. 'I'm the boiler and you are the stoker,' he said to me. That riled me sometimes because it seemed to me that I did all the work while he just sat there. Then I thought that I should hate to sit on my arse for hours and hours on end, squeezing words out of my head, and that it was work after all, not so easy as some suppose. He was right of course. It's his business to write and it's mine to keep things going so he can write. For one thing, what would happen to all of us, to him, to Sylvie, the house, and to me, if he doesn't keep it up? As a matter of fact, I would be all right. He bought an annuity for me some years ago, enough for me to live on. Did you know that? He said that he wanted me to feel free— not tied in any way."

Peter looked at Una and smiled, but before she could speak he said, "It's Mr. Holt, him and this house I'm thinking of. Perhaps he has some money put by, perhaps we could do more with the orchids, it's quite a nice little business as it is, but that would be chicken-feed compared to what he is used to. Mr. Holt likes his comforts and would hate to go without them now whatever he may think. For instance, for years the only drink here was beer and now, look at us—whisky, wine, brandy after dinner—not that Mr. Holt drinks much as a rule. It's only lately that he has said that drink helps him. If he dries up, as he is always afraid of doing, if one day he finds that he can't write any more, where will we all be?"

"But don't you want him to be happy?" Una cried. "Isn't he to have any life of his own except his work? He looks a different man since I came here, you can't deny it."

"I don't say that you haven't done him good," Peter said. "He was looking hipped, not himself, when you turned up, bored and restless, like he gets when he needs a break. Something must have gone wrong with his last bout of London. He hasn't been himself since he came back. But now he has had enough. He is ready to settle down and get on with it. When it comes to it, all he really needs, here in the woods anyway, is to be let alone to write in his own way. All else that comes along, the orchids, even Sylvie, is extra. I know him better than anyone else does, that's why I say to you, don't waste your time. The best thing you can do is to go back where you belong before you get hurt. I could get your car out and going anytime now, the roads are clear."

Una buttered a piece of toast carefully before she looked up at

163

Peter again. Then she said, "Poor Peter. Do you know what I think? I think that you ought to have a holiday, a good long rest away from this house. No one is indispensable, you know. That's the trouble isn't it? You want to be indispensable to someone, to Mr. Holt. All this refusing to have proper electric light, or an easier furnace, or an Aga instead of that ghastly range, is not because you like work but because you want to be important. 'Peter the indispensable, Peter the glutton for work.' I believe that you are nearly as jealous of me as Sylvie is. It's no use you trying to get me out. I'm not going. He needs me. I belong here now and I'm staying."

"Quite a speech," Peter said. "Why don't you look out for yourself and leave me alone? I know what's in your head, and I tell you straight that it's no use. Mr. Holt, he isn't the marrying kind, he's no family man. If he had wanted a wife and children he would have seen to it long ago. If you want to know, he said to me once how lucky he was not to have a devoted wife helping him on with his career, driving him to do work he didn't want to do. A confirmed bachelor, that's what he is now, if ever he was anything else. No, it's too late for that. Forget it, Miss."

"You talk as if he were a hundred," Una said. "Why shouldn't he begin a new life and be happy? I could make him happy. Not for a week but for always."

"I don't suppose you are the first woman to think that," Peter said. "I see that it's time I talked more plainly."

He walked across the room, fetched the dressing-table stool and putting it beside her sat down.

"I'm sorry for you," he said, "and I'm only talking for your own good. You have looks and plenty of guts. You could amount to something on your own, if you had any sense. It's a shame, that's what I have been saying to myself all this week. I'm surprised at Mr. Holt. A young girl like you, and brought up properly I can see, whatever you pretend. What's your mother doing, letting you run loose like this at your age? Mr. Holt, he's no good to you, none at all. He's slippery as an eel over women. He uses them as springboards when he needs them and takes off, refreshed, as you might say, and goes back to his work here in this house. How do I know? He has talked to me, hasn't he? I'm his friend as well as his servant by now. He and I, we have talked about everything under the sun, women among the rest of it. Smile if you like, but if you think you are different from any other woman you are riding for a fall. Take my advice and go while the going's good, and that's before he puts you out, which he will do on some pretext or another, and sooner than you think."

Una pushed her chair back and stood up. "This is a most extraordinary conversation," she said. "It has gone on quite long enough. I have only listened to you because in this house you are, as you say, more of a friend than a servant, or that is what Mr. Holt thinks. I think you are rude, impertinent and spiteful and that you take too much on yourself. Pick up that tray, please, and get out of my room!"

Her face was flaming. She put her hands to her cheeks and walking to the window stood with her back to the room.

Peter watched her thoughtfully. Then he shrugged his shoulders and, standing up, picked up the tray.

At the door he said, "Very well, Miss, play it your own way. Don't say that I didn't warn you. Wait and see—"

3

The spring of sweet water in the woods flowed out of a cleft between two rocks at the head of a narrow glade. Perhaps there had once been a small landslide here when a part of the hillside had slipped away, leaving the exposed shelf of rocks and the open space between the trees. In summer the grass was a vivid green and the miniature waterfall, less than two feet high, falling from the shallow basin in the cleft, splashed a half circle of wild flowers before disappearing into the grass. Ferns grew between the rocks and, in autumn, blackberries ripened on the sun-warmed stone. In winter the cleft was often hung with icicles but the water always bubbled up between them and into the basin which never quite froze over, making a perpetual drinking-place for bird and beast.

This was the spring where Sylvie liked to drink, although it was over a mile away from the house. She would approach it joyfully, bounding up the hillside towards the clean scent of its water which would taste faintly of iron on her tongue. She would thrust her long muzzle between the grass and the flowers, letting the cool drops fall on her brow, and then lift her head to lap noisily from the basin until she had drunk her fill. This morning, soon after the sun rose, she came to the spring furtively, her tail dragging on the snow.

Half the glade was in dazzling sunlight and half in the sharp-edged blue shadow of the trees. She crouched for a long time in the fringe of shadow, looking over her shoulder, as if making sure that she had not been followed, and searching the familiar glade with suspicious eyes. When she moved out into the sunlight, she looked dark and menacing against the deep purity of the snow. This was not the sleek well-cared-for graceful Sylvie that Jerome and Peter knew but a gaunt wild creature. The pale hair of her throat and chest was clotted and stained; her coat was stiff with snow and full of pine needles and twigs, as if she had been rolling frantically in an effort to cleanse herself, as indeed she had. She walked slowly, almost clumsily, her head lowered and her ears laid back until, scenting the water, she broke into a heavy trot as if her thirst had suddenly become unbearable.

The waterfall had dwindled to a thread veiled by a curtain of ice. Ice covered the stony basin except for a dark star of open water at its centre. The snow below and around the spring was marked by the tracks of birds but nothing moved in the woods while Sylvie drank until a jackdaw, planing down from the trees, perched on the rock above her head and watched her inquisitively, turning his grey-naped black head in the sunlight. Sylvie knew that he was there, but she did not look up. She drank deeply and silently, as if she were not only satisfying an inordinate thirst but washing away all remembrance of the night. When at last she lifted her head, it was to lick gratefully at the icicles that lined the cleft as if she could not have enough of coldness and cleanness. She did not know that now the water in the basin was faintly coloured or that the snow below the spring where she had stood was marked by spots of blood.

The jackdaw hopped nearer and Sylvie, who disliked these bold teasing birds, stepped back. On any other day she would have rushed at the jackdaw, barking frenziedly, half in play, but to-day she only snarled silently, wrinkling her muzzle and showing her teeth, and turned her back on him. Climbing up on the shelf of rocks, she stretched herself out in the sunlight, lowered her head to her paws and, forgetting the jackdaw, careless of her fears now that her thirst was satisfied, trusting the woods once again, she fell deeply and innocently asleep.

When she awoke, the shadows of the trees were short on the snow. Stretching and yawning, she shook herself and stood on the rocks looking out across the valley. She was still dishevelled and dull coated but the dazed furtive look had gone from her eyes; she no longer crouched unhappily but stood with something of her usual bold arrogance and pride. Sylvie had left her guilt at the spring and was now at peace, appeased, herself again. When she left the rocks she moved lightly, holding her head high.

The shortest way to the house was down and across the slope of the hillside to her right but she crossed the glade, returning on her own tracks. She did not know why she felt compelled to double and turn between the trees, weaving an elaborate pattern of her tracks in the snow, as she had done since the first streak of dawn had shown her the fields far beyond the village on the other side of the valley and the huddle of staring sheep.

An hour later she crossed the snow-cleared road well above the entrance to the lane and plunged into the woods, apparently going across country to the village; but she was on her way back to the house and soon circled back and crossed the road again, moving uphill through the spruce plantations towards the scent of home. She skirted the lawn, keeping in the trees out of sight of the windows, passed behind the sheds and the greenhouses until she reached the garage; there she paused, looking up at the house. Nothing moved behind the curtained windows, and she came out into the open, paused again, one paw raised, and then ran down the path to the back door, as if she were returning at the sound of Peter's whistle from her usual morning run in the woods.

4

Jerome frowned down at his typewriter, re-read a few lines on the half-filled page, and sat back in his chair. He lit a cigarette and looked round his room. Peter had made up the fire a short time ago and had put a fresh pot of coffee over the spirit lamp on the table. The sunshine of the last few days still persisted in the window and laid a bright square on his rugs. The orchids stood on their table. The room was as it had always been and as he liked it, but something was missing.

For the last hour or two, and he saw by the china clock above the fireplace that it was now five minutes past eleven, he had been unable to concentrate as he usually did when he was working on a play. His whole mind was not involved as it ought to be if he were to keep up the pace which he thought was the essence of his success as a playwright, the striking while the iron was still white-hot. A part of his mind, a mere fraction, but enough to act as a brake on the rest, was busy with something else, a small niggling worry and a sense of loss.

He got up and poured himself a cup of coffee and carried it to the window and looked out at the woods. The trees across the lane were, at first glance, as they had been for the last three days, unmoving under their burden of snow and pierced by sharp sunshine; the snow-powdered purple of the hills touched the same blue sky; but when he looked more closely he saw that there was a difference: the white was perhaps less, the dark green of the trees more, and there was a softening, a blurring.

"A thaw," Jerome said aloud, as he drank his coffee. "I believe that it is beginning to thaw." As he spoke he glanced down at the windowseat, but it was empty. He swung round, and there was no familiar shape on the hearthrug. His unanswering audience, his echoing-wall, his shadow, had gone. Giving a last worried look into the woods, he put his cup down on the table and went back to his work.

A Winter's Tale

As he put a fresh sheet of paper into his typewriter, Jerome told himself that Sylvie had only been with him for three years, that before she came to the house he had always worked alone. True writing, any truly creative work, he supposed, must, and should, be a lonely business, bleaker than birth, as lonely as death. As he thought this, he smiled at himself but he knew that it was partly true. It had been a mistake to allow even Sylvie in this room. If he had left her with Peter the first day she had come to the house instead of taking the small warm appealing creature with him into his workroom and putting her down on the cushion in his chair by the fire, telling her to be still and as quiet as a puppy can be, he would not now feel this disturbing sense of absence, of something wrong with the room. It was a diminution of his powers to admit that he needed anyone or anything. Nothing except himself should be necessary when he was working.

You are arrogant and pompous, he told himself, and picked up his wooden owl.

The door opened and Una came round the screen into the room. She was carrying a book and was wearing a grey pleated skirt and a thick white woollen sweater with a broad collar. Her hair was loose and in spite of her high heels, her gold bracelets, her careful make-up, she looked a diffident schoolgirl unsure of her welcome. Jerome looked at her as if he had never seen her before and scowled; but as he saw her eager ingratiating look change to one of alarm, he could not help smiling. Reassured, she came across the room to him.

"What is that?" she said. "Oh, I see—it's your famous owl. I have heard about that, it goes everywhere with you. Why didn't I see it in the flat? It's your mascot, isn't it, or your lucky charm?"

"It's my private inspiration," Jerome said, putting the little wooden figure down behind his typewriter and taking off his spectacles. "Never mind about him—what are you doing here?"

"I came to say good-morning, and to see that you were all right." Una bent down and kissed his cheek. "Don't you want to know how my arm is? It's much better. Peter has dressed it again."

She perched herself on the arm of his chair and leaning against his shoulder said, "Do you know that Sylvie has run away? Peter says that she has been out all night. He is in a state about it."

"I know," Jerome said shortly, turning to his typewriter again. "She will come back in her own good time."

"That's what I told him. Poor Peter, you know what he is like about that dog. Have you had any breakfast? Peter says that you are writing a play."

"I'm trying to write a play."

"How exciting! But wouldn't it have been better to finish your novel first? More tidy—"

"Tidy! What an extraordinary thing to say. Now listen, Una, run away, that's a darling, or I won't write anything."

"Peter said that I mustn't interrupt you, but I'm only saying good-morning. Do you know, I have never seen this room before?"

She walked to the fireplace, looked briefly up at his snow-picture and, turning round with a self-conscious swirl of grey skirts as if she knew very well that he was watching her, looked curiously round the room. "So this is the lion's den," she said.

"You sound disappointed." Jerome sat back resignedly in his chair. "What did you expect?"

"I don't know. A few bones—laurel wreaths lying about, piles of dusty books and papers, signed photographs. This is a very ordinary room, except for the orchids, and so neat."

"A workroom should be neat, especially early in the day."

"A workroom? I should call it a study, or a studio, or even a writing-room, although it does look like any old room. Still, I suppose I should consider myself honoured to be here."

Una looked at him, smiling and holding her head on one side. "No one could call you neat or ordinary this morning," she said. "Your hair is standing on end, you haven't shaved. You have put that jersey on inside out. Now you look even more like a real writer than you did last night in your velvet jacket. Don't be cross. I was only teasing."

"I'm not cross. Writing is a gloomy dishevelling even grubby business, why I don't know. Ask any writer—but I'm not going to talk to you, Una. Run away, please."

"I will just see if that coffee is really hot. Shall I pour out another cup for you?"

"Leave it alone or you will have Peter after you. Now listen, Una, I must work. Why don't you go for a walk?"

"I don't want to go for a walk in the snow alone."

"I expect that Peter could find you something to do in the greenhouses, there is always a lot to do there."

"I'm tired of the orchids, and anyway Peter would never let me touch one."

"Then go into the sitting-room, I expect that there is a fire there."

"There is. I have been sitting there for more than an hour. I couldn't stand it any longer. I want to be here, where I can be near you. You would let Sylvie stay."

"Sylvie is quiet. She can't talk."

"I won't say another word. I will sit on the windowseat in the sunshine where you can't see me and read—I have brought a book. I won't disturb you. Let me stay, Jerome."

"If you manage to efface yourself as Sylvie does, I will forget you are there. You will soon grow tired of it."

Una leant over his shoulder. "Let me read a few words first . . . 'A house in the woods . . . May and Giles . . .' Is it about us?"

"Certainly not."

"What is it called?"

"Never mind. Go and sit down, Una."

"I believe that you only let me stay in the room because Sylvie isn't here. It must feel odd without her. Is that it, Jerome?"

Jerome did not answer. He hunched his shoulders, put on his horn-rimmed spectacles once again, and began to type.

"Now you don't look a bit like a lion," Una complained. "Or

even an eagle in his eyrie. You look just like your old owl."

When Jerome only typed faster, she smoothed his hair, and tiptoed with exaggerated care to the window-seat.

For ten minutes by the clock, the only sounds in the room were the gentle crackling of the fire and the staccato sound of the typewriter, broken by long pauses and the rustle of paper. Then Una put her book down on the window-seat and began to play with her bracelets, pushing them up and down her unbandaged arm, while she stared out of the window. Presently she sighed, put a cushion behind her back, took up her book again, flipped over a few pages and let it slide to the floor. As she bent to pick it up, she looked guiltily at Jerome. He did not turn his head and, uncrossing her legs, smoothing her skirts, she stood up and tiptoed to the orchid-table to examine the plants and then wandered over to the bookshelves.

"Can't you sit still?" Jerome said suddenly.

Una jumped. "You couldn't possibly have heard me move," she said indignantly. "I have been as quiet as a mouse."

"Mice make most irritating little noises and are never still for a moment."

"I have been perfectly still for hours."

"You have never stopped fidgeting. You don't know what it means to keep still. Can't you curl up on the window-seat, shut your eyes, and go to sleep?"

"Sleep? At this hour? No, I can't. I can't even sit on the window-seat any longer, it's too cold. I'm frozen. Just feel my hand."

Jerome looked up at Una and, sighing, leant back in his chair.

"It is no use," he said, as he took her hand in his. "Really, my dear, you would be happier in the other room. What a cold little paw."

"I will sit in that chair by the fire."

"No. I would see you there every time I looked up."

"Am I so terrible to look at?"

"You are looking very pretty this morning. That white and grey makes you look like a pretty little pigeon, very strokable and sweet. No, you are far too distracting. I wouldn't get anything done with you there under my nose."

"You won't get round me like that. You don't mean a word of it. Where does Sylvie sit?"

"On the hearthrug in winter, but you are not Sylvie."

"No, I'm not," Una cried. "That's the trouble, isn't it?"

Jerome stood up. "Now, listen to me, my little blonde limpet," he said gently, "I must work. Haven't you anything of your own to do? Don't tell me that you are one of those tiresome women who sit on the bank knitting while their husbands fish, or follow them round while they play golf, when the poor chaps would much rather be on their own."

"How do you know that they don't like having their wives with them?"

Jerome laughed and put his hand under her elbow. "I only know that I don't want anyone, even you, my little fidget, when I'm trying to work," he said.

"Sylvie always stays with you when you are working. Peter told me so. If she does, why can't I?"

"You are not Sylvie," Jerome said. "Don't be absurd, Una. I have been astonishingly patient but I have had enough of this. I must get on. I shall ignore you and trust your pride will prevent you from staying where you are obviously not wanted."

"I haven't any pride. I love you too much."

Jerome sat down in his chair. "Love?" he said. "Be careful, my dear. I am beginning to be very tired of that word. It seems to me that it is only another word for possessiveness and jealousy."

As he pulled his typewriter towards him, there was a knock on the door and Peter came into the room. He stood against the black and gold background of the screen and looked at Jerome.

"What is the matter now?" Jerome said irritably.

"I came to tell Miss Una that her luncheon is on the table by the fire in the sitting-room."

"But it's only twelve o'clock," Una said, "and I had my breakfast late."

Peter ignored this. "Better hurry up, it's an omelette and you don't want it to spoil," he said. "I have put the rest of last night's wine by the fire and there is coffee in the percolator." He looked across the room at Jerome again, and Jerome, meeting his glance, said, "Go on, Una, it's the least you can do—Peter seems to have taken a lot of trouble and his omelettes are worth hurrying for."

When Una, carrying her book and holding her head high, had gone, he said, "Well, what is the matter? You know better than to interrupt me like this. Am I never to have any peace?"

Peter looked round the screen to make sure that the door was shut, then he came close to Jerome and said, "Come with me to the kitchen, Captain. Come at once. It's serious. I have something to show you."

5

Peter had spent a busy morning. As always when he was disturbed in his mind, he had found himself extra work to do. Not only had he polished the furniture in the sitting-room and waxed the hall floor before Una came downstairs soon after ten, but he had checked the depleted stores in the storeroom and scrubbed the kitchen floor. He was in the kitchen on his knees when the telephone rang.

Drying his hands on his apron, Peter walked slowly to the dresser. To be in touch again with the farm had seemed an achievement, convenient at the time, and on any other day he would have been glad to have news from the village, to speak to Mr. Vipan at The Crown or to Mrs. Truman at the shop, but now he picked up the receiver reluctantly and his 'Hello' was surly and gruff. It was only the exchange at Woodstreet, making sure that the line was in order again. Peter put the receiver back on its cradle as soon as he could, as if it were red-hot.

Forgetting his bucket and brush, he stood by the table drumming his fingers on the white scrubbed surface, and stared out of the window at the trees. As Jerome had done, he had noticed the first signs of a thaw but, at that moment, this meant nothing to him. He put out a hand and touched one of his orchids without knowing what he was doing. His thoughts were far from the kitchen, deep in the woods. He would not have heard the faint scratching at the back door if he had been really engrossed with his work, as he usually was at this time of the day, but this was the sound for which he had been waiting for the last ten hours, even in his uneasy sleep. He hurried across the kitchen and through the porch and pulled the door open. Sylvie pushed past his legs as she always did when he let her in from a run in the woods and, without giving him any greeting, without even acknowledging his presence, walked into the kitchen and threw herself down on her bed.

Peter shut the back door and bolted it, a thing that he had seldom done before in the day-time. As he knelt beside Sylvie and put his hand on her head, he looked up at the clock, noting that it was half past eleven.

"Where have you been?" he said, trying to keep his voice steady.

Sylvie moved her tail languidly, sighed, and stretched herself comfortably on her bed.

"Don't you go falling asleep as if nothing had happened," Peter told her sternly. "Sit up and look at me."

Obediently she sat up, yawning a little and looked into his face. Her eyes were clear and empty, unclouded by remembrance. Never before had they seemed to him more limpid and innocent. He saw that the uneasy watchfulness of the last days had gone from Sylvie, that somewhere in the woods she had rid herself of her troubles and was now calm and appeased.

"What have you done?" he beseeched her, and ran a shaking hand over her rough and dirty coat and down the caked hair of her throat and chest. As he took his hand away and looked at the red stain across his fingers, the telephone rang again.

Peter leapt to answer it as if he were afraid that its loud peal would rouse the house and reach through the thick walls into Jerome's workroom.

"Yes," he said into the mouthpiece. "It's Peter. What's that? No, I haven't. No, out of order until a few minutes ago."

As he listened, Peter's eyes followed Sylvie as she rose from her bed, shook herself, and approached her filled plate which had waited for her on the sheet of paper behind his armchair all night. She ate ravenously with none of her usual hesitation and nicety, gulping down the chopped meat and crunching the biscuits as he had not seen her do since she was a half-grown long-legged puppy.

"Terrible," Peter said into the telephone. "Last night? It's been years since such a thing happened in these parts, isn't it?"

The voice gabbled excitedly in his ear and Peter frowned.

"Sylvie?" he said. "She's here, beside me."

He listened intently.

"Of course she was," he said. "What do you mean?"

"I do know," he said. "What are you getting at, Tom?"

"Sylvie?" he almost shouted it into the receiver. "How can you think such a thing of Sylvie?"

Now the voice was more conciliatory.

"You had better be careful what you are saying," Peter said. "Mr. Holt wouldn't like that at all."

He looked at Sylvie again as he answered and tried to keep his voice even. "No, I couldn't be mistaken. She sleeps in his room, I tell you."

He waited, then interrupted, "You will be saying next that someone saw her," but the voice went on.

"No, they couldn't have, could they?" asked Peter. "There are other dogs in the valley, aren't there? The field beyond the woods you say, Braddock's? That's all of three miles away."

Peter was getting angry. "No, you can't speak to Mr. Holt," he said. "He's working. Of course it's serious, it's shocking, but it's as much as my place is worth to disturb him before three o'clock. Ring him up then, if you must, but it will be a waste of time."

"Tracks? I shouldn't think that would help much. It's beginning to thaw."

"Well, let us know how you get on. Come up and see her for yourself if you don't believe me."

Now the voice was uncertain, even apologetic, and Peter said, "I'm glad to hear you say that, Tom. You all know Sylvie, she wouldn't hurt a fly."

He listened a moment longer and then said impatiently, "So long now, good-bye."

Peter laid the receiver gently down. Sylvie, having licked her plate clean, was now drinking from her blue bowl. As if she felt his eyes on her, she looked across the room at him and waved her tail. Then yawning again, she shook herself, climbed on to her bed and, flopping down with a contented sigh, closed her eyes and was asleep.

Peter sat down in his armchair and, resting his elbows on his knees, put his head in his hands. He was trying to think, to make up his mind what to do. When he lifted his head he did not look down at Sylvie sleeping trustfully beside him, but round the kitchen as if the familiar room, the red purring range, his beloved flowers by the window-sill, his pipe and tobacco pouch and pile of papers, could help him.

When he stood up, he walked straight to the porch, put on his duffle-coat and gum-boots and picked up the stiff broom. As he opened the back door, he saw Sylvie's tracks coming towards the house from the direction of the garage. He followed them until they disappeared into the woods and stood, hesitating again, looking back at the house; no one was standing in the window of Una's room. He walked a short way into the woods through the deep softening snow and, moving backwards as he went, began to brush Sylvie's tracks and his own footprints away, bending down to smooth the brush marks in their turn with his hands. When he was back at the garage, he shrugged his shoulders then, tucking the broom under his arm, walked to the house stepping carefully in Sylvie's tracks, obliterating every mark that she had made in the snow. As he swept round the back door, as he had already done earlier that morning, he whistled tunefully and kept a sharp eye on the peaceful snowy woods, as if he expected them at any moment to disgorge a horde of angry men armed with shot-guns. "Have to send her out later for a trot round the house, look odd otherwise," he said to himself, as he kicked off his gum-boots in the porch.

When he returned to the kitchen, he took a bowl from the dresser, filled it with warm water and set it down on the floor beside Sylvie's bed; then he fetched her comb and brush, some rags and two old towels. He stood looking down at her while he rolled up the sleeves of his sweater, then paused again as if a new thought had struck him. He stood there, rubbing his chin, blinking and muttering to himself in an agony of indecision; it took him five minutes by his cuckoo-clock on the wall above him to make up his mind.

"I'll chance it," he said out loud. "If it comes off—two birds with one stone."

He was not at all sure what he meant by this last remark, but he was grinning his lop-sided grin as he opened the hatch and looked into the sitting-room. He was not surprised to see that Una was not there.

"I thought so," he said to himself. "Well, now we'll see Miss Know-all."

Quickly he had set about his preparations for Una's early luncheon, putting knives and forks, salt and pepper, butter and bread and glasses into the hatch; then, shutting its sliding doors gently so as not to rouse the sleeping Sylvie, he had left the room to lay the table by the fire.

When he had come back to the kitchen he had looked up at

the clock; it was then a quarter to twelve, and he had set his omelette pan on the fire and begun to beat up the eggs, separating the whites from the yolks, using the beater with more than his usual thoroughness and care. "At least she shall have a good omelette," he had said to the kitchen. "Considering everything, it's the least I could do. It's in my heart to feel almost sorry—poor little cocksure Miss Clever. Poor silly little toad."

Jerome came into the kitchen with Peter close behind him. "*What* is all this?" he said, irritably.

"Hush!" Peter whispered, putting his hand on Jerome's arm and jerking his head in the direction of the sitting-room. "Talk low. She's next door. We don't want her to hear. She mustn't hear a word. Better whisper." He darted to the hatch, pushed the bolt across, and pointed at Sylvie's bed.

His manner was so dramatic and conspiratorial that Jerome could not help smiling, angry and puzzled though he was. "Well, you old mountebank?" he said, obediently lowering his voice. "Sylvie is back, just as I said she would be. Do you have to drag me from my work to tell me that?"

"Come closer and take a good look at her."

As Jerome approached her bed, Sylvie roused herself from her deep dreamless sleep. She sat upright on her blanket, blinking and yawning. It was so unlike her to wake in this sluggish heavy fashion, that Jerome said, "She doesn't know me. What is the matter with her?"

At the sound of his voice Sylvie stood up, waving her tail in glad recognition, but as Peter said, "Tired out, that's what she is," she paused, doubtful and bewildered, staring up at him as if she were making an effort to remember something that had slipped far down into her mind. Jerome bent down to touch her head and she shrank back on her haunches again.

"Sylvie!" Jerome said, and knelt down by her bed. "She is filthy," he said accusingly to Peter. "What is that on her chest?"

"Don't touch her," said Peter. "That's blood."

"Blood? Has she hurt herself?"

Jerome looked up at Peter, who slowly shook his head. "That's not her blood," Peter said. "Two sheep were killed last night on the other side of the valley, just behind Braddock's farm. Their throats were torn out. Tom Barton rang up from the village. He wanted to know where Sylvie was."

"Sylvie! I don't believe it," Jerome said, sitting back on his heels. "Who is Tom Barton? The telephone is out of order anyway."

"Tom's the new constable, came here after Cruchman left, must be a year now," Peter said patiently. "The exchange rang through just before he got on to me. I said that Sylvie was right here beside me, that she had never stirred all night. I said that she slept in your room."

Jerome stood up. He put his hands in his pockets, and stared down at Sylvie. "Did he believe you?" he asked.

"He wanted to speak to you. I said that you were working and that he could ring again at three. He will believe you all right, he'll have to. You must say that Sylvie was in your room all night, that she was still there at eight this morning, and stick to it. They found the sheep early. Saw the rest of the flock huddled together at the other end of the field and went out to look. They think they know when it was done. Their own dogs raised hell just before dawn."

"Braddock's is miles away," Jerome said. "Hunting dogs out to kill go in pairs. It can't have been Sylvie. There are other dogs in the valley. She got that blood on her when she stumbled across a hare or a pheasant and killed it out there, although I find it hard to believe even that of her. She has never killed anything before. Do you remember when she found that leveret? She brought it straight to me."

"Try and follow the tracks, they will," Peter said, "but that won't help them much, at least I hope not. It's beginning to thaw."

"Then you think that it was Sylvie? It's not possible. It's absurd. Sylvie!"

"You know very well that it was Sylvie," Peter said. "She was out all night. She was beside herself, rushing out into the darkness like that, and you know why. Your fault, this is. Drove her to it you did, you and that—"

"Shut up," Jerome said. "Stop that ranting. I must think. What can we do?"

"Do? We must lie like hell. Do you want Sylvie shot? They are out there now with shot-guns, searching the woods, calling at all the farms, rousing the valley. You know what these farmers are. Sheep country this is, and the sheep are in lamb."

" 'Once a sheep-killer, always a sheep-killer,' that is what they say," Jerome said, looking down at Sylvie. "Once a dog has tasted blood—I don't know what I ought to do."

Peter looked at him incredulously. "What are a few sheep compared to Sylvie?" he said. "You couldn't have her shot, you can't mean it."

"Of course not," Jerome said impatiently. "She is my dog. But do you know what this means, Peter? It means that Sylvie will never be able to run loose in the woods again as she has always done, never be free. Perhaps to Sylvie that would be more terrible than death. I ought to send her away, find her another home."

"I wouldn't let you do such a wicked thing," Peter said. "This is Sylvie's home. You know her. You know very well that she wouldn't live long without you. If you took her to the flat, she would pine for the woods and for this place. No, it wouldn't do —would you be willing to stay in London for always? Keep her in for a while, watch her, take her out on the chain. But I don't think we need do even that. I think, I know, that Sylvie will never do this again, never, if you give her a chance to settle down and forget it. She was not herself last night. A madness came over her. All this week she's been wild with jealousy, although she held herself in and tried to understand. Then, on top of everything, you go and beat her. You're to blame for this, not Sylvie."

Controlling himself, and glancing over his shoulder at the hatch, Peter said, "What's done is done. If Sylvie so much as touches another sheep, so much as runs one, you can do what you think right. But she won't do it again I tell you. Settle down to your work, let us be here as we always were, the three of us, calm and comfortable, and Sylvie will forget this like a bad dream. Look, she's forgotten now. She's asleep again."

Coming close to Jerome and putting his hand on his arm, Peter said in a rapid, urgent whisper, jerking his head again towards the hatch, "Get that girl out. Send her packing, that's the only thing to do. Time she went, anyway, now that it's beginning to thaw. You want to work, don't you? You need to write that play —it's been too long since the last and that's been worrying you, hasn't it? Then you can get back to your book in peace. You won't write anything with her around, getting in your hair. Can't you see that?"

Peter shook Jerome's arm, and then said more slowly, "Those two are a danger to each other now. Once an Alsatian has taken a dislike, gone for anyone, that person isn't safe. That girl won't be really safe with Sylvie ever again and she's still more dangerous to Sylvie. She must go before Tom or anyone else has a chance to talk to her. She won't keep her mouth shut, glad to make trouble she'll be. She knows that Sylvie was out all night. I told her so myself."

Jerome jerked his arm away. "What an idiotic thing to do," he said. "Why did you have to tell her that?"

He looked up and met Peter's eyes. The two men stared at one another. Jerome looked away first and, seeing the bowl of water and Sylvie's brush still waiting on the floor, he said, "Why couldn't you have cleaned the blood off Sylvie before you fetched me? You might have left me a little doubt. Surely that would have been the wisest thing to do? It would have made it easier."

"Perhaps it would," Peter said. "I thought you ought to know just how things were."

"I know exactly what you thought," Jerome said furiously.

The hatch rattled sharply and Una's muffled voice said from the sitting-room, "Why have you locked this, Peter? I have finished. I have put everything in the hatch."

"Just a minute, Miss. The bolt must have slipped," Peter said loudly.

"Who have you been talking to?"

"Been talking to Sylvie."

"She has come back then? I told you she would."

"Sylvie's been back for hours."

"Good, then you needn't worry any more. Shall I tell Mr. Holt?"

Peter looked at Jerome, who shook his head violently. "Mr. Holt knows, Miss," Peter said. "I told him. He won't want to be disturbed again."

"I won't disturb him. I'm going to read and sleep here on the sofa until tea-time."

"Good idea," Peter said, and he added softly, "Pleasant dreams!"

Jerome caught hold of his arm. "Stop grinning like that," he whispered. "I know very well what is in your mind. I'm sick and tired of this and of all of you and that includes Sylvie. I'm going

189

back to work and nothing will stop me. If Barton rings up put him through to me but see that I'm not worried again by any-one, by anyone do you hear?"

"I hear you," Peter said as Jerome walked to the door. "Re-member what I said though, Captain, 'The sooner the better.' Better hurry back to your room now or she may catch you in the hall."

As the door shut behind Jerome, Peter knelt by Sylvie's bed and wrung out a cloth in the bowl.

"Come now," he said soothingly. "Let me get this muck off you. Let me put you to rights and then we can forget all about it. It won't be long now. He's got the idea, swallowed it hook, line and sinker. Sit up, my beauty, and let your old Peter see to you."

6

All that afternoon, from soon after midday until nearly five, the house was calm and peaceful in its setting of trees and snow. There was no wind and the blue smoke from its chimneys went straight up into the air. The sun, slowly sinking towards the west, shone down on it from a sky that was still without a stain or cloud. From the surrounding trees the snow began almost imperceptibly to loosen its grip and slide away, but from the windows of the house it would have been difficult to see any change. No one came up the lane from the gate or over the hill from the farm. The telephone was silent and the house's three human inhabitants, as if by mutual agreement, kept well apart and were occupied in their own ways.

Sylvie slept on in her bed by the kitchen range, the sleep of exhaustion and peace. She did not even raise her head when Peter, his work finished, stood looking down at her before he left the kitchen for the greenhouses, first for his short siesta and then to work again among the orchids. Once in his basket chair facing the glass inner door and the central tiers of plants, he put his unlit pipe between his teeth, opened a ten-day-old paper on his knees, and leaning back, shut his eyes. He did not sleep but let himself sink to a lower level of consciousness where all was pleasantly blurred, free of sharp outlines and troubling thoughts. He had done what he could for Sylvie and Jerome and now had ceased to worry. Sylvie was back; this fact was enough for the present. As for the immediate future, he was content to leave it to Jerome; knowing him as he did, he had no doubt at all as to what would happen in the next few hours.

Una slept curled up on the sofa in front of the sitting-room fire. When she woke she stretched herself and yawned, much as Sylvie had done, and putting on her shoes, wandered into the hall. She glanced uncertainly at the closed door of the workroom, listened for the faint sound of the typewriter, turned away and slowly climbed the stairs. In her own room she switched on the lights, sat down in front of the dressing-table, and looked at her reflection critically. If she had only known it, she had never looked better, more nearly beautiful. She was pale and there were delicate blue marks under her eyes, but her eyes were large and dark while her face had lost its sharpness and was softer, fuller, and lit by that almost spiritual radiance that comes to some women during an intense and satisfying love affair. She frowned at her reflection and taking off her white sweater creamed and massaged her face and neck, brushed her hair and manicured her nails. Taking more trouble than she had done for days, she made up her face again, smoothing rouge on her cheekbones, drawing a blue line along her eyelids. Her concentration on this task was so complete that she might have been a painter absorbed in what he felt was his masterpiece. The result pleased her and she sat for a long time with her hands in her lap, looking at herself in the glass. It was half past four and her window was dark when she put on her sweater again, combed her hair and pinned it on top of her head, put scent behind her ears and went downstairs lightly and happily, sure of herself once again.

As for Jerome, he was far away in another world. He was no longer conscious of the room or even of himself. His brain was running as smoothly as the well-cared-for engine of a racing car. The pile of typed sheets at his left grew on the table. He hummed gently to himself as he worked, a happy tuneless busy sound. At times he nodded his head as if agreeing with an inner voice. When he paused in his typing to lean back in his chair and light a cigarette, his brain raced on. Once Peter, before going to the greenhouses, came silently into the room and laid a plate of sandwiches beside him but he took no notice and when the telephone rang soon after three o'clock he got up and answered it automatically, his mind elsewhere.

Tom Barton, the policeman, spoke to him from the village. Jerome listened, taking in the meaning of the words but refusing to give them any importance, shrugging them off as a bird shrugs rain-water from its protecting feathers. "No," he said into the mouthpiece while his eyes, still seeing a very different setting, looked vaguely round the room. "Of course I do. Absurd, I tell you. In my room all night. My man Peter can confirm it. He let her out at eight o'clock. I'm very sorry about all this but I'm busy now."

When he put the receiver down, Jerome stood by the table for a few minutes looking towards the window, but he was not thinking of Sylvie. He walked a few steps across the room, turned and walked back, stretched his arms, sighed and sitting down in his chair ate a sandwich before he began to type again, as if this interruption had never been. Words came from his brain and fingers on to the page, not in an even flow but in sudden spurts followed by a pause. In one of these pauses, he heard a faint scratching at his door. This familiar sound did not disturb his thoughts. As he had so often done before, he pushed his chair back, crossed the floor, opened the door letting Sylvie into the room, shut it again, and was back in his chair picking up his sentence where he had left off.

Sylvie did not greet him. Knowing her place, she slipped smoothly into it again. She went straight to the hearthrug and lay down. Her coat was smooth and shining, her ruff silver-clean and brushed. She rested her dark head on her paws and watched him with half-shut calm eyes. Jerome had forgotten that earlier in the day it had seemed to him that something was missing from his room. He accepted Sylvie's presence as he had her absence. After hours of effort he had reached the point when nothing was necessary to him except himself. As the sun sank and the woods darkened round the house, he worked on, still riding on a wave of his own words. When just before five, Una carrying a tea-tray walked into the room, she cried, "Why, Jerome! You are working in the dark."

The fire had sunk and in its red glow the shadowy room was like a cave of which Sylvie was the guardian spirit. Jerome could see his typewriter well enough to put in a fresh sheet of paper and that was all he needed to see. When Una put the tray down on the table by the fire and switched on all the lights, he blinked up at her, looking once again like a ruffled owl.

"Darling, you will blind yourself," she told him severely. "Surely you could spare the time to put on the lights?"

Jerome took off the spectacles he had not needed for the last hour and scowled. "I could, if I wanted to," he said. "I touch-type, as you know."

"Well, it's less gloomy like this, isn't it?" Una said. "Will Sylvie let me make up the fire or will she object if I go near her? I should like her to know that I have forgiven her, that there are no hard feelings."

A Winter's Tale

Sylvie had lifted her head as Una came into the room. Now she lowered it again and shut her eyes. There was something insolent about this complete indifference and Una said sharply, "She doesn't look much the worse for her adventures. I wonder where she has been and what she has done."

Jerome swung round in his chair. "Why should she have done anything?" he asked aggressively. "Sylvie has been in the woods."

"I know, but she looks so pleased with herself. She looks quite different. She isn't worrying about you and me any more. I wonder what happened out there in the woods. What a pity she can't talk."

"A pity? I don't think so. For me Sylvie's silence is one of her chief attractions."

"I suppose by that you mean that I talk too much? Isn't that what you mean? Perhaps you would like me better if I were dumb, like Sylvie?"

"At this moment, yes, I would."

Jerome leant back in his chair and looked at Una's painstakingly arranged hair, and at the careful heavy make-up that he so much disliked to see on her small delicately boned face.

"You are looking very smart," he said disagreeably. "What have you been doing to your face? Rather a waste of time and trouble this evening, I'm afraid. Pour me out a cup of tea, now that you are here and then—"

" 'Run away, I'm busy,' that's what you are going to say, isn't it?" Una said, as she filled a cup and carried it to him, putting

195

it down beside his typewriter. "It's after five," she said. "I think that you have been shut up in this room long enough, but I suppose it's no use my saying so."

"None at all." Jerome picked up his cup. "Where is Peter?" he said. "He should know better than to let you bring in my tea."

"It was Peter's idea that I should bring it to you. He met me in the hall, gave me the tray and opened your door for me. If you must know, he said, 'Go on, Miss, he won't bite you. Do him good to have a break. You talk to him for a bit.' "

Jerome stared up at her and then looked past her at Sylvie. He handed his empty cup to Una and smiled. "I see," he said. "Well, now it's up to me. Listen, you persistent little nuisance, if you are not out of this room in two seconds, I will put you out."

Una laughed at him. "How ferocious!" she said. "You just try!"

"I mean it, Una."

"No, you don't. If you must work, go on then, I won't stop you, but I'm tired of being alone. I will sit quietly in that chair and smoke a cigarette. You needn't take any notice of me."

"I can't write with anyone else in the room."

"Why not? Jane Austen could. She wrote all her books on the corner of the table in the family sitting-room."

"This is too much," Jerome said, pushing his chair round to face her. "What has Miss Austen to do with it, you would-be erudite little donkey? But I'm not going to start a literary discussion with you, if you think I am. You have wasted enough of my time as it is."

He pulled his chair up to the table and put a new sheet of paper into the typewriter. "Nor am I going to the trouble of putting you out of the room by force," he said. "You would probably enjoy that."

Una flushed. "That's a horrid thing to say," she said. "What *is* the matter with you, Jerome?"

When he did not answer but only hunched his shoulders and stared down at his hands, she put his empty cup down on the tray and coming close to his chair said, "After this week, haven't I a right to want to be near you? Look at me, Jerome. Answer me."

Jerome did not look up. "You have no right at all," he said. "May I remind you that I didn't ask you to come here? You forced yourself into my house—"

"You will say next that I forced you to make love to me."

"Well, I could say something like that, couldn't I?"

Una stepped back. In the silence, Sylvie lifted her head and looked anxiously towards the writing-table.

"I don't believe it," Una said at last. "This isn't you, Jerome. There is something behind this. You are trying to make me do something—why?"

"I'm only trying to make you let me work in peace."

"There is more to it than that, or you wouldn't be so brutal."

Una looked wildly round the room. "What has happened?"

she cried. "I don't believe that this week has meant nothing to you. I refuse to let you spoil it. We love each other—we could be so happy if you would only let us be."

Jerome looked up at her. "Love?" he said. "There we go again. Evidently we don't mean the same thing by the word. I have loved you all this week. I have spent a whole week of my time on you. Now I have had enough. I have something else to do. It's as simple as that."

"Is it? What about me?"

"Well, what about you? You have had what you came for, haven't you? I never promised you anything else. I even warned you."

"I came because I loved you," Una said. "I thought that you were a man—"

"Well, you ought to know by now if I'm a man or not."

"Must you try to cheapen and spoil everything?" Una cried. "I meant a human being not a scribbling monster. Do you mean to say that this play, those words on paper, mean more to you than I do? More than flesh and blood, than life?"

"There is no need for melodramatics," Jerome said coldly, and he looked down at his table again. "I want to work, and I'm going to work. Please go, before I lose my temper."

Una put her hands up to her face, pressing them against her temples in an effort at self-control. Then she said quietly, "I have been a fool, interrupting you like this, making a scene. Of course you want to work, it *is* important. I'm going now. I will wait in the sitting-room. I will be there if you want dinner. If not I will be upstairs in our bed. You must get some sleep sometime. Yes, I will wait for days if necessary."

She leant across the table and touched his hand. "I'm sorry, Jerome," she whispered.

Jerome looked down at her hand and hesitated; then he pushed his chair back and stood up.

"There is nothing to be sorry about, for either of us," he said briskly. "Everything comes to an end, that's all. Time you went, my dear."

Una looked up at him unbelievingly. "Are you turning me out?" she said. "Out of this house, I mean?"

"You will have enough sense to go of your own accord."

"I suppose you would like me to go now, to-night? It doesn't matter to you that it's dark out there, cold and dark, that my car is still in a drift?"

"Tomorrow morning will do. I am not throwing you to the wolves."

Una backed away from him. "You might as well," she said furiously. "I won't go, I won't I tell you. Set your dog on me, why don't you? Tell her to see me off. She has won, hasn't she?"

Jerome put out a hand to her, placatingly. "Don't be so childish, Una," he said. "What has Sylvie to do with this? It's nothing to do with either of you. Why can't you believe me when I say that I have work to do, work that will take all my time day and night for weeks?"

"You and your work!" Una cried. "To hear you talk, one would think that no one had ever written a book or a play before. The world is full of writers, they are two-a-penny these days, but they don't all have to shut themselves away in a forest before they can write a word. Your precious work doesn't give you the right to lord it over that wretched Peter, that dog, and me. A pompous conceited puffed-up bully, that's what you are!"

"That's enough," Jerome said, and Una, taking one look at his face, darted behind the armchair and standing with her hands gripping the velvet back, cried.

"Don't touch me! I'm going, I can't go fast enough, but before I go, I'll tell you a thing or two—it's time someone did. You only hide up here in the woods to make yourself more interesting and important, and when you are in London you might as well be here. You go about with the same old crowd, people who eat your food and drink your drink and tell you only what you want to hear. You ought to go out in the world and find out what real people, young people, are thinking and doing. You are old but it's not too late. I don't suppose that any one under thirty has read a book of yours, and the young will tell you that in a few years there will probably be no writers left, a few real poets of course, and people who write for television but certainly no novelists, the world doesn't need them any more. As for your plays, they are clever and witty but where will they be in a hundred years or even twenty? Even if you were another Shakespeare that doesn't give you the right to behave like God!"

Una paused to push her hair back from her face and to get her breath, and Jerome laughed.

"Dear me," he said mildly, "what a tirade! Incoherent, a little naïve, but your meaning is clear. You should see yourself standing there, spitting like an angry little cat. If you think all that of me I wonder why you came here."

"If you think it was because you are a writer you are quite wrong."

"I had thought that perhaps it was because a well-known writer of plays, even one despised by the young, might be thought capable of giving an ambitious if not very talented young actress a leg up the ladder—but playwrights are two-a-penny these days, so it couldn't have been that."

"That's the sort of thing you would think. I fell in love with you the first time I saw you. Why, I can't imagine. I hate you now. I hate you and I hate myself."

"Oh, Una, don't—my dear child," Jerome said, looking at her white distraught face. He tried to reach her, but she slipped past his outstretched arm and, breaking into noisy tears, ran round the screen and slammed the door.

Jerome stood in the middle of his room staring at the black and gold screen. He took a few steps towards the door as if he would follow her. Then he shrugged his shoulders and turned back to the fireplace. Kneeling down on the hearthrug, he made up the fire, arranging the logs carefully. He noticed, with surprise, that his hands were shaking. Sylvie, who had risen to her feet to stand listening to the raised voices and to look from Jerome to Una in perplexity, lay down again flattening herself on the rug, as if she wanted to make herself as inconspicuous as possible.

"Lie down," Jerome told her sternly although she had made no move towards him. "Lie down. Leave me alone."

Dusting his hands on his trousers, he walked to his writing-table and sat down heavily, leaning his head on his hands. The room was very quiet. After a few moments he sat up, put on his spectacles, and began to type, slowly at first but soon with assurance and speed, on the blank sheet of paper that was waiting for him.

7

The weather changed that evening. Soon after dark, clouds rolled up behind the hills and spread across the sky above the valley. It was a little warmer and for the first time for several days the wind could be heard moving round the house. Peter, wrapped in his duffle-coat, stood at the back door watching the stars slowly disappear and listening to the woods which had shaken off the icy trance of the last days and were now full of invisible movement and alive with night sounds.

He had spent longer than he usually did dozing in his basket chair and when at last he roused himself, he had walked up and down the aisles between the plants picking out in his mind's eyes the orchids he would cut the next day if the thaw persisted and he was able to drive the van to Woodstreet, where the lorry would be waiting to take the long-delayed consignment of cut flowers to the florists in Maningham, fifty miles away. Peter had known that he ought to prepare the boxes for the orchids while he had some spare time, but he had found that he could not settle down to anything. Twice he went back across the yard to the kitchen to see if Sylvie were still safely sleeping on her bed. The second time, he had found her standing by the door into the hall. After he had let her out and had watched her run to Jerome's door, he had not gone back to the greenhouses but had busied himself in the kitchen until it had been time to put on the kettle for Jerome's tea.

Now, as he looked up at the sky, Peter was thinking that it was unfortunate for his orchids that the thaw and Jerome's new play should have arrived at the same time; he could expect little help in the cutting or the packing, delicate careful work that only he and Jerome could be trusted to do. He thought that in one way it was a pity the girl had to go at once. She was ignorant and she had no feeling for the flowers but she would have been another pair of hands, small and light hands that he could have used. Peter, until that moment, had forgotten Una. Feeling no compunction he had watched her carry the tea-tray into the workroom and had lingered between the kitchen and the hall, listening to the raised voices in the room until he had seen Una come out, slamming the door behind her, and rush upstairs. Now he wondered uneasily where she was and what she was doing.

He slid the hatch back gently and peered into the sitting-room. The lights were on but there was no one there. Above his head the cuckoo-clock chimed the half-hour, half past six. The empty bed with the ruckled blanket reminded him that it was nearly three hours since he had let Sylvie out into the hall. He knew where Sylvie was; it was time that she went out of doors for a run; but first he must find out if his stratagem had succeeded, if Jerome had not weakened, and if the girl were already packing or perhaps only weeping in her room.

This thought did not appear to give Peter any pleasure, although he smiled a little grimly to himself. Nor did he leave the kitchen at once. He looked up at the clock again and began to make his preparations for dinner, making up the range, fetching the chicken ready for roasting in its pan from the larder, putting the potatoes he had peeled that morning into a saucepan. He went into the storeroom and, switching on the light, took down the last tin of peas and a jar of preserved fruit. The next day, if the thaw went on, he would go to the village in the morning for supplies. The next day, with luck, the house would be itself again, the work would go on smoothly without interruptions or alarms, and life would return to normal. Meanwhile, there was the evening and the night to be lived through. Feeling suddenly exhausted, Peter put the tins and jar down on the kitchen table and, fetching a glass and his own bottle of whisky from the dresser, poured himself a stiff drink and sat down in his armchair. He was an abstemious little man and seldom wanted more than the one whisky and water he allowed himself with his dinner.

"It's been a hell of a day and it's not over yet," he said aloud, looking at Sylvie's bed.

The hall door opened and Jerome peered into the room. He looked dishevelled and cross; his dark hair was on end, his clothes rumpled, and his face had taken on the sallow unhealthy tint that came from hours of fierce concentration. He scowled at Peter and, shutting the door behind him, slouched into the room. Peter half rose from his chair, but Jerome waved him back and fetching one of the straight wooden chairs from the table planted it by the range and sat down. A soft scratching at the hall door brought Peter to his feet. He let Sylvie into the room and then, glancing at Jerome's face, took a glass from the dresser and poured out a whisky for him. The two men sat on each side of the range, not looking at each other, nursing their drinks, and Sylvie ignoring her bed, sat upright between them, her back to the room, staring into the red coals behind the bars.

There was no sound in the kitchen except the gentle purring of the range, the sound of the wind, and the ticking clock on the wall. Presently Jerome looked up and, meeting Peter's eyes, jerked his chin towards the hatch. Peter shook his head re-assuringly, and Jerome stretched himself in his chair.

"I always said that this was the best room in the house," he said. "Do you remember that winter when we could only afford to keep this one fire going? We ate here at this table, didn't we? And we brought our mattresses down and slept here every night for nearly a week. There was snow too, then."

"We kept what oil we had for the stove in your workroom,"

Peter said. "You worked in your greatcoat and the mittens Mrs. Robbins knitted for you. I can see you now."

Jerome sighed. "Those were the days," he said.

"You didn't think much of them at the time, if I remember rightly," said Peter. "You will be saying next that it's better to travel hopefully than to arrive, which is something I never did believe. Have another drink?"

Jerome held out his glass. "If I hadn't to work half the night it would be a good idea to get drunk," he said.

Peter looked sharply at him and shook his head. "That wouldn't help anyone or anything," he said, "at least, not tonight. If you ask me, you will need to keep your wits about you. Tomorrow now, that would be different, might do you good."

"You think so? What about the play?"

"Once you are settled and easy in your mind, that will come in its own good time," Peter said. He looked past Jerome to the window. "Listen to the wind, it's making itself heard but it's a different wind, all the bite has gone out of it. It's in the south. I shouldn't be surprised if it brought rain."

He glanced at Jerome, who sat with his head bent, looking down at his drink. "Go fast, the snow will, now that it's begun to go," Peter said. "The roads must be a mess but they'll be passable tomorrow. I'll clear the drift by the gate after breakfast. The way should be open then."

Jerome did not answer and Peter picked up a notebook from the table beside him. "I rang up Cooper this afternoon," he said. "They can take all we can give them. I thought that I might get six boxes off tomorrow afternoon, if I cut first thing. Two boxes of the Cattleyas, I should think. The Cymbidiums take up a lot of room—there's one very big awkward spray, and then there are the Cyps—quite a show we have. That Odonto-glossum's a picture. I'll put it in your room tomorrow.

Jerome looked up. "It will mean a lot of work," he said. "This bad weather couldn't have come at a worse time as far as the orchids are concerned."

"Can't be helped," Peter said cheerfully. "No one can help the weather. Luckily everything comes to an end, as is only right and natural. Snow doesn't lie long in these parts."

"Why don't you ask Mrs. Robbins to send up one of the boys with Alvin tomorrow morning?"

Peter shook his head. "It's Alvin's day off tomorrow, and any-way we can't trust him too much with the plants. I'll manage. I have managed all this week haven't I? The orchids haven't seen much of you.

"I had better spare an hour or so to help with the packing," Jerome said doubtfully.

"You get on with your own work first," Peter said. "See how it goes tomorrow when your whole mind is on it. I'll bring you the consignment notes to sign, of course."

He got up from his chair and, pushing Sylvie to one side, opened the oven door and slid in the pan.

"Mrs. Robbins sent this roaster up late this morning," he said. "I wasn't expecting Alvin today, thought they had enough to do on the farm. He came but I took care that he didn't see anyone except me. I'm a bit behind-hand with dinner. This won't be done till nearly eight o'clock. You had better have some soup first, having had nothing to eat except sandwiches all day. Shall I bring in a tray as usual?"

Jerome stood up slowly and put his empty glass down on the table. "No," he said. "I will have dinner in the sitting-room. Make it half past eight, then I can do another hour's work first. Get up another bottle of the Chambertin, open all the tins that are left, light the candles. I want to do this decently, with a flourish."

Peter said nothing, and Jerome said, "You needn't look at me like that, damn you. She is going in the morning. She could hardly go tonight. Can't you see without being told that this is a farewell feast?"

He walked to the door and as he opened it he said over his shoulder, "Keep Sylvie with you now. Take her out on the chain —I'm not taking any chances—and then give her her dinner. I'm going back to work. Better call me soon after eight, I will need a drink to fortify me, only one, I promise you. Knock on the door, it will be locked, and make sure that I hear you."

As the door shut, Peter pursed up his mouth and shook his head disapprovingly. He looked down at Sylvie, who turned her head towards the door but made no move to follow Jerome.

"Well, Sylvie," Peter said, "that's that, or is it? I wish it was this time tomorrow."

He fetched her plate from the larder and as he began to cut up her meat on the table, he glanced across the room at her where she sat upright on the rug before the open range.

The firelight outlined her head and ears with a gold radiance. As if she felt his eyes on her, she turned to look at him.

Suddenly Peter flung down his knife on the table and cried, "Look at you! Sitting there, quiet and happy. How can you, Sylvie?

He stopped abruptly, staring at her. No one could guess, he thought. No one but me saw how she looked this morning when she came back from the woods, slinking, wild—

Sylvie's calm gaze did not change. Slowly she turned back towards the range and Peter picked up his knife.

"Here's your dinner ready," he said, in the usual monotonous slurred voice he kept for her. "Eat it up, and I'll get on with my work. Work—it always comes back to that, seems to me. I only know one thing for certain now—that I'll never be sure of anything again."

He put the filled plate down behind the armchair, looked up at the clock, sighed, and rolled up his sleeves.

8

At ten minutes to eight Jerome, having changed his coat, washed his hands and combed his hair in the downstairs cloak-room, hurried across the hall with Sylvie at his heels and opened the sitting-room door. He was tired and rather apprehensive, but he held his head high and squared his shoulders as if he were confident and even pleased with himself which, in a way, he was. It would have been easier, perhaps wiser, for him to have eaten his dinner in his workroom and not to have seen Una again; but he had answered Peter's third knock, torn himself from his work, and voluntarily let himself in for a difficult and disturbing few hours. His mind was still occupied with his play, but he knew that he must try and forget it for a while and use all the charm, tact and persuasion he was capable of if he wanted to avoid another scene with Una. For some reason that he did not clearly understand, it was important to him that this affair should end gracefully without tears or recriminations.

His sitting-room seemed reassuringly quiet and peaceful. Its shaded lights, dim colours, his books and gramophone, the orchids, the brightly burning fire, promised a comfortable evening like any other. The curtains were drawn across the windows. The drinks were waiting on their tray on the sofa table. Peter had already laid the dinner table which stood in the middle of the room. Jerome glanced approvingly at the clean white cloth and the silver candelabra, with candles waiting to be lit.

Una was sitting in the armchair close to the fire, nursing her bandaged arm. She looked up quickly as he opened the door and he saw colour rise in her face. She was wearing her red dress and all her bracelets again, but her hair hung loosely to her shoulders and she had not made up her face at all; even her lips were pale. He saw with both pity and exasperation that her eyelids were pink and her cheeks still a little swollen and soft with tears. He had never seen her looking so nearly plain and he was touched. His resolution wavered. In all their short time together he had never been nearer to loving her, and it was all he could do to prevent himself from hurrying to her and pulling her up from the chair into his arms.

A soft pressure against his legs reminded him that he was still standing in the doorway holding the door knob. He moved and Sylvie pushed gently past him into the room; as he shut the door, she walked quickly over to the fire. He saw her wave her tail politely, recognizing Una's presence, and then settle herself in her own place on the other side of the hearthrug close to his chair. Una, who had half-risen, sat down again and turned her head away from him.

Jerome said, "Hullo, so there you are, Una," as if he had been searching for her all over the house. He followed Sylvie to the fireplace and stood on the hearthrug with his hands in his pockets, rocking himself backwards and forwards on his heels and looking down at the girl.

"Hasn't Peter given you a drink?" he said.

Una shook her head. Her hands were held tightly together in her lap.

"What will you have, a sherry as usual? Or would you rather have whisky this evening? It would do you good."

"Nothing, thank you."

She spoke stiffly, like an offended child, and Jerome, exasperated by her refusal to look at him, said, "Oh, come off it, Una! What is the good of sulking?"

"I'm not sulking. I don't want a drink, or anything else from you."

"Not even dinner? Peter will be disappointed. He is making us a very special dinner, a feast."

Una looked up at him. Her face was suddenly eager, alight with a quick hope. "A feast?" she said. "Why?"

He did not answer, and she said, "I see. You have told Peter that I'm going. This is his way of celebrating. A Thanksgiving dinner, I suppose. Well, they always have a good meal after a funeral, don't they? Baked meats, or something."

Jerome looked down at her set white face and angry eyes. "Does it make you any happier to take it this way?" he said mildly. "There is no need, you know. If something comes to an end it doesn't necessarily die. I mean, there need not be a corpse to wrangle over, or to mourn."

He walked to the drink table and poured out two whiskies. "Here you are, drink that and you will feel better," he said, as he bent down and put the glass into her hand.

"How like a man to think he can smooth anything and everything away with a good strong drink," Una said. "To behave as badly as he likes and then to put it right with a whisky and soda."

Jerome moved away from her. "How like a woman to make the worst of what can't be helped," he said lightly, "to refuse to pour oil on troubled waters and to stir up as much storm and pother as possible. Why spoil what we have had, Una?"

He sat down in his armchair and put a hand on Sylvie's head.

"That dog means more to you than I ever did, doesn't she?" said Una. "I can't spoil what we have had because we have had nothing, nothing worth having."

"If that were true, I should have thought that you would be anxious to go as soon as you could, but it isn't true and you know it. We have had a great deal, a week that I will always remember with joy and gratitude. Why should you feel so full of resentment because it can't go on forever? The best things in life, the most poignant and beautiful, are the briefest, the most short-lived. Think a bit and you will see that it's true. As for Sylvie, she means as much to me as a dog can mean. I don't see why you should grudge her that."

Una laughed. She tossed her hair back and looked at him scornfully. " 'The most poignant and beautiful,' only a writer could talk like that. Are middle-aged men always such pompous humbugs? 'Joy and gratitude!' I suppose you think that I should be grateful to you?"

Jerome sat back in his chair and watched her thoughtfully over his glass. "Why not?" he said. "You came here because you wanted to come. You made your wishes plain. You have been happy, really happy, for a whole week. That is more than a lot of people can ever say. It's no use trying to make a villain out of me. I have done you no harm."

"You only say that, don't you, because you know that you weren't the first man that I had ever slept with?"

213

Jerome did not answer. He looked away from Una to the fire. Then he said gently, "Please, Una, listen to me and take that heavy unbecoming look off your face. What I'm trying to say is that if only you will take this in the right spirit, you will go away from this house none the worse, but richer, richer in experience and knowledge as well as in memory, as I will be. I mean it, Una, pompous or not. You will make a better wife to some man one day because of this week, as long as you suppress your devastating honesty and never tell him a word about it. Don't look so disgusted. It's true, Una. Why, you are prettier, softer, richer than you were when you came. Even your name suits you now."

"My name? What do you mean?"

"When I first knew you, I thought that Una was too round and soft and female a name for such a spiky little person. I don't think so now."

Una stared at him. "You really are a shocker," she said weakly. "A cynical selfish egotist, but I know that at the moment you mean what you say." Her eyes filled with tears and she said forlornly, "The trouble is that it takes two to make an end of this sort of thing and I don't want us to end. I don't see why I should have to go. I don't see why it shouldn't last forever. That's the trouble. I simply don't see *why*."

Jerome swallowed the rest of his whisky and stood up. He walked across the room and poured himself out another drink. When he came back to the fireplace he did not sit down but stood on the hearthrug again between Sylvie and the girl.

"I have tried to tell you about my work," he said. "I have never talked about it so much before, but you won't listen, or you won't believe me, when I say that I must live here on my own if I'm to go on working."

"Why should I believe it? I know that there are plenty of writers who are happily married and who write none the worse for it."

"You don't know that. Perhaps they would be better writers if they hadn't married, or better husbands if they weren't writers. That's not the point. The point is that I know what is best for myself and for my work. I have made my life and I'm too old to change it. It wouldn't do, Una. I'm not a marrying man."

"How do you know until you have tried? You wanted to marry once—you wanted to marry Martha Cleghorn. Everyone knows about it, it's no use frowning at me. But I'm not asking you to marry me. I'm only asking you to let me stay with you."

Jerome put his glass carefully down on the chimney-shelf and knelt down on the hearthrug beside Una's chair and took her hand in his.

"Stop trying to understand, my dear," he said, "and give in with a good grace so that there will be nothing ugly to remember. Just take it from me that it wouldn't do. I would be no good to you. We would be at each other's throats, quarrelling in a few months, or even weeks. If we part now while we still love each other we will be lucky. It is very terrible, very ugly, to hate someone you once have loved."

"Hate? I could never hate you," Una said. She lifted his

215

hand and held it against her warm cheek. Jerome sighed, and suddenly she flung his hand away.

"I don't believe a word," she said. "You are only trying to make me go quietly because you are afraid of a scene. There is something behind all this, something to do with Sylvie. Something that has made it necessary for you to get rid of me quickly. I have felt it all day—"

"Can't you leave Sylvie out of this?" Jerome said. "If anything has brought this to a head, it's my play."

"I don't believe it. It's Sylvie. Look at her sitting there smug and pleased with herself! You and she and Peter all know something that I don't. If she could speak I would shake it out of her!"

Sylvie, at the sound of her name, had raised her head. Now she looked uneasily at Jerome, whined softly, and got to her feet.

"Lie down!" Jerome said to her. "You keep out of this."

As he turned back to Una and tried to take her hand again, Peter knocked on the hall door and, opening it, looked into the room.

"What about your dinner?" he said. "It's nearly half past eight."

Jerome stood up and felt for his glass. "Why didn't you say so before?" he said. "I hope that chicken isn't spoiled. We are quite ready."

"I'm not," Una said as Peter shut the door. "I look a sight. If I must eat with you, I'm going upstairs to do something to my face. I saw that Peter had laid the table for two but I didn't think that you would come after the things you said to me. I didn't think that you would have the nerve."

"Your face is all right as it is. You needn't worry."

"I couldn't sit opposite you like this. I have some pride. I must—"

"Go down with the colours flying? You little goose! Don't you know that it will be years before you will need to worry about your face. Jerome put out his hand to pull her to her feet.

Una ignored his hand. As she stood up she said, " 'Little goose, little donkey, limpet, kitten, cat'— You call Sylvie, 'my girl.' "

She ran from the room into the hall and up the stairs, leaving the door open behind her.

Jerome sighed, and looked round for a cigarette. Then he walked to the hatch and, sliding it back, said, "Hold everything Peter. She will be a few minutes. As for me, work or no work, I'm going to have another drink."

Dinner was nearly over. It had been a surprisingly successful and cheerful meal. Jerome put his fork and spoon down on his plate and looked gratefully round the room. It had done its loyal part by appearing at its best, by being warm and comfortable and ordinary as he had hoped it would be. For a moment or two he saw it and the dinner-table, with its white cloth and candles and its two seated figures, himself in his velvet jacket and Una in her crimson dress, as if he were watching a scene from his own play, from the wings or the auditorium itself. He was grateful to Sylvie for effacing herself and being content to sit unnoticed beside him, and grateful to Peter who had produced a fair dinner with what materials he had; the clear soup had been strong and hot, the chicken tender, and the peaches flambé in brandy had at least pleased Una.

Jerome had waited on Una himself, taking the food from Peter at the hatch and putting her plate before her, pouring wine into her glass, hovering round her as if she were an important and honoured guest or a convalescent needing extra care. At first she had refused to talk and had sat with her head bent, her pale silky hair shining in the candlelight, her face sullen. He had wanted to lean across the table to shake her but he had exerted himself, as he seldom troubled to do for anyone, to charm and please her. Encouraged by the amount he had drunk, he had talked fluently and easily, mainly of the theatre, of plays and dramatists, producers, actors and actresses he had known and worked with, flattering her by asking her opinion, making her laugh in spite of herself at his brand of theatrical gossip and at his improbable stories.

When she slowly responded, straightening her back and lifting her head to look across the table at him and, at last, talking herself, even arguing with him, he had felt so pleased and triumphant that he had shouted to Peter to bring another bottle of wine. As he watched the colour come into her face and her blue eyes, which each held a small reflection of the candles, begin to sparkle and shine, he told himself that he had better be careful: he imagined that he had caught a warning look from Peter when he took the wine from him at the hatch. At once he began a careful retreat, trying to put a subtle distance between himself and Una, to become with every word he said less the lover and companion of the last week and more the middle-aged well-known man talking to a young and adoring girl. He was still caressing and pleased with her, but also slightly amused, slightly condescending. It seemed wiser to him to let her talk of her own work and ambitions which, until that moment, he had never pretended to take seriously. He listened gravely and indulgently although he had heard it all before, from her first day at the London School of Drama to her last fight with her mother and her new hopes of television. He looked surreptitiously at his watch under the tablecloth and then round the room. Soon he was thinking of his play, going over that last scene in his mind.

"You are not listening, Jerome," Una said. "I don't blame you, this must seem dull, very small beer to you, but you asked for it. What are you thinking of, or shouldn't I ask?"

"I was thinking, my dear, that there might possibly be a small part for you in my new play."

As he said it, he knew that he had made a mistake. All his charm had been for nothing. Una looked at him and said abruptly, "Is this a bribe?"

He stood up and carried their used plates to the hatch before he answered. When he came back to the table he did not sit down but stood behind his chair, leaning his arms on the chair back.

"What a thing to say, Una," he said. "Why spoil everything? You looked so pretty and happy. I thought that you were enjoying your dinner. Peter must have taken a lot of trouble."

"I was enjoying it," Una said. "It was a good dinner. Exactly the same as the one we ate the night I came, except for the soufflé. You haven't answered me, Jerome."

"I am not going to answer anything so absurd."

Una took a cigarette from the box on the table. When she had lit it, she said. "Hasn't it occurred to you that I might talk when I got back to London? I can think of a lot of people who would be interested to know all about this house and the way you live in the woods. The papers for instance—it would make a good story. 'My week of love with a well-known playwright.' 'The secret life of Jerome.' After all, no other woman, even Martha Cleghorn, has ever been here. You told me so yourself."

Jerome smiled. He took a cigarette and lit it deliberately, taking his time before he answered her. "Surely that would do you more harm than it would do me?"

"Perhaps it would, but an angry woman wouldn't worry about that, would she? You had better not laugh at me, Jerome. I might do it."

"You might, but you won't."

A Winter's Tale

"Are you so sure?"

"Yes, I'm quite sure."

Una pushed her chair back and walked away from him to the windows. She pulled the curtains back and leaned her head against the black panes. "Listen to the wind moaning away out there," she said. "It's odd how you can feel the snow even when you can't see it. It's still there but it's slipping away. I don't want it to go. I liked the snow. 'Our millions of white feathers,' do you remember, Jerome?"

Jerome lifted his head sharply. "Of course," he said, remembering something that had eluded him. "Of course—it began then, that was it. Yes, Una, I remember. Come back to the fire. It's cold at that end of the room."

"Snow is exciting," Una complained. "Now there will be nothing but dreary old rain and slush. Rain is so dull."

"That depends on where you are," Jerome said, as he came up behind her and put his hands on her shoulders. "Now in the Sahara—"

Una twisted away from his hands and wandered over to the fire, stopping on the way to look down at the orchids on their table.

"I will always hate orchids," she said. "Conceited, arrogant things."

"I will remember never to send them to you after a first night," Jerome promised. "Not even in a nice little box or wrapped in cellophane. Come and drink your coffee and stop wandering about like a lost soul."

"I feel like a lost soul. I will be lost without you, Jerome. What am I going to do?"

Una turned round suddenly to face him and held out her hands. "Can't you see that I mean it?" she said. "You mustn't laugh at me."

Jerome took her hands in his and said. "I'm not laughing, I'm far from laughing, but this isn't a tragedy, and in your heart you know it isn't. I'm not going to play it as if it were to please you."

He put his arm round her shoulders again and drew her towards the fire. "I will tell you exactly what you are going to do, but first come and help me clear this table and get it out of the way. We don't want Peter in on this scene, do we? Come, my dear, blow out the candles, while I put all this in the hatch. We haven't got all night."

"Haven't we?" Una said. "I don't see why not," but she did as she was told and held the silver candelabra while he folded the cloth.

"That's better," Jerome said, as he pushed the table back. "Now, put that down on the bookshelves and go and sit by the fire. I will fetch the coffee."

He slid the hatch door back and looked into the kitchen. The coffee tray was waiting in the hatch with the spirit-lamp lit under the Cona. The brightly lit kitchen, seen through the frame of the hatch, looked cosy and safe and inviting. The red arm-chair was drawn close to the range but Peter was sitting at the kitchen table eating his own dinner; he looked up inquiringly.

"Will you want anything else tonight?" he said, and as Jerome shook his head he put down his knife and fork and, getting up, came to the hatch.

"I ask because I'm going to the greenhouses when I have finished my dinner," he said. "I thought I would put in an hour or two getting the boxes ready for tomorrow, for one thing. I won't have time in the morning what with Miss Una's car to see to."

"A good idea, if you have the energy," Jerome agreed. "Don't worry about me. I expect that I will work most of the night."

"I'll put sandwiches and a flask of coffee in the study before I go," said Peter. "What about Sylvie?"

"Sylvie can stay with me. She always does, doesn't she, when I'm working?"

"She ought to go out for her run. Shall I take her now?"

"No, it's too early. I will let her out last thing."

"Let her out? I thought you said—" Peter looked past Jerome into the room and made a warning gesture which Jerome disregarded.

"What an old worrier you are, Peter," he said. "I will keep her on the chain, of course. I will take her a quick run round the house before I start work. Do me good. Clear my head."

Peter looked at him doubtfully and Jerome said, "Leave Sylvie to me. I will see that she doesn't run wild tonight. The valley sheep can graze peacefully under the moon, if there is one. Don't you trust me?"

"Hush, the girl will hear you!" Peter said softly. "Trust

you? I don't know that I do—" He took Sylvie's heavy chain out of his pocket and laid it on the hatch. As he picked up the two empty wine bottles he said, "Be careful, Captain."

Jerome laughed and picked up the coffee tray. As he turned to carry it to the fire, he heard Peter shut the hatch gently behind him.

Una was standing in the middle of the room. He saw that she had pushed the big sofa up in front of the fire and set the stool ready for the tray. She looked past him at the closed hatch.

"What's all this about Sylvie?" she said. "Why shouldn't she go out by herself as usual? What is that chain doing there?"

"Pour out while I fetch the brandy," Jerome said, putting the tray down on the stool between their chairs, but Una was not to be diverted. "You had better tell me, hadn't you?" she said, as he took the brandy bottle and glasses out of the cupboard.

Sylvie was already back in her place on the hearthrug, sitting upright and watching every move Jerome made, as if she had seen him looking at his watch surreptitiously all evening and was now wondering if it were worth while settling herself to sleep. When he sat down in his armchair and picked up his cup, she stretched herself out on the rug, turned her face towards the flames and shut her eyes. Jerome looked down at her and for the moment forgot Una. It suddenly seemed to him that Sylvie was different, not the Sylvie he had known. He was puzzled. She could not know, what he had not yet really admitted to himself, that never again would she be free to roam through the woods at her will. Was there already about her the dull resignation of the prisoner? She looked heavier in spite of her thinness, coarser, more ordinary. It seemed to him that she had lost her air of fineness, almost of spirituality, that he knew had come from her efforts to understand and to be more than she could be. He saw that something had gone from Sylvie and he doubted if it would ever return.

He sighed deeply and, setting down his cup, reached for his brandy glass. Una was talking earnestly, leaning forward in the chair opposite him. "You might as well tell me," she was saying, "I heard what you said to Peter—something about sheep. Sylvie was out all last night. Did she go after the sheep? Did she chase them or something? You and Peter have been so secretive and mysterious all day."

Jerome did not answer, and she said, "Now she mustn't go out alone. She must be kept on a chain. Poor Sylvie, she won't like that. She is used to being free. That would be cruel, Jerome."

"Better to be kept on a chain than to be shot at sight," Jerome said angrily, and he drained his glass. "Do shut up, Una."

"Shot? Who would shoot Sylvie? I don't believe it."

"Any farmer in the valley would after last night, if he caught her at it again."

Una stared at him. "At it again?" she said slowly. "What did she do? Has she hurt a sheep? Did she kill one? Jerome, how horrible!" She looked down at her bandaged arm and said, "I was right to be afraid. What are you going to do about her, Jerome?"

Jerome roused himself. "Do? Nothing," he said briskly. "Sylvie is my dog. She was not herself last night. Perhaps I should not have beaten her. We will keep her on the chain for a day or two just as a precaution. Now Una, you must forget all this, pretend you know nothing about it—Peter would never forgive me. This is none of your business. You will never see Sylvie again after tonight. She is nothing to do with you."

He looked at her anxiously and said, "Don't look like that, smile at me, Una. This is our last evening together. Let's forget Sylvie and talk of something else. Let's talk about you. What were we saying while we cleared the table?"

Una, who had been staring down at Sylvie as if she had never seen her before, looked up almost unwillingly. She did not smile at Jerome but she turned in her chair, so that she could no longer see the Alsatian lying between them and, tucking her legs under her, said, "Very well, Jerome—you were telling me what I was to do with myself when I got back to London, what was to happen next."

"So I was," Jerome said. "Drink your brandy. It will help to make you comfortable and sleepy. Well, you will have a good night's sleep. Then, in the morning Peter will bring you breakfast. You will pack in a leisurely way and put on your thickest clothes. You will walk down the lane with Peter carrying your suitcase. At the gate on to the road you will find your car, clear of snow, filled up with petrol, nicely warmed, ready and waiting. You will drive away, without a look back, and be in London before dark."

Una put her cup down on the tray and picked up her glass. "I see," she said, "and you? What will you be doing?"

"I will be working away, poor me, striking while the iron is hot."

"You won't be there to see me go? You won't say good-bye?"

"Much better not, don't you think so? We will say good-bye to-night in this room."

Una looked down at the glass in her hands. "And then?" she said in a colourless careful voice. "I'm back in London. What do I do then?"

Jerome leant back in his chair and looked over Sylvie's head into the fire. "I suggest that you ring up your unfortunate mother and tell her what you think best. Then I should go about a good deal, if I were you. See your friends, buy some new clothes, have a good time."

"And then?"

"Then you will live happily ever after," Jerome said, smiling at her. "You will either make something of yourself on your own, take your work seriously, do as I advise and try and get in with some repertory company and learn your job thoroughly before you think of television or radio. Or you will marry and have children. I don't see why, with your iron determination, a bit of luck and lots of hard work, you shouldn't do both and have the best of both worlds."

"And you? Where will you be?"

"Oh, I shall watch your progress from afar, with interest."

"Shall we meet?"

"Why not? At cocktail parties, at first nights perhaps. I will come and see you act. As I said, I may be able to help you."

"I see," Una said slowly, lifting her head to look at him, "And now what are you going to do, this night, I mean? No, don't tell me. I will tell you. In a few minutes, when you have finished your brandy, you will give me a kiss, a nice light one, and get yourself out of this room as quickly as you can, taking Sylvie with you. You will hurry across the hall and shut the door. Perhaps you will lock it. You will say to yourself, 'Thank God, that's over. She is going without too much fuss or bother. I managed that quite well, it might have been worse.' Then you will sit down at your typewriter and at once you will forget all about me, as if I had never been."

"I won't forget you, Una," Jerome said. "I couldn't if I tried. After this week I know too much about you."

"What do you know, I wonder?" Una said. Holding her glass with both hands she put it to her lips, tilting her head back.

"I know a lot of things," Jerome said, smiling to himself. "All sorts of little intimate things, such as the way you stand when you are not thinking, with one toe turned in; that you like far too much sugar in your tea, that your left breast is a little larger than your right, that you like to wear warm soft furry things; that you sleep with one hand under your cheek and your mouth so closely shut. No, I won't forget. As a matter of fact, I never forget anything. I can't afford to."

"What do you mean?" Una said, sitting up to stare at him.

"You won't write about me, will you? You won't put me or us, or any part of us, into a book or a play?"

"If I did, you wouldn't recognize yourself, my naïve dear."

Una put her empty glass down on the tray. Her hand was trembling. She sat on the edge of her chair and said, "I wouldn't put it past you. There is nothing you wouldn't do. You take everything that comes along and you use it, like one of those awful plants that sits with its mouth open waiting for wretched flies, or like some octopus with horrible grappling arms. You are not a human being. You are a monster, a scribbling monster, that's what I said before."

"Gently, Una," Jerome protested. "There is no need to upset yourself or to get scarlet in the face with indignation. I am what I am, and nothing will change me."

"I suppose you will say next that you are a writer, as if that excused everything?"

Jerome said nothing and Una cried, "Is it worth it? That's what I want to know, Jerome? Is it worth it to you?"

Jerome put his empty glass down on the tray and stood up suddenly. He took a cigarette from the box and lit it before he answered her. "It must be worth it, mustn't it?" he said at last. "I wouldn't do it otherwise." He looked down at her and said gently, "But sometimes I don't know."

He knelt down on the hearthrug and put another log on the fire. The sparks flew upwards and the rising flames lit his face. Beside him, Sylvie lifted her head and pressed it gently against his arm. He put his hand on her head, fondling the length of her warm soft ears. As he turned to Una, the girl said suddenly:

"Here we are, sitting by the fire, with our brandy and our cigarettes, with the wind moaning outside, exactly as we did on the first night I came here. Was it only a week ago? I was so happy. I didn't think that it would all end so quickly, I didn't think that it would ever end. I suppose I didn't think at all."

She turned her head and looked round the room as if she had never seen it before. Then she leant forward in her chair and said, "Tell me Jerome, please, quite truthfully, what were you thinking that first evening when we sat here after dinner. I want to know. It's important to me."

Jerome sat back on his heels on the hearthrug and looked up into her face. He smiled and said, "Why, Una, how should I know now? I expect I thought how pretty you were looking in your red dress, how sweet and young you were, what a lucky fellow I was, something like that. I know that I said to myself, 'Bless the snow.'"

"Peter told me that I came at the right time, when you couldn't work, and that if I had come when your writing was going easily and well, you would have got rid of me somehow that first day, snow or not. Is that true? Don't lie to me, you know I hate lies."

Jerome said nothing and Una cried, "Of course it's true. I did the trick, didn't I? It worked, like a dose of salts! I suppose I should flatter myself that I set your mind working again. You thought that first evening, as you sat there watching me over your glass, 'This is a bit of luck, a woman is what I need to set me going, a few nights should do.' You thought that, didn't you, didn't you—or something like it."

"Hush!" Jerome said. He put his hand on her knee and said again, "Hush, Una. Don't, my dear." She pushed his hand away and said, "Don't touch me. Go away. What a fool I have been. You may be a genius, I don't know or care. I only know that you are utterly selfish and ruthless, incapable of loving anyone. You are not worth worrying about."

Jerome patted her knee gently. "Have it your own way," he said. "Perhaps you are right. Anyway, there is nothing more to say."

He stood up and looking down at her again said, "All the same before I go, and as I won't see you again, just one word of warning or advice, because, believe it or not, I want you to have what you want from life, to be successful and happy. You have youth, looks, intelligence, some talent, and a great deal of will power, but if you want to please and use men, as normal women do, you must learn that men do not want to hear the truth about themselves, that truth is the last thing they want from women. The women who succeed in life are the sly and artful ones who hide their motives, cover up, keep things comfortable and never, never tell the truth, not to a man anyway."

He laughed, and said, "Cheer up, Una, no need to look like that. In the long run we have probably done each other a lot of good. Well, my dear, no use prolonging this. Let's say 'Good-night.' "

Jerome walked quickly to the door with Sylvie at his heels; as he reached it, he stopped suddenly, felt in his pocket, and came back to her.

Una had risen to her feet. She stood on the hearthrug, staring after him. She seemed very young and forlorn and helpless, standing like a schoolgirl with her arms at her sides and her feet apart. Above the crimson wool of her dress, her face was unnaturally white.

"I have been carrying this round all evening," Jerome said. He held out a small round package, knotted in one of his silk handkerchiefs.

"What is it?" Una said as she took it reluctantly.

"A farewell present. Something I wanted you to have."

"I don't want anything from you," Una said. A hot uncomfortable blush spread across her face and neck. "I don't want paying."

"What an asinine thing to say," Jerome said. "It isn't a fur coat or a diamond necklace. Come on, have a look at it. It will make you laugh."

He took the little package from her and, unknotting the handkerchief, held out a small glittering object on the palm of his hand.

"What is it?" Una said again, and put her hands behind her back.

"It's a lucky charm. Indian or Chinese, I would say, but I don't know where it came from. I have had it for years, ever since my uncle died. All this time it has been waiting for you in an old jewel case in my room with some chessmen, Victorian brooches and old coins. Perhaps it belonged to my mother, or my grandmother—I don't know. Look, Una, it's carved out of old ivory and inlaid with gold and it has two emeralds for eyes. It could be an owl, couldn't it? It looks a very wise downy old bird. Hang it on your bracelet with all those other dangling things. It will remind you of me."

"Why should I want to be reminded of you?" Una said. She glared up at him and struck suddenly at his arm. The little trinket bounced from his hands and into the flames.

Jerome stepped back and shrugged his shoulders; but Una, giving him a horrified glance, fell on her knees on the hearthrug. "Quick! Quick!" she cried, "I can't bear it. Quickly before the fire spoils it. There it is, I can see it, at the edge, by that log. Where are the tongs?"

Jerome said, "Oh, Una!" and began to laugh helplessly, while Sylvie, excited by the sound of Una's raised voice and the tension in the room or perhaps thinking that this was a game of some strange form of hide-and-seek, ran madly round the room, rearing up to look on the bookshelves, leaping on to the chairs and down again.

"Stop it, Sylvie!" Jerome said. "Don't you start—I have had all I can stand of female hysterics for one evening. An impossible pair, that's what you are."

"I have got it," Una said triumphantly. "Give me that handkerchief. Look, it's quite all right, only a little dirty."

233

She stood up holding the charm in her cupped hand. Sylvie ran to her and stood on the hearthrug waving her tail and looking up expectantly.

"No, Sylvie," Una said. "This is not for you. This is mine." Her hair hung over one eye; she tossed it back and smiled up at Jerome. There was a streak of wood-ash on one cheek. Her eyes were shining.

"Poor Jerome," she said. "Don't look so bewildered. I'm all right now. I give in. It's over."

Una looked down at her hand and said, "I will keep this with me always. When I get back to London, I will send you a present, then we will be quits. I will look everywhere until I find a little cat, a cheap little china one. You can put it on your writing-table and think of me sometimes." She put her arms round his neck and kissed him.

In relief and gratitude Jerome kissed her back. Her arms tightened round his neck and, suddenly suspicious, he held her away from him and looked down into her face. He was tired and overstrained, and he knew that he had drunk a little too much. The room was too warm, the fire too bright; Una's scent made his head swim, not unpleasantly; he could not think clearly but he knew that this sweet reasonableness was not like Una, this surrender too sudden. She smiled up at him, a little tremulously, and her eyes slowly filled with tears.

"Una," he said, and she laid a finger across his mouth. "Don't say anything," she whispered. "There's nothing more to say. It's over now, don't worry. You can go back to your treadmill, as Peter calls it, but first say good-bye to me properly, here, now."

She tightened her arms round his neck and pressed her body against his. As he put his arms round her, he felt her tremble uncontrollably and knew, although he could not see it, that her face wore the blind lost look he had come to know well. He let his cheek rest on her silky hair and said, pityingly, "Hush, Una. No. It won't do."

At once she gripped him fiercely and, lifting her head, cried, "Why not? You needn't stay long. I know you want to. Be kind, Jerome."

"No," he repeated. "No, Una," but she must have known that he had capitulated, that nothing could now keep him from her, not even the small triumphant purring sound that she could not suppress. She clung to him for a moment longer, as if she were listening to the thudding of his heart, as if she knew that now the same wild surge of longing consumed them both.

Jerome thought confusedly, 'Why not? Poor child—anything else would be graceless—an act of grace, that's what it will be, brief and thankful. This is the right, the inevitable way to end it.'

As Una released him and, stepping back, undid the cord round her waist, he wondered fleetingly if she had pushed the sofa up in front of the fire with this scene already clear in her mind, but the faint chill of this thought vanished almost immediately—a snowflake descending into a fire.

235

He took his coat off and threw it on the chair. "Wait, Jerome," Una cried, as she always did, but now he would not wait. "Don't be silly," he said and pushed her hands away.

As he felt the answering flare rise in her to meet him, a sound, indescribably shocking, jerked them apart. A low howl, long, mournful and despairing, rose in the room.

"It's Sylvie!" Una cried. "We had forgotten her. She knows— Put her out. Put her out!"

Jerome swore furiously and sat up. He saw Sylvie standing with the Alsatian's crouching stance, her tail between her legs, in the shadow behind his armchair. Her long head was raised, her muzzle pointed to the ceiling.

Shocked and cold with dismay, he shouted at her, "Be quiet! Be quiet, damn you!"

"Put her out at once, Jerome," Una pleaded. "She will forget all about us when she can't see us. She will run up to her bed." She gave a sudden nervous laugh, and at once put her hands over her mouth.

Jerome turned on her savagely, "Don't you dare laugh," he said, and Una cried, "Be quick then, put her out. It will be all right, Jerome. I promise you—"

Jerome leapt to the door and flung it open. He was shaking with anger and shame. "Out, Sylvie!" he said.

Sylvie flinched at the cold rage in his voice. She hesitated, looking at him with a supplicating, humble look. "Out!" he said again, and took a step towards her. She flinched again as if he had struck her, but stood her ground. As his fingers gripped her collar, she growled warningly.

"Sylvie!" Jerome cried, and took his hand away. At once, without another glance at him, she walked to the door and out into the hall.

Jerome shut the door behind her and turned back to the room.

9

No echo of Sylvie's despairing cry reached Peter in the warm glass-enclosed world of the orchid-houses. He had put in a good two hours' work in the packing room and then had walked up and down between the benches to make sure that all was well, looking lovingly at his charges resplendent under the electric-lights, before leaving them in peace to the remaining hours of darkness. When he turned out the lights and shut the door on them soon after midnight, he was whistling happily. Turning up the collar of his coat against the sudden cold, he followed the snow-covered path to the side door and entered the silent house. He hesitated for a few moments in the kitchen and did not glance at the hatch, but he stood in front of the door into the hall and even went so far as to lay his hand on the doorknob before he decided not to open it. He had put the flask and sandwiches on the table in the workroom hours ago after banking up the fire, and he had no excuse to disturb Jerome who, once he had settled down to a night's work, would resent any interruption. There was no reason why Sylvie should not be safely with Jerome, lying in her own winter place in front of the fire. Peter went into his bedroom and was soon fast asleep.

The cuckoo-clock in the dark and empty kitchen chimed one as Una eased herself cautiously from under Jerome's arm and off the sofa, and stood up on the hearthrug in front of the sitting-room fire, which had sunk to a red glow. The room with its shaded lights was dim and warm, and it was very still. She dressed with silent furtive haste, and then bent to pick up her bracelets from the rug where Jerome had thrown them. The gold links made a small hard clinking sound as her hand closed over them and she froze, still half-crouched beside the sofa, but he did not move. Una straightened herself slowly and stood looking down at him while she folded the bracelets carefully in her handkerchief and put them in the pocket of her dress.

He lay on the sofa, one arm doubled under him and the other stretched out across the place where she had been. His jersey was wrinkled across his back and his feet in fawn socks were pressed uncomfortably against the sofa-arm, but the heavy even sound of his breathing told her that he was still deep in sleep. His face was turned towards her on the cushion, with his mouth half-open; his dark hair stood up at the back of his head. He looked as dishevelled, unlovely, and as helpless as only a middle-aged half-dressed sleeping man can look. There was no expression on Una's face as she stared at him.

The velvet jacket was lying on the floor by Jerome's armchair;

238

she lifted it and spread it carefully over him before she picked up her shoes and, holding them in one hand, walked on stockinged feet to the door.

The hall was dimmer than the sitting-room although the hanging light in Peter's lantern was still on. The porcelain stove shone whitely, sending its warm breath through the house. As Una shut the door behind her, something moved in the shadows beyond the stove, between her and the stairs. She stood still, and saw that it was Sylvie.

Sylvie walked slowly out into the centre of the hall until she stood directly under the light, which swung slightly in the draught that came from under the front door. The cold air brought with it a reminder of the dark woods, and the hall was no longer only a hall; the chequered pattern of light and shade flickering over the polished floor might have been made by some cold moon shining through the leaves of a primeval forest; it showed Sylvie's lowered head and gleaming eyes. Una shrank back against the sitting-room door.

The girl and the dog confronted each other while round them the house waited silently. The darkness at the top of the stairs advanced and retreated as the light swung. The shadows gathered round the stove. Somewhere, deep in the house, a clock ticked on moving slowly towards morning, but neither Una nor Sylvie heard it.

Una was the first to move. Keeping her eyes on Sylvie, she pushed herself away from the door and took a step, not towards the stairs but to the front door. Sylvie growled softly, and Una stood still. She could have shrieked for help, knowing that Jerome might reach her in time, but this did not occur to her. Her mind held only one purpose. Setting her jaw grimly, watching the dog, she edged carefully towards the door and Sylvie slowly followed her until the door chain, which Peter had fastened hours ago, was under Una's hand. She unhooked it and felt for the large old-fashioned key. As she turned it and groped for the latch, the wind swung the door wide open. Wind and night were in the hall bringing the cold promise of the forest, the wild freedom of the trees. The light swung wildly, the shadows danced.

"Out, Sylvie!" Una whispered as she struggled with the door, but Sylvie did not move; lifting her head she stared into the darkness.

"Out, Sylvie," Una beseeched again, clinging to the door-handle. "Quick. Now's your chance!"

A fresh gust of wind filled the hall; as if that were a summons that could not be ignored, Sylvie started forwards and a shadow slipped past Una out into the night. As if she could not believe that Sylvie had really gone, she held the door open a moment longer, but now the hall was empty and there was nothing under the light.

Una turned the key again and fastened the chain with cold and shaking fingers. Then, as quietly as a thief, she crept up to bed.

Jerome woke and stretched. He did not know what had pulled him up from his depths of sleep, but it seemed to him that some-where a door had shut. He sat up, swinging his feet to the hearthrug, and smoothed his hair. The fire was nearly out. His watch had stopped. He had no idea how long he had slept, but he knew that it was very late.

He stood up and, as he lit a cigarette, he looked round the room from the crumpled sofa cushions to the curtained windows. The brandy bottle and glasses were on the tray; the orchids stared blandly back at him from their table. Of Una there was no sign, and he was grateful to her for leaving him to wake alone, for accepting that this was indeed their good-bye.

He passed his hand over his forehead experimentally, as if he expected to feel an ache there, but apart from a slight muzziness and a thickness on his tongue he had never felt better. He supposed that he should be feeling guilty at losing so many hours of work, but he did not. He knew that these hours of love and sleep had been well spent, that they had been perhaps exactly what he needed if he were to work through the next days as he planned to do. This act, for whatever motive it had been done, for grace, gratitude or desire, had been the right one both for himself and for Una. He had risen from the particular sofa like a giant refreshed, and now there was nothing to keep him from his writing-table.

"Bless the girl," he said to the silent room and, picking up his jacket, he went out into the hall leaving all the lights burning.

In the cloak-room he washed his face in cold water, rinsed out his mouth and combed his hair, noting as he did so that his eyes in the mirror above the basin looked, at this unnatural hour, clear and bright. Hanging his jacket on a peg, he took down his old tweed coat and slipped it on. As he crossed the hall again, he stopped suddenly under the light and then went to the foot of the staircase. Putting his hand on the bottom post of the banisters, he said softly, "Sylvie?"

There was no answering sound or movement from the dark landing above and he said, a little louder, "Sulking, Sylvie? I'm not coming up to fetch you, if that is what you want. Come down when you have forgiven me. You know where I will be."

He hesitated again, shrugged his shoulders, and turned towards the door of his workroom.

Jerome did not know why he felt impelled at that moment, when he longed only to sit down to his work, to walk the length of the hall to his front door or why he opened it, undoing the chain and turning the key, as Una had done. The wind leapt at him from the darkness chilling him as if he had been plunged into a cold bath but, holding the door open, he stared out into the night. The waning moon had not yet risen and at first he could see nothing except darkness, and he heard nothing except the sighing of the trees. Then, miles away, high in the woods above the house, he thought that he heard the old dog fox call once and, in a rift in the clouds, he saw a few cold stars dance across the sky.

Shivering, he shut the door and hurried back to the familiar warmth of his room where the flask of coffee was waiting to ease him into the smooth-flowing current of work that he confidently expected to carry him, oblivious of everything and of everyone, far into the hours of another day.

Part Four

I

The telephone ringing in the kitchen brought Peter out of his bed. He knew that it had been ringing for some time; its shrill warning note had been a part of his dreams; but, as he sat up in the darkness, he thought that it was the alarm telling that something was wrong in the orchid-houses.

Still half asleep, he switched on his bedside light and reached for his old silver watch. It was not the middle of the night as he had supposed but nearly six o'clock. He threw his bedclothes off and, muttering angrily, bent down to grope for his slippers. Only then did he realize that the loud insistent ringing in the kitchen could have nothing to do with the orchids. Wide awake at once, he flung his door open and hurried on bare feet to the dresser.

The room was dark but the moonlight, shining on the snow outside the window, cast a faint unearthly radiance on the ceiling. Peter lifted the receiver and an unfamiliar truculent voice spoke in his ear.

"What?" Peter said. "What's that? Yes, this is Mr. Holt's house."

The voice spoke again and Peter, as he listened, began to shiver as if the cold of the stone floor under his feet had reached through his whole body to his heart.

"No!" he said, in a shocked whisper; but the voice had not finished what it had to say and he could only listen. When at last he dropped the receiver, he looked wildly round the silent room and then ran out into the hall where the lights were still on. The door of Jerome's workroom was locked. Peter threw himself on it, twisting the doorknob, beating on the panels with his fists.

Jerome unlocked the door and stood scowling on the threshold. His hair was on end and he was sallow with weariness. The warm close air of the room flowed round the black and gold screen and past him into the hall.

"What is the matter? Have you gone mad?" he demanded sternly but, as he looked down at the small distraught figure in blue and white striped pyjamas, his expression changed.

"Why, Peter—" he said uncertainly, but Peter interrupted him.

"You let her out!" he shouted. "After all you said! I might have known it. You let her out into the woods."

"Don't shout at me," Jerome said. "Sylvie? I didn't let her out. I put her into the hall, sometime after dinner. She took herself up to her bed. She must have."

He put his hand out and took hold of Peter's arm. "You are shivering," he said, more gently. "Come in here to the fire."

Peter shook the hand off. "Then who did?" he cried. "Who let her out? They shot Sylvie. She was shot out there."

Jerome stared at him. "I don't believe it," he said flatly, "I won't. Not Sylvie."

He came out into the hall, shutting his door behind him. "What are you trying to tell me?" he said. "That Sylvie is dead?"

Peter made a strange moaning sound. "They don't know," he said. "They rang up directly they got back to the farmhouse. Braddock's it was. She must have gone back to the very same field. They were up, getting ready to milk. They heard their dogs giving tongue and went straight out. There she was, plain in the moonlight, standing over a sheep, and the rest in a huddle by the gate into the yard. They saw her plain, Jim Braddock said. No mistake. They all know Sylvie. She didn't move, he said. Just stood with her head up and waited for them. 'I could have walked up to her,' that's what he said, but his son fired, got her high up, and off she went then back across the fields to the woods. He gave her the second barrel. They saw her fall and get up again and go on into the trees. They let her go. 'No use following in that half-light,' he said."

Peter stopped as if the words were choking him, and looked up at Jerome.

"She was hurt bad, that's what they think, but they don't really know," Peter said slowly. "There was blood, drops of it, going away across the snow. 'If she can keep going, she'll make for home. Better go out and look for her, she's yours,' that's what Jim Braddock said."

"What is their number?" Jerome asked. "Never mind, I will find it. Go on in there and sit down by the fire."

He opened his door, pushed Peter through it, and turned towards the kitchen. Half-way across the hall he hesitated and then ran up the stairs, switched on the landing light, and looked down at Sylvie's empty bed. He knelt down and put his hand on her blue blanket; it was smooth, cold, untouched. When he stood up, his face was grim, set in hard ugly lines. He looked at Una's door, took a step towards it, and hurried back down the stairs and into the kitchen.

When he came into the workroom again, he was carrying Peter's dressing-gown. Peter looked up from the chair by the fire but, after one glance at Jerome's face, he turned his head away.

"Put this on," Jerome said. "There is still some coffee in that flask. Drink it up at once."

He went to the window and pulled the curtains back. The waning moon shone down on the sea of dark trees, its cold light already paling on the hills before the promise of dawn.

"Hurry up," he said over his shoulder. "Drink that and get

dressed. Braddock says that they will start out their end directly they have finished milking."

"Anything new?" Peter croaked, as he put down his cup and stood up.

Jerome shook his head. "It's just as you said. They only know that they got her with both barrels. They think that when she went away she was running on three legs."

"Perhaps it's not so bad as they think," Peter said as he walked to the door. "Moonlight is tricky. Perhaps they were further off than they thought. Sylvie's coat is so thick. Dogs can lose a lot of blood—"

His voice trailed away. "What are we going to do?" he said. "What can we do?"

"We are going out to find her," Jerome said.

"But, if she can, she will come straight home here to this house," Peter objected. "We should stay here, one of us anyway."

"She didn't come back yesterday for hours," Jerome said. "She went somewhere to lie up, to rest, to recover—"

"It's hopeless!" Peter cried. "There's miles of trees. Where could we begin to look?"

Jerome turned away from the window. "You didn't let me finish," he said. "I was going to say, 'and to drink.' I know where Sylvie went that first time and where she will make for today. I will take you straight there. It's only a mile or so from the house. We can go by the path along the side of the hill where the snow will be lighter for most of the way. It shouldn't take us much more than an hour."

"You go," Peter said. "I still think that one of us ought to stay here in case she comes. It's taking too big a chance."

"It's a chance we have got to take," Jerome said firmly. "I think that I will need you, Peter."

Peter looked at Jerome's face. "All right," he said. "I'll go. No need to look like that, Captain. We don't know anything yet. I had better take the sled, we'll need it to bring her back on if she's badly hurt. A blanket and some towels too. And my First Aid box, there's some brandy in it."

He hurried to the door and, glancing over his shoulder, stopped short. Jerome had gone to the cupboard by the fireplace. Peter saw him open it and take out the Lüger.

"What's that for?" Peter said loudly. "It's loaded. Put it down."

"You go and get dressed," Jerome said gently. "We mustn't waste any more time, but before we go we should have some tea and something to eat. It will be a climb. We must make up the furnaces too, no need to let the orchids or anything else innocent suffer for this. Yes, take the sled and your First Aid box, and a spade or a pick."

"No!" Peter cried, but Jerome pushed the pistol into his pocket and turned to the window again. "I will be along to help you in a moment," he said. "Put on long boots and the thickest gloves you can find. Hurry up."

Peter stood where he was, looking at Jerome's back. He tried to speak, but the words would not come. Then he went away round the screen and across the hall to the kitchen.

Una saw him go. She stood in her white dressing-gown at the

top of the stairs, looking down. She had slept heavily for a short while, had woken to see the moonlight shining between her curtains and to hear an owl call desolately down the valley, and had slept again, a light, uneasy sleep torn by strange and disturbing dreams. The sound of Peter's fists beating on Jerome's door had woken her. Sitting up in bed, she had listened to the voices in the hall. She was putting on her dressing-gown when she heard Jerome run up the stairs, and she had stood quite still, frozen with fear, hardly breathing, until she heard him go down again. Now she sank down on the top step and, putting her cheek against the cold wood of the banister, watched his door.

It opened and he crossed the hall to the cloakroom. When he came out again, he was carrying his sheepskin jacket, a scarf and his old green hat. He stood immediately below her under the brass lantern, as if he were trying to remember something he had forgotten, or as if he were turning over something in his mind. His shoulders sagged wearily and his head was bent. Una rose stealthily to her feet, careful to make no sound, but before she could decide to go back to her bed, Jerome walked down the hall below her and into the kitchen.

Una crept down the steps to the turn in the stairs. Now she could see the whole length of the hall. She heard voices again and movement in the kitchen. Doors opened and shut. She heard the clink of china, a tap running, and she heard Peter stoking the furnace. She waited for what seemed a long time but was only a few minutes, holding on to the banisters. Suddenly the kitchen door opened again and she shrank back.

"Better take your big torch," Jerome's voice said. "It will still be dark under the trees. I will fetch mine as well." He walked out into the hall, followed by Peter. Both men were wearing long rubber boots and looked bulky, incongruous in the hall, in their heavy coats and scarves.

"It's on the top shelf," Peter said. "I'll get it. I know where it is."

Peter hurried towards the cloakroom and Jerome turned his head and looked up at the stairs as if, in the turmoil of worry and preparation, he sensed an island of cold waiting stillness. He looked straight at Una. She flinched, but stared back at him.

"Here it is," Peter said. "You forgot your gloves," and stopped. He shut the cloakroom door carefully behind him and looked from Jerome to the girl.

The colour came back into Una's face. She put her hair back with one hand and ran down the last steps.

"What is it?" she said breathlessly. "What has happened?"

Jerome's voice stopped her at the foot of the stairs. "What you meant to happen," he said.

Una gasped. They saw her mouth open and shut soundlessly, but she recovered almost at once and said, with an air of bewilderment, "I don't understand. Why are you dressed up like this in the middle of the night? Peter too—"

"It was you," Peter said suddenly. "You let Sylvie out."

Una glanced at him, and then turned to Jerome. "Sylvie was in the hall," she said. "You went to sleep, there on the sofa, and forgot to let her out for her run. I let her out because she asked to be let out. Was that wrong?"

"And locked and bolted the door behind her," Jerome said. "Stop it, Una. You knew. I told you, God help me. I didn't drink so much that I can't remember what I did. Were you banking on that? It's no use. Don't lie. You let her out on purpose."

Una lifted her head. Her face whitened again as she saw the look in his eyes. "Very well. Yes, I did," she said defiantly. "Did you really expect me to go meekly away and leave her with you here in this house, to let her win? Yes, I let Sylvie out."

Peter started forward, lifting his hand, which held Jerome's heavy torch. "You— You—" he stuttered, but Jerome caught his arm.

"Leave her alone," he said. "It's done, and no one can undo it now. Come on, we haven't time to waste on her."

Holding Peter's arm, he marched him down the hall to the kitchen door and shut it behind them both.

Una stared after him. As she heard the back door slam, she sat down on the bottom step of the stairs, buried her face in her arms, and began to weep.

2

The sun rose as Jerome and Peter left the path that had taken them up and across the hillside through the dark and silent woods. They had not spoken a word since they had left the house as dawn was breaking. Round them the woods, still mysterious with night and the last light of the sinking moon, had shown no sign of life; the only sounds had been the squelching of the soft snow under their feet, the sound of the sled's runners and their own laboured breathing. Jerome walked in front and Peter, pulling the sled, had all he could do to keep up with him. When they plunged down-hill into the trees where the snow still lay thickly, Jerome turned to help Peter, but was waved away by a curt gesture.

"Get on," Peter said. "I can manage. Get on, and don't you miss the way."

Although he did not raise his voice, the words echoed strangely through the early morning snowy peace of the woods. Jerome did not answer; he turned into the trees again, stumbling through the drifts between the trunks, knocking the soft melting snow from the branches. It had been late summer when he had last come this way with Sylvie running in front of him through the green sun-shot resin-scented flickering half-light under the trees towards the tinkle of falling water. He stood still and listened, suddenly afraid that he had indeed missed the way; the spring was silent now, sealed with winter, and he had no eager guide. Then he saw that the trees ahead were thinning, showing the morning sky. He walked on a few steps and knew that he had found the clearing; here was the narrow open space that he remembered, and the grey rocks, snow-sprinkled now, above the spring.

The sun, well up above the dark tops of the trees, was dazzling on the open expanse of snow. The sky was a brilliant arch of blue. All trace of the wind and cloud of the evening before had gone. It was too fine, too clear to last, and the new warmth in the air presaged rain to come. As Jerome's tired eyes went from the waiting ranks of trees across the sunny snow-filled glade, it seemed to him that never before could there have been an early morning more achingly alive not only with the promise of a new day but with all the days of the year to come. For him the wintry air of the little clearing was suddenly redolent with the coming seasons, warm with the scent of summer flowers still under the earth.

Peter clutched his arm. "There she is!" Peter cried. "Look, she's lying over there in the snow, against that rock."

Sylvie lay in the sunlight below the shelf of rock, which was her usual resting place, and a few feet from the spring whose thread of water fell almost imperceptibly into the dark centre of the basin. From a distance she looked as if she were asleep. The sunlight caught the silver hairs of her coat and her long head rested on her front paws. On the rocks above her, a jackdaw, startling black against its snowy background, stared down at her inquisitively. As the two men appeared through the trees, the bird retreated, but it did not fly away and was soon back on its rocky perch again to watch the scene with its bright bold eye. Sylvie did not move as Peter, dropping the sled ropes, ran heavily towards her. Jerome followed more slowly, walking in Peter's footsteps as if he were unwilling to desecrate the white peace of the snow more than he need.

"She's alive," Peter called joyfully. "She's breathing. Her eyes are open," and then Jerome heard him catch his breath.

"Let me see," he said gently and knelt down beside Peter.

There was no need for him to disturb Sylvie or to touch the blood-clotted silver and black hair of the body that seemed not only misshapen, with its awkwardly flung out hind leg, but so much smaller than he remembered it. He saw the shattered hip and the wounds on back and shoulder.

"How did she get so far?" Peter said hoarsely. "Must be all of two miles."

Jerome could not speak. He pulled his glove off and laid his hand on Sylvie's brow. At his touch, she slowly lifted her head and looked up at them.

"She can move," Peter whispered. "Perhaps it's not so bad after all. Did she reach the water? Did she drink? I must get her some water before we do anything else. Why didn't I bring a bowl? I'll bring some in my hands. No, give me your hat, that will do." He jumped up and hurried to the spring.

Sylvie looked at Jerome. He thought that she recognised him, but he was not sure. In her eyes, which were unclouded, a strange light came and went, a gold-green secret radiance that glowed and retreated, seemed to pulse as if at some inner command, and then to ebb; Jerome looked into them with awe, watching what he knew was life itself changing, yielding, becoming something else.

"She reached the spring," Peter said above him. "The snow is all trampled round. There's blood. I have brought her some more water." He put the hat down on the snow close to Sylvie's head, dipped his fingers into the crown and held them out to her.

"There's nothing we can do," Jerome told him. "Hush. Don't worry her."

As he spoke Sylvie began to pant, drawing her lips back from her teeth, showing her tongue. A shudder ran through her body. "She's in pain," Peter cried. "Terrible pain. I can't bear it. We must do something."

"Yes, we must," Jerome said. "There is only one thing we can do."

"No!" Peter cried, seizing his arm. "Let's get her back to the house. Let's try. I can ring up—"

"You know it's no use," Jerome said roughly. "Don't make it harder. Go and sit down over there on the rocks. Turn your back. No need for two of us. She is my dog."

Peter made a strangled sound, a harsh and choking sob. He touched Sylvie's head and, getting to his feet, stumbled away as Jerome took the Lüger out of his pocket.

The report sent the jackdaw wheeling indignant up into the

blue of the sky. Peter took his hands slowly away from his ears, but he stayed where he was crouched on the rocks, facing the woods. The echoes died away, and Jerome, rising to his feet, lurched blindly across the clearing into the fringe of the trees. Peter heard him retching violently.

Peter stood up stiffly and, moving like an old man, walked back to the sled. He opened his First Aid box and took out the small bottle of brandy. Jerome his back turned to the clearing, was wiping his face with his handkerchief when Peter reached him.

"What's that?" Jerome said. "Brandy? No, I don't want it."

"Better drink it, there's only an ounce or so there," Peter said. "Come on, get it down."

He watched Jerome put the bottle to his lips and tilt his head back, and looked searchingly into the unshaven haggard face, where now a little colour had returned. Jerome met his eyes. "Thank you, Peter," he said, and gave the empty bottle back to him. "Fetch the spade and pick," he said, "and bring me that blanket. We will bury her here, in sight of the spring."

As Peter went back to the sled, Jerome followed him and took the blanket from his hand. "Stay here a minute," he said. "Don't look." He walked to the rocks and spread the blanket over the dark heap that lay below them.

When he turned back to the glade, he said in his normal voice, "This is the best place, I think, a few yards from that big tree." He took the spade from Peter and began to scrape the snow from the grass. "The ground will be stone-hard," he said. "We will have our work cut out. You had better bring that pick here."

The sun climbed up the sky as the two men laboured. The jackdaw returned to his usual perch and, turning his head from side to side, seemed to listen to the sound of steel on the half-frozen earth. Jerome had taken off his coat and soon Peter was working in his jersey with the sleeves rolled up.

The pick rose and fell. They worked in silence until Jerome straightened himself and dropped his spade. "This is deep enough now," he said. "You will have to help me lift her."

Peter threw his pick down. Tears were running down his devastated face. He cried in a choking voice, "I could kill that girl. I could kill her, do you hear?"

"I hear," Jerome said wearily. "It's no use talking like that. It can't help Sylvie. Come on, let's get this over."

The jackdaw had been joined by another of its own kind and now a carrion crow suddenly appeared on the rocks. The three black shapes watched with avid curiosity as Jerome and Peter carried the heavy blanket-covered shape to the grave and laid it down as gently as they could. As Jerome picked up the spade, Peter ran furiously at the birds, waving his arms but making no sound; then he stood dumbly, with his arms hanging at his sides while Jerome shovelled in the earth.

When it was finished and there was nothing to be seen except a slight unevenness in the ground, Jerome scattered earth and snow over the blood-stained place where the body had lain. He picked up his hat and crammed it deep into a crevice in the rocks. The Lüger lay in the snow where he had dropped it. He bent down and picked it up, looked for the spent shell and ground it into the earth with his boot. Then walking into the middle of the glade, he extracted the clip and unloaded the pistol. Holding it by its butt, he swung his arm with all his strength and sent it whirling up and out and down into the trees.

Peter nodded approvingly, picked up his coat and put it on, and wound his scarf round his neck. Jerome came up to him and took his arm, and together they walked back to the sled; as they reached it, Jerome turned, and they both looked back. The clearing was sunny and quiet, still and empty now that the birds had gone.

Jerome looked up at the calm blueness of the sky and across the snow to the spring. Peter saw his lips moving and the withdrawn considering absent look that he knew well come into his eyes.

" 'Receive each mild spirit,' " Jerome said softly to the silent glade and the woods. He frowned, and shook his head. "Pure?" he said consideringly. "Rare? Wild?"

He considered again, standing with his bare head bent while his hand tightened on Peter's arm. "No," he murmured. "Who am I to change those words?" and, lifting his head, he said, still softly, as if he were speaking to himself but clearly enough for Peter to hear him: " 'Receive each mild spirit, new worlds to inherit.' "

He turned his head and looked at Peter. "Yes," he said. "That is right for Sylvie, after all; but perhaps you and I should say, 'More geese than swans now live, more fools than wise.' "

Peter snatched his arm away. "Shut up! Shut up," he cried. "You and your words! Can't you keep quiet even at a time like this? Turn everything into words, even this, that's what you do. I have had enough. I can't stand any more. I'm leaving, leaving you for good."

His voice broke. He stared at Jerome, moved his arm in a clumsy horrified gesture, including the glade and the rocks, the dark trees and the sky. "Not here," he whispered. "Not in this place. Let's get back to the house."

Throwing the spade and the pick on the sled and seizing the ropes, he made off towards the trees and the way that they had come. Jerome pulled his heavy coat over his shoulders and walked slowly after him.

3

The house was as it had been all the last week in its setting of trees and snow; the curtains were drawn back from the windows; smoke rose from its chimneys; it gave no sign that anything out of the way had occurred, but already the day was changing, clouds were coming up over the hills and the snow was melting fast.

When Peter, after leaving the sled on the path and taking his boots off in the back porch, went into the kitchen with Jerome close behind him, he saw at once that not only had the debris of their quick early meal been cleared away and the cups and saucers washed and dried, but a cloth had been spread on the table, a fresh meal set out, and the coffee percolator was bubbling on the brightly burning range. He stood still, looking from the newly swept floor to the orchids neatly arranged on the window-sill; then he hung his coat on its hook behind the door, sat down in his armchair beside Sylvie's bed and put on his slippers.

Jerome hesitated in the doorway, looking at Peter. He too, had seen the table ready and waiting in the clean neatness of the kitchen and, as Peter had done, he ignored it. He pulled a chair up to the range and slumped down on it, leaning his head on his hand. The two men sat in silence while the cuckoo-clock above them ticked away the minutes.

Suddenly Peter got to his feet and opening the hatch looked into the sitting-room. Jerome lifted his head and Peter, glancing at him, said, "The fire is lit. The room has been tidied, but there's no one there." It was the first time he had spoken for over an hour.

"Where are you going?" Jerome said sharply as Peter walked to the hall door and opened it.

"Only to make sure that there's no one in the hall. There isn't. The light has been turned off, that's all."

Peter turned back to the kitchen and looked up at the clock. "Only half past ten!" he said. "Seems like years." He went to the range and picked up the percolator. "Better have some coffee, seeing that it's here," he said. "Silly not to, I suppose. We both need it badly. Do you want anything to eat?"

Jerome shook his head and Peter, looking at the carefully arranged bread and butter, the cold chicken and ham on the dish, said violently, "I couldn't touch a crumb of it. Stick in my throat, it would, like poison. Why did she do it? It beats me. What did she think was the use?"

He fetched fresh cups and saucers from the dresser, refusing to see the tray waiting on the table. "I wonder where that girl has got to," he said. "Hiding in her room? Or could she have had the sense to take herself off, to go right away? That's too much to ask, I suppose."

"I'm afraid it is," Jerome said wearily. "She couldn't manage her car by herself, for one thing. She has no petrol. We will have to deal with her soon. Forget her now, she can wait."

As Jerome took the filled cup from Peter's hand, he looked up into his face. "Peter—" he began, but Peter interrupted him.

"Don't say anything," he said. "No need, or use. I'm through. I'm going."

"But where will you go after all these years?" Jerome said gently. "Have you thought—"

"That's my business. You don't have to worry about me. Thanks to you, I have my own money coming in regular. I have a right to that after all these years. I don't want anything else from you."

"Very well. If you must, you must," Jerome said. "I don't blame you. I would do the same, if I were you. There is nothing more to be said."

263

Putting his empty cup down on the top of the range, he stood up. "I'm going to the workroom," he said. "I will write a letter to Michael now. He will arrange to send you your money if you give him an address. He will probably ring up today when he finds the line is in order again. If he does, don't answer. I couldn't speak to him or to anyone else today. I will write to Mr. Stone too. Go to him or to Michael if you need any help. They would always do anything they could for you. How are you going? You had better take the van. I can fetch it back from the station later."

"I don't want the van," Peter said. "I can walk to the gate and get a bus."

"Just as you like," Jerome said. "Please switch the exchange to the extension in my room. I must ring up Braddock's. That's one thing I must do." He did not look at Peter, but picked up his sheepskin jacket and walked slowly to the door. Before he reached it, he stopped and, rubbing his hand over his face, yawned deeply. "God, I'm tired!" he said. "I'm all in. Extraordinary, isn't it, how at the worst times, when the mind and spirit are almost extinguished, the body asserts itself? What wouldn't I give for a bath and a shave!"

"The water will be hot. I made up the furnace," Peter said. "What's stopping you?"

"That girl. I couldn't go upstairs while she is still in the house. I won't see her again."

Jerome turned round and looked directly at Peter. "Do one last thing for me," he said. "Remember these fourteen years, and go upstairs and tell her to pack, if she hasn't packed already. Get her out of the house and to her car."

There was a moment's silence. Then Peter said shrilly, "You have a nerve! Me? Why me? I doubt if I could keep my hands off her. What are you thinking of?"

"I'm thinking that I could trust you to see her safe and un-harmed out of this house. I couldn't trust myself."

Peter said nothing, and Jerome cried, "I mean it, Peter. You and she are not involved. Do this for me. Do it quickly. Get her away at once."

"I should have to go down to her car and dig it out," Peter said slowly. "Then there's petrol and water, and her luggage. I must pack my box and leave it to be called for. I'm only taking a suit-case with me."

"Alvin will help you with the car," Jerome said. "He must be about somewhere."

"He isn't here today. Today is Wednesday," Peter said. "It's a week. Only a week, since she came."

He looked up at the clock again, and sighed. "It'll take the best part of two hours, what with one thing and another, I should think," he said. "You had better go and shut yourself in until the coast is clear. There may be a scene."

"Thank you, Peter," Jerome said, but Peter had turned his back on him.

Jerome hesitated, looking at the small familiar figure, at the back of the neat grey head. Then he went out into the hall and shut the kitchen door quietly behind him.

4

By midday, low clouds, heavy with the threat of rain that did not come, hung over the valley. Melting snow dripped steadily from the trees, freeing the dark-green furry branches from the burden they had carried all the last week, but snow still lay between the tree trunks and down the length of the lane. The slate roof of the house, clear of snow, glistened blue and damp in the dull light. Close round the walls was a band of grass-green but beyond it the familiar whiteness stretched away to the woods. When, at nearly two o'clock, Peter and Una left the back door and following the path past the orchid-houses and the garage turned into the lane, the clouds had lifted slightly to show the hills and a few gleams of watery sunlight lightened the sombre winter landscape and the dark woods round the house.

Peter led the way, pulling the heavily loaded sled which he had covered with a tarpaulin. He wore his cap and gum-boots and his loose duffle-coat pulled on over his dark blue overcoat and suit; his shoes and a soft hat were in the pockets. He and the sled had been down earlier to the gate with tins of petrol and water; the marks of their passage were two deep furrows in the soft snow. Now the going between the high banks was even worse than it had been; the sled sank to the top of its runners at every step he took; he jerked it along grimly and looked straight before him down the lane.

Una, in an old pair of boots that he had made her wear, struggled along in his wake. She had put on her fur coat over her white sweater and dark green trousers, which were the exact colour of the spruce trees; her fur gloves made her hands look like the paws of a small bear. He hair was tied back in a short fair pony-tail that bobbed behind her as she walked. Her exposed forehead and ears made her small chin look sharp and her nose pointed. Her face was white and expressionless and her red-rimmed eyes were sunk in her head. She looked, at that moment, older than she would probably look in twenty years' time.

Peter, turning his head to glance at her uneasily, quickly looked away again. He did not want to remember that last scene in the hall when she had clung to the handle of Jerome's door calling out to him that she was sorry, beseeching him to forgive her or at least to let her see him once more. When only the silence in the room had answered her, she had sunk to her knees against the door and Peter had been forced to pull her to her feet, almost to drag her through the kitchen. He had expected some sort of a scene when he carried her suitcase down the stairs behind her, but he had not been prepared for such a demonstration of grief and despair. When, after his first journey down to the car, he had knocked on her bedroom door to tell her to pack, he had found her sitting dressed by the fire, the room neat, her fur coat lying on the bed and her suitcase already packed and wait-

267

ing. He had not wasted any words on her, but had told her bluntly that she was to leave the house, that he would be back for her in an hour's time to take her to her car. She looked at him composedly and had asked only one question: "Is Sylvie dead?" and when he had nodded, unable to speak, she had said, "I thought so. I saw you both from the window coming back from the woods alone." He had taken the key then from the inside of her door and had locked her in, but no sound of protest had followed him as he hurried down the stairs to begin his own packing.

It was cold, with a raw damp coldness between the steep banks of the lane. Peter looked round again briefly and said in spite of himself, "You should tie your scarf round your head. It won't help to get neuralgia, will it?" Una plodded on, as if she had not heard him, and Peter remembered the way she had pulled herself together directly he had closed the back door behind them both. She had waited with her back turned on him while he put her small box and suitcase beside his own on the sled, and before he had finished fastening the tarpaulin the sound of her weeping had ceased. She had allowed him to help her on with the gumboots and then, holding her head high, she had followed him down the path.

When they came to the steepest part of the lane directly below the house, Una stopped at the bottom of the steps that led to the front door and put her gloved hand on the iron balustrade. She looked up at the closed front door and Peter, who had stopped when she did, saw her eyes go to the windows of Jerome's workroom. He looked up, too, although he knew that there would be no one standing behind the window-seat to watch them go.

Peter gave the sled ropes an angry pull. "Better get on, hadn't we?" he said. "You have a long way to go before night."

Una took her hand reluctantly away from the balustrade. "Why should you worry?" she said coldly, turning her gaze from the house to him. "I'm going. That's all you need to think about," and blinded by fresh tears that she could not keep back, she stumbled after him, unable to see the path that he had made for her in the snow.

As they reached the corner by the clump of fir trees, Peter looked back for a last glimpse of the house. It sat secretive and grey and solid against its dark background of trees. The windows, catching the yellowish, struggling light in the western sky, were shining and blank.

"Don't stop!" Una cried. "Go on, don't look back. There is nothing there to see."

She wiped her eyes on the back of her fur glove and looked at him defiantly. "You heard what I said to him in the hall," she said. "I said that I was sorry. I said that I would never forgive myself. Do you want me to say it all over again to you?"

"What you say can make no difference," Peter said, and then more gently, as he glanced at her small white ravaged face, "Come on, we are nearly there."

He walked on, jerking the sled behind him, and said over his shoulder, "Look, you can see your car. Yes, there she is, waiting for you. Most of the snow had gone off her and I hardly needed

269

to use the spade. I filled her up, tank and radiator. The battery isn't so bad. I had to crank her, of course, and she took quite a bit of starting. Then I backed her out on to the road and ran her awhile to warm her up. She's ready and facing the right way. She should start for you now, like a bird."

As he talked, they covered the last few yards to the gate; Peter sighed with relief. He opened the car doors and Una sank down on the front seat. She sat up almost at once and took off her gum-boots, threw them on the snow, and put on her shoes. As Peter put her box and suitcase in the back of the car and picked up the crank handle, she moved over into the driving-seat. While he walked round to the front of the bonnet, she fastened the fur collar of her coat closely round her neck, smoothed her hair, and put on her driving gloves.

Peter swung the handle and the little car spluttered, coughed, and started into life. "Gently, don't flood her," he shouted. He stood, listening, holding his head on one side, until the engine settled down and hummed contentedly; then he put the handle down on the back seat and slammed the door for the last time.

As he stepped back, Una rolled the window down and beckoned to him. Putting his hands in his pockets, Peter moved warily up to the car as if he expected her to make some violent movement. He looked down into her white face, framed in the dark fur collar, and slowly shook his head.

"I shouldn't say anything if I were you," he said gently. "Much better not."

Una met his eyes. The expression on her small face changed

and hardened. She lifted her chin and, looking away from him, wound the window up and put the car into gear. The red car jerked, leapt forward, and vanished down the road.

Peter stood with his hands in his pockets, looking after it and swearing to himself. Then he picked up the discarded boots and threw them into the front of the sled. He pulled out his suitcase from under the tarpaulin and set it down on the snowy ground while he took off his duffle-coat and cap, changed from his boots into his shoes, and put on his hat which he had owned for years and only worn a few times. When he was ready, he stowed boots and coat in the sled, pulled it to the side of the lane and bent to adjust the tarpaulin. Before he picked up the suitcase, he looked at his watch; it was getting on for three. The bus to Woodstreet would pass the bottom of the lane in a quarter of an hour. Carrying the heavy case, which pulled his shoulder down and gave him a lop-sided air, Peter trudged up the road from which the last trace of snow had gone to meet it.

5

It was dark when, three hours later, Peter came back to the house.

The sun that evening had set into a bed of clouds, staining the sky with colour long after it had gone. Seldom had such a sunset been seen over the valley; stars were showing in the rifts between the clouds before the last fiery streaks disappeared; when Peter turned in at the gate at the bottom of the lane, a faint glow still persisted over the hills. The wind was rising, sending a whispering and stirring through the trees. A few drops of rain fell.

Peter did not look up as he passed under the dark bulk of the house. The melting snow had turned the lane into a stream of slush and mud and, after retrieving his coat and boots, he had left the now useless sled where it was by the gate. He carried his heavy case and his blue overcoat and was breathing deeply, as if he were exhausted. As he reached the garage and saw the glass-houses gleaming palely under the dark sky, he quickened his pace and lifted his head but, at that moment, there was no thought of the orchids in Peter's mind.

He had left the bus a mile out of the town, rising suddenly to his feet among the surprised passengers, demanding to be put down at once, refusing to wait until the next stop. When the conductor, as he handed down his case, had asked him if he were feeling ill, Peter had not answered. He had not heard the question and was walking back up the road as fast as he could before the bus was out of sight. He had walked three miles, stopping to rest every few hundred yards because his feet, in the shoes he was not used to, were hurting him, before a lorry had picked him up and carried him into the valley and to the gate.

He opened the back door and entering the kitchen, switched on the light. He was met by an empty silence. He stood in the doorway, looking round and blinking in the sudden brightness. The neglected meal was still on the table, pushed to one side; the coffee percolator stood on the floor by the range which was nearly out; an empty cup and half a loaf of bread were on the table by his chair with an ashtray full of cigarette butts. Sylvie's bed and drinking bowl had been taken away.

Peter shook his head disapprovingly but looked with gloomy satisfaction at the kitchen's dishevelled state and, putting his suitcase, overcoat and hat into his bedroom, where his locked and corded trunk stared at him from the middle of the floor, hurried down the passage to the furnace-room. The furnace had been stoked but coal and wood were scattered about untidily. He bent down and picked up a hatchet and piece of scorched blue blanket, and knew where Sylvie's bed had gone. When he went back to the kitchen, he looked for her brush and comb but they, too, had been removed and her collar and chain were missing from their hook on the wall. Peter sighed and took off his old coat and hung it on its own peg behind the door. Then he opened the hall door and peered out.

The hall was dark. No sound came to him from the rest of the house which seemed to him to have the air of a house that has not been lived in for a long time. A cold tide flowed down the stairs from the rooms above where a window must have been left open. Peter shivered as he stood in the doorway. He could not bring himself to go down the hall, knock on the door, and tell Jerome that he was back, which would have been the most sensible thing to do. He listened intently, hoping to hear the sound of the typewriter although he knew that it could not be heard from the end of the hall. He shut the door gently and turned back to

273

the kitchen, muttering uneasily to himself. Suddenly he took down his coat, threw it round his shoulders and, banging the back door behind him, hurried down the path round the side of the house on to the lawn.

Light from the lamp on Jerome's writing-table shone out into the darkness. Peter walked slowly toward the uncurtained window. A thin scattering of snow still lay on the grass and behind him the trees stirred and sighed. He saw that Jerome was sitting at his table behind the shaded lamp, his head bent, his shoulders hunched, as he had sat for so many hours over the years. Peter smiled a little grimly, as he peered into the dim firelit room, knowing that his doubts and haste had been unnecessary.

Clutching his coat round him, he came nearer until he was standing at the edge of the square of light cast by the lamp on the lawn. Now he could see the typewriter and Jerome's moving hands and hear the muffled sound of the keys, rising and falling, going on and on.

"You old bastard!" he muttered, with affection and wonder and, smiling his wry smile again, he turned away.

Walking to the edge of the lawn and standing with his back to the house and his hands in the pockets of his old coat, he stared into the darkness in the direction of the spring. The invisible woods, alive with the wind, stretched before him to the hills. As he listened to the sounds of night, the soft rustlings and stirrings, and breathed the cold damp wood-scented air that carried with it so much that his senses missed, his fingers found in his pocket the small whistle he had always used to call Sylvie back from the woods. He took it out and hesitated, turning the small cold thing round and round in his hand. Then he put it carefully into the fob-pocket of the suit he still wore, lifted his arm in a gesture of farewell towards the hills and the spring, and walked back to the house over the lawn where now the last trace of Sylvie's quick and eager feet had disappeared.

A NOTE ABOUT THE AUTHOR

Jon Godden *was born in Bengal, India, in 1906. Her parents had lived for many years in India, and she herself has spent time alternately there and in England. She is the eldest of four sisters, the second of whom is Rumer Godden, the novelist. Jon Godden started to write in 1938 when she was living in Calcutta, and her novels have received high praise on both sides of the Atlantic. She now makes her home in Kent.*

A NOTE ON THE TYPE

The text of this book was set on the Linotype in Fairfield, a type face designed by the distinguished American artist and engraver Rudolph Ruzicka. The bolder version of Fairfield likewise displays the sober and sane qualities of a master craftsman whose talent has long been dedicated to clarity.

The book was composed, printed, and bound by H. Wolff, New York. The paper was manufactured by P. H. Glatfelter Co., Spring Grove, Pennsylvania. Typography based on designs by George Salter.